The
Devil's Lady

WORDSWORTH ROMANCE

The Devil's Lady

LINDEN HOWARD

WORDSWORTH EDITIONS

The paper in this book is produced from pure wood
pulp, without the use of chlorine or any other substance
harmful to the environment. The energy used in its
production consists almost entirely of hydroelectricity
and heat generated from waste materials, thereby
conserving fossil fuels and contributing little to the
greenhouse effect.

First published by St. Martin's Press, Inc. USA

This edition published 1994 by
Wordsworth Editions Limited
Cumberland House, Crib Street, Ware,
Hertfordshire SG12 9ET

ISBN 1 85326 510 1

Printed and bound in Denmark by Nørhaven

Chapter One

I lived with my Aunt Veronica until 1892; Aunt Vee, as I called her, was a remarkable woman, and I realise now that she was years ahead of her time. She was tall and handsome, forthright in speech, sharp of tongue, and warm of heart.

Mine was a happy childhood and girlhood; I never dreamed how completely my pleasant, well-ordered life would change, with the coming of the Stranger, soon after my nineteenth birthday; but through the time that followed his coming, I had reason to bless Aunt Vee's upbringing, the principles she had implanted in me, the imprint her personality had left upon me; those things were a small candle-flame in the darkness that gathered around me.

My mother had died when I was a baby. Her name was Victoria Elisabeth, and she was Aunt Vee's younger sister. I had a photograph of her in a silver frame; her face was as round and innocent as a cherub's, she had a full mouth, like a Cupid's bow, and laughing eyes; her fair hair curled slightly, and there was a dimpled softness about her, belied by a wilful chin and a waywardness in the tilted head.

The waywardness must have been in much evidence when she eloped with my father, Daniel Fairfax, in the face of family opposition; my maternal grandparents disapproved strongly of him. Once, I asked Aunt Vee why they didn't like him.

"For one thing, they knew nothing about him. He said that he had quarrelled with his family and cut himself off from them; but his story did not satisfy papa. It was obvious that Daniel came from a good background, he was educated, well-bred—and very charming; but he did not follow a profession, and apparently did not possess the means of keeping your mother in the comfort to which she was accustomed. Our papa, as I have often told you, was a man of substance, and hoped that both his daughters would marry well."

"YOU did not marry at all, Aunt Vee," I pointed out.

"No, dear. Some women are born to be old maids," she answered drily. "I was thirty when your mother ran away with the man who became your father. I thought it most romantic."

"Were you sorry that YOU didn't meet someone like my papa, Aunt Vee?"

"Not really, dear," she admitted candidly. "I have never considered marriage to be a woman's crowning bliss, and have enjoyed the independence that papa's money has given me. I wanted to be a lady doctor, but papa put his foot down very firmly on the subject." She sighed. "I was in a difficult position; because of Vicky's runaway marriage, mama became ill and depressed and I was needed at home."

"I suppose grandpapa was very angry with my mama?"

"At first; however, he said that his door would not be closed against Vicky, should she need to return home. Daniel was another matter, and not to be admitted to the house, according to papa. We heard little from your mama, after her marriage. One or two letters with a London postmark and no address. She wrote that she was blissfully happy and regretted nothing. Then there was a long silence. Mama grieved openly; papa said that Vicky had made her bed, and if it was not to her liking, she must toss and turn as she would."

Aunt Vee paused, with great dramatic effect, before she continued:

"Then your mama came home; alone. She had been away two years. The spring had gone from her step, she looked old and tired. Life had been difficult, financially, she admitted. Now Daniel was seriously in debt; he had borrowed money on a large scale. Papa offered help, for Vicky's sake; but she said it was no use—Daniel had left her, having written a note declaring himself unworthy of her, saying it would be better if she returned to her family and made a new life for herself. He said, in his note, that he would always love her; but he had to go away, otherwise he faced a prison sentence; he was worthless and mama was to forget him. She never heard from him again."

"How sad!" I said.

"How impossible!" Aunt Vee retorted drily. "How ill-timed. He left on the very day your mama planned to tell him she was expecting YOU!"

Aunt Vee never minced words, nor used genteel phrases like 'an interesting condition' or 'a delicate state of health'. She used the right words for things.

"Your mama was two months pregnant, dear. She returned to her home after seeing her doctor and found the note from your papa. So she came back to us; it caused great consternation; but at least, she WAS properly married, and therefore not quite a prodigal daughter. Papa insisted that Daniel must be found and made to face his responsibilities, but your Mama refused to entertain the idea. There was a great to-do about it, but papa was adamant, and eventually, he traced Daniel's father; *his* name was Damon Fairfax and he lived in a big house in Hampshire. Papa wrote, telling him the circumstances. Old Mr. Fairfax replied that he had not seen his estranged son for several years, and had no idea where he was; as for any child of such an obviously ill-advised marriage, that was not *his* responsibility, he pointed out.

"The letter made papa very angry; he wrote several more letters, but old Mr. Fairfax did not reply to any of them. Your poor mama refused to be drawn into the quarrel; she was in a strange state of mind, as though she was not really with us at all. I have sometimes thought that she was still living inside the two years that she had spent with Daniel, and could not free herself from their spell. I daresay that sounds strange to you, Catherine."

"Did you ever see the place where old Mr. Fairfax lived?" I asked, once.

"Yes, dear. It was very large, like a Castle, standing in a big park. There were tall iron gates set in the wall; I took you there when you were three years old, and lifted you up to look through the gates. I remember the lodge-keeper came out and stared at us. You would not remember that; it was just after your mama died."

Her eyes filled with tears.

"I loved your mama dearly, even though we were not so close after her marriage. She spoke to me with great affection of Daniel, but I must confess *I* did not entertain any kind feelings towards him. I watched your mama slipping away from us, as though she had no will to live."

"She had ME, Aunt Vee!" I said, hurt.

"Yes, my love; but you were a baby, demanding her time and attention, not old enough to be a comfort to her. You are not like her, in looks. You are not like your papa, either. He came to the house, once or twice, before he married your mama and I remember he was fair and quiet. Perhaps you resemble your grandfather."

I would like to have been pretty and softly-rounded, like my mother. I was tall, with strongly-marked features, too wide a mouth, and a great deal of thick brown hair with bronze highlights, that I found difficulty in taming. As for the daintiness I yearned to possess, to my shame, my waist was twenty-three inches, not eighteen and Aunt Vee refused to allow tight lacing, declaring that it was not good for young figures to be confined into a corset.

Soon after my mother died, Aunt Vee's mother died, too; her father lived only a few years afterwards, suffering a seizure, through which Aunt Vee nursed him devotedly.

I loved my spinster Aunt. She gave me security and affection; her honesty and plain speaking, her orderliness about life were to stand me in good stead in later years.

After the death of my mother's parents, Aunt Vee moved away from Bristol, declaring that country air was better for a child; I think the truth was that the old family house at Clifton, high above the Avon Gorge, held too many sad memories for her. So we came to live in a sleepy little town on the borders of Wiltshire and Dorset, when I was seven years old; we were both happy and content there.

Our house was small and pretty, at the top of the High Street, with a small flagged courtyard in front, in which stood stone urns filled with geraniums; at the back, there was a wild garden that Aunt Vee never pruned much because she said it would spoil its character; so hollyhocks, lupins, delphiniums and roses crowded along the path under the crooked apple trees. The garden led to a river; on many a summer afternoon, I sat on the river bank, eating apples, dipping my bare feet in the water and reading. People said such behaviour was extremely hoydenish.

In winter, we sat by the fire and read our books; or we painted, two happy amateurs with our separate easels. Twice a year we went up to town to shop, to go to concerts, to look at Art Galleries and Churches and famous buildings, a knowledge of which was essential to a full education, Aunt Vee declared. I was always glad enough to come back again to the sleepy town, the comfortable house, and our funny little maid, Duffy, who had come from a neighbouring farm, to look after us.

Aunt Vee taught me to sew; I made my own dresses, designing them myself, and Aunt Vee created the most marvellous hats for us, which we wore to Church on Sundays, secretly delighted to know that everyone believed they were expensive London creations. I learned to cook, and play the piano, and keep house, to arrange flowers, and to entertain people. Aunt Vee insisted that I should THINK about life and have opinions of my own.

"Young women are not supposed to have opinions; or, at least, not to air them!" I pointed out doubtfully.

She simply smiled at me, and said calmly:

"*You* are not like other young women, dear!"

"In that case, I shall *never* get a husband!"

She looked at me thoughtfully, then nodded.

"You will. *You* need a husband, Catherine; you are not self-sufficient, as I am. But he must be a man to match you; you will have no respect for a man who will always let you have your way—and no time for a man who will *not* let you have your way! Your temperament is much more like mine than like your mama's! Choose your husband carefully! Let there be a clash of wills, sometimes! Without such clashes, life is a bowl of cold porridge!"

I laughed.

"What a strange remark!" I said.

"Remember it!" she answered calmly.

So the pleasant days became weeks and months, gathering themselves into years; and I have set down my early life, that it may be understood how strange and sharp was the contrast when everything changed.

The Stranger came into my life when I was almost twenty years old; he arrived on a Spring afternoon, when the trees were frothed with delicate green and all the birds were singing in the trees.

It was time for the annual Spring-cleaning ritual, and Duffy, Aunt Vee and I were hard at work, in pursuit of a winter's accumulation of dirt and cobwebs.

I was wearing an old print dress and had hidden my hair under an ancient cap of Aunt Vee's. I had just tied an apron around my waist, when we heard the sound of horses' hooves outside; moments later, there was a thunderous knocking at the front door.

The sound was both imperious and impatient; Aunt Vee almost toppled from the stepladder, as we looked at one another in consternation.

"We are not expecting visitors!" she said, astonished. "Duffy! You must say we are not at home!"

The knocker rose and fell again before poor little Duffy had scuttled to the front door. I was suddenly angry; who was it, I wondered, who dared to announce their arrival in such an autocratic manner?

Aunt Vee and I stood still, listening.

"I wish to speak to Miss Catherine Fairfax."

It was a man's voice. Rich, deep, resonant, a voice once heard never forgotten. A blind man in a crowd of people would recognise it instantly.

"Sir?" Duffy didn't stand a chance. "I am to say—that is—Miss Fairfax is not at home. Nor is Miss Sheldon."

The deep voice was arrogant. "My visit is a matter of too much urgency to be fobbed off with the excuse behind which young ladies withdraw when they do not want to receive callers. I wish to see Miss Catherine Fairfax at once!"

Duffy stood uncertainly at the open door, nervously

swallowing and smoothing down her apron. I looked at my Aunt. Twin spots of colour burned in her cheeks; she braced herself and pulled the half-open door wide open, stepping into the hall, with great dignity.

Automatically, I followed her. Duffy looked back at us, with an audible sigh of relief. The stranger stepped past her and stood in our hall, seeming to fill the whole house with his presence.

He stood over six feet in height and the caped coat he wore accentuated the broadness of his shoulders.

His face was that of a soldier of fortune; two deep grooves ran from his nose to the corners of his mouth, and there was a puckered scar on one cheek. His Roman nose added to his look of arrogance; his wide, full-lipped mouth had a hint of sensuousness. With his high cheekbones and slightly foreign air he reminded me of an old-time pirate about to plunder a rich Spanish galleon. His jet-black hair, springing back from his forehead in glistening waves and curls, was heavily streaked with silver. He gave an impression of hard, muscular strength married to a careless grace of movement that would make him stand out in the most distinguished gathering; but his eyes were his most disturbing feature.

They were a brilliant green, cold and clear as lake water; above them, his thick black brows had an upward slant that gave his face a sardonic expression.

Here was a man, I thought, who could effortlessly charm the birds from the trees. I distrusted him and felt hostile towards him.

His eyes flicked quickly over Aunt Vee, who stood there, with her lips pressed tightly together; he gave me a more leisurely scrutiny, and I was suddenly aware that I was still wearing the faded cotton dust cap. I put up a hand and pulled it from my head; in doing so, I loosed several pins and my hair tumbled around my shoulders.

Acutely embarrassed, I glared angrily at the Stranger. A flicker of amusement crossed his face, as he stared back at me, coolly unperturbed.

"May I ask who you are?" Aunt Vee asked him shortly. "And the nature of your business? *I* am Miss Sheldon, and this is my niece, Catherine Fairfax."

"I am Troy Merrick," the Stranger answered her, equally crisp. "Your niece is my cousin by marriage because my wife, Selina, is a Fairfax by birth. Her father was the eldest son of Damon Fairfax. Damon had a younger son, Daniel, who made a runaway marriage with a young woman named Victoria Sheldon."

"She was my sister!" Aunt Vee said faintly; for a moment, she looked bemused. Then she recovered herself, and gestured towards the parlour which was reasonably tidy.

"Bring a tray of tea for us, please, Duffy," she murmured.

When Duffy would have taken his coat, Troy Merrick waved her away and tossed it carelessly on a chair. Not the action of a gentleman, I thought indignantly. He sat back, quite at ease; I sat stiffly on the edge of a small chair, consumed with curiosity.

Aunt Vee was mistress of herself again.

"I did not know that Damon Fairfax had more than one son," she said, shortly.

"He had two." Troy spoke precisely, his eyes still on my face. "Charles—Damon's eldest son—and his wife, Stacey, were killed in a coach accident when Selina was a baby. Since then, she has lived with her grandfather. He is an old man, now, and sick. He wishes to meet his other grandchild."

I spoke for the first time, ignoring Aunt Vee's warning look.

"Why should he wish to make *my* acquaintance so late in his life?" I demanded. "When my mother's father wrote to him, telling him that Daniel had married my mother, and that she was expecting a child, Damon Fairfax rejected the idea that any child of what he called an 'ill-advised marriage' could be of interest to *him*!"

"True," Troy agreed calmly. "Damon Fairfax has lately uncovered a conscience that he obviously did not know he possessed, and is aware that he treated your father badly. He wishes to make amends."

"In what way?" I demanded.

"He asked me to try to trace his unknown grandchild. This I have done." Troy's eyes never left my face. "He sends a message, Miss Fairfax. He wants you to go and stay at Sandleford."

"Indeed I shall not!" I told him angrily. "My grandfather has ignored my existence, for twenty years. Now he decides that he will graciously favour me with an invitation to visit him. No doubt his conscience DOES prod him, Mr. Merrick! So it should! *I* see no reason to pander to this sudden whim of his to acknowledge me!"

"My dear Catherine ..." murmured Aunt Vee, taken aback.

"It was you who taught me to say what I think!" I reminded her.

I saw the gleam in Troy's eyes; obviously, he was enjoying the furore he had caused.

"Is it your pride that is hurt?" he asked me smoothly.

"Naturally. As my sense of justice is outraged," I retorted.

"What of your wife?" Aunt Vee asked. "What are her views on this sudden change of heart of her grandfather's?"

"I don't think Damon consulted her on the matter," Troy replied, with a careless shrug.

I sat there, silent, thinking: *I have a cousin. She is this man's wife.* I would like to see Sandleford Park; I would like to have those gates opened for ME, so that I can walk up to the great house beyond them and know I *belong* there, by right of birth.

I looked at Aunt Vee; she seemed tired. Perhaps the spring-cleaning had been too much for her. Or perhaps she feared I would be lured away from her by the tempting prospect this astonishing man dangled in front of my eyes.

"Tell me about Damon Fairfax," Aunt Vee said quietly to Troy.

"There is little more to tell." Troy Merrick seemed suddenly wary. "As I have said, he is old and sick. Eccentric. Obsessed by two things: that Sandleford is a house of misfortune because of the old legend that surrounds it; and obsessed, also, by the fact that he was unjust to his younger son." The piercing green eyes met mine challengingly, and I felt an extraordinary sensation, as though Troy Merrick possessed a compelling magnetism that could hold people spellbound.

"Sandleford is an impressive house," Aunt Vee said. "Once, I took Catherine to see it, when she was a small child. I held her up to look through the gates."

"Now she may go freely through those gates whenever she pleases," Troy replied.

I shook my head and stared at the wall above Troy's head. Duffy, round-eyed with curiosity, brought in a tray of tea and a cake I had baked that morning.

In silence, Aunt Vee poured the tea. I was acutely aware of those eyes that held me prisoner; but I would not look at this man. I feared and distrusted him.

Aunt Vee said briskly to Troy: "I should like to know more of this desire of Damon's to meet his grand-daughter; in what way does he hope to make amends for the fact that he has ignored her existence all these years?"

Scarlet with shame, I glared at Aunt Vee; she smiled blandly at me, quite unperturbed. I reminded myself that she never minced matters. As for Troy, his face was suddenly withdrawn; the clear eyes were full of secrets. His voice was cool.

"I must tell you, Miss Sheldon, that Damon Fairfax is not a rich man; in fact, he is almost penniless. The house had fallen into a sad state of disrepair, until my marriage to Selina. I had it restored as a wedding gift for her, because she is greatly attached to the place. Did you hope that Damon's remorse might take some practical form where Catherine is concerned?"

"Yes," replied Aunt Vee matter-of-factly. "I have little to leave my niece, when I die."

"There is no reason at all for this discussion!" I cried, furious and embarrassed. "However, as my grandfather seems so set on my paying him a visit, I will do so!"

"Would you have agreed to come if he was a rich man?" Troy asked me mockingly.

"No!" I said shortly.

"Money is a most useful commodity, Miss Fairfax!"

"Certainly it is. I have enough for my needs. I don't need Fairfax money! Next week, I am going to the Cotswolds to visit an old school friend for a few weeks. When I return, I will write to you and you may suggest a date for my visit."

."Thank you." He stood up and bowed; his voice, his face, his gestures, all mocked me, I felt.

"The invitation to Sandleford will naturally include you, also, Miss Sheldon," he said.

He sounds as though HE is Master of Sandleford, I thought. How strange. My grandfather is the Master there.

"Tell me about the legend of Sandleford," I said, curious.

"There is no time now. Selina will tell you the tale."

He picked up his coat, said he hoped I would enjoy my holiday, and took his leave of us.

Aunt Vee and I went to the front door, Duffy hovering excitedly behind us. Outside the house stood a handsome, maroon-coloured coach, decorated with fine gold brushwork and drawn by a pair of matched grey thoroughbreds.

The coachman, waiting impassively for his Master, wore the same dark-red livery. Damon Fairfax might be a poor man, but Troy was not, I reflected. He had the air of a man on whom wealth sits almost negligently.

Troy was seated in the coach. The coachman climbed on to the box, picked up the reins and urged the horses forward. For a moment, Troy's face was framed in the window. All the life had gone from it; it was as sombre and brooding as a winter's day, just before the first snows begin to fall.

In spite of the warmth of the afternoon, I shivered. He was disconcerting. He had a kind of restless energy, a tremendous, exciting vitality; and he had depths that seemed cold and frightening.

I watched the carriage roll away; Troy did not wave to us. I wondered if he would tell my grandfather that I looked a sorry sight, in my print dress, my hair dishevelled, my face flushed from my exertions.

Like a servant girl, in fact, not a young lady.

"What an extraordinary man!" Aunt Vee murmured.

"I didn't like him," I replied firmly.

"He is not a comfortable man to be with," she admitted, "but one could never ignore him. I must confess I am excited at the thought of a visit to Sandleford."

"*I* am not, in the least," I said carelessly.

It wasn't true. Curiosity raged like a fever in me, in spite of resentment at being summoned to meet a man whose conscience was troubling him.

We talked about nothing except Troy's visit. I think Aunt Vee was rather sorry that I was going for my annual visit to Anne Jessop, first. She was intrigued and excited, speculating endlessly as to what Sandleford would be like.

Anne thought it terribly romantic. What a foolish word, I thought! Though I didn't want Fairfax money, I was secretly rather sorry that I hadn't suddenly become an heiress. Nevertheless, I was a person of importance in Anne's eyes, because I had a grandfather who lived in a house almost as big as a Castle.

Four lazy pleasant weeks flowed by; all too soon, it was time for me to return home. Anne kissed me goodbye, and said I must be sure to write and tell her about my new relations.

Aunt Vee greeted me delightedly. She had been busy, sewing new gowns to wear. I sat down and wrote a formal little note to Troy, asking him to name a date for our visit.

As I sealed the envelope, I thought about his wife, Selina. He had spoken little of her. It must have been a dull life for a young woman, living in straitened circumstances with only her grandfather for company. Would she resent my coming to Sandleford, after she had been the only grandchild for so long?

I waited impatiently for Troy's reply; it came a week later, and was a great shock to me. Damon Fairfax had died the day after my letter had arrived at Sandleford.

Aunt Vee was upset; I felt a curious sense of loss, although I could not pretend to be grief-stricken for a grandfather I had never known. I sent a letter of condolence from Aunt Vee and myself, in which I wrote that, no doubt, Mr. Merrick and his wife would not now wish the visit to take place.

Troy's reply was brief; he said that he was sailing for Australia,—'unexpectedly' was the word he used—and would write to me as soon as he returned. Most certainly he and Selina wished me to visit Sandleford, with Aunt Vee when he came back to England; he was sorry that Damon Fairfax had died without meeting me.

The summer months passed happily enough. I was the same as I had always been; no, that was not quite true. Something was altered within me. I found myself thinking about Troy; I wondered if his wife had gone to Australia with him. There were times when I thought I could not bear to wait so long to visit my father's home; other times when the whole episode of Troy coming to see me seemed blurred and unreal.

Summer became Autumn, and still there was no word from Troy. Aunt Vee remained cheerful. It was a long and tedious voyage to Australia, she pointed out to me.

November was a sad, grey month of misty skies and leafless trees. I felt curiously depressed and could not think why; I confided in Aunt Vee, and she said:

"I am sure that Troy means us to visit Sandleford, if that is what troubles you, dear."

"I am not in the least troubled. I wouldn't go if you were not coming; and I am very happy here with you," I told her.

She cupped my face in her hands and kissed my forehead. Usually, she was an undemonstrative woman, but I never needed reminders of her great love for me, and knew she wished I had been her daughter.

"I am proud of you, Catherine," she said softly. "You are intelligent and though you are not as pretty as your mama was, you have character. You hold yourself proudly, and look the world in the face. You are honest and kind."

"You taught me to be so, Aunt Vee."

"I had a willing pupil. You are quick-tempered and stubborn, impulsive and outspoken. I have the same qualities and age has scarcely tempered them. You will never be a dull person; neither will you be meek and submissive, thank Heavens!"

We piled logs on the fire and ate our simple meal; outside, the air was thin, reminding us that winter was at our heels.

When the clock struck ten, I kissed Aunt Vee goodnight; she was reading a volume of poetry and I thought she looked tired.

She said a strange thing.

"Your happiness is precious to me. They say hate reaches out from beyond the grave to exact vengeance for old wrongs; but *I* believe that love, not hate, is stronger than death and survives it!"

I thought it a strange remark; but she would not enlarge upon it. Upstairs, I undressed and brushed out my heavy hair. Then I leaned my arms on the window sill and stared at the black sky, pierced with brilliant stars. I saw the friendly lights of the town, twinkling below me. I knew that everything was going to change, very soon; a way of life I had known for so long was about to end for ever.

Often, in the time to come, I was to know that feeling; as though the darkness gathered itself into forms and shapes that closed around me, and brought with them a wind that blew coldly.

I was wakeful for a long time, that night. When, at last, I slept, my sleep was shallow and troubled by fragments of dreams that made no sense.

At dawn, I was awakened by someone shaking me violently. I sat up and blinked into Duffy's white, distraught face.

"Oh, Miss Catherine, do come quick!" she sobbed. "She's still asleep in her chair and I can't rouse her! I'm feared there's summat wrong with her!"

I went quickly downstairs, my heart hammering, my legs like tissue paper. In the sitting-room, the logs had burned themselves down to grey ash, and Duffy's cleaning things were scattered on the hearth.

Duffy had pulled back the curtains. In the pitiless morning light, I saw Aunt Vee sitting in her chair, where I had left her the night before.

I touched the cold cheeks and quiet hands. I had never seen death before; but I knew Aunt Vee was dead.

Like a sleep-walker, I bent and picked up the book she had been reading; it was lying face downwards on the floor.

I read the words on the open page.

"Fear no more the heat o' the sun,
Nor the furious winter's rages,
Thou, thy wordly task hast done,

Home art gone and ta'en thy wages ..."

I put my head in my hands and cried as though my heart would break.

People were kind, in the sad weeks that followed. Dr. Greyling declared that Aunt Vee had died peacefully from a heart attack. Anne Jessop came to me at once; Duffy did all that she could, running the house single-handed, for I had no heart for any of it.

Mr. Jarley attended the funeral with me; he came back to the house, afterwards. He was my Aunt's solicitor, a middle-aged bachelor; she trusted him implicitly and he had often dined with us.

He looked uneasy, as he sat drinking the tea that Duffy had brought.

"Your Aunt was a happy woman," he said. "She lived a full and useful life. She died as she would have wished; she had a heart condition and knew that she could die at any time. She refused to allow Dr. Greyling to tell you the truth; she did not wish you to be made unhappy before it was necessary. I think you should go away for a while; I understand that Miss Jessop would be delighted to have you with her for Christmas."

I shook my head, and he said firmly:

"You cannot stay here alone. I have something to tell you, Catherine; there is no way of breaking this gently. Your Aunt was in debt when she died. She liked to live well and her capital has been dwindling for years. Some of the investments she made were ill-advised, but she was a strong-willed woman, not to be dissuaded when she had made up her mind about something."

"You mean I shall have no money?" I faltered.

"I am afraid not. This house must be sold. Your Aunt left you her jewellery, that is all; and she appointed Troy Merrick to be your guardian until you are twenty-one."

I stared at him in complete disbelief.

"*Why?*" I whispered.

"She believed he would be the most suitable person; I cannot say I agreed with her. However, she was adamant.

She came to see me, and changed her Will after he called on you both, last Spring. Until then, *I* had been her choice as your guardian." He sounded hurt.

"I am sorry," I murmured, remembering the conversation between Aunt Vee and Troy concerning money. I had been embarrassed, and we had never mentioned it afterwards.

Now I realised she had named Troy as my guardian because he was obviously a man of some wealth and position. She had been so anxious that I should be provided for but I did not relish the idea of charity from Troy Merrick.

The thought of visiting Sandleford with Aunt Vee was one thing; living there as Troy Merrick's ward was another thing altogether.

"*Must* I go to Sandleford to live?" I asked.

"I am afraid so, Catherine. It is probably for the best, you know. Your Aunt knew that you would be left in very straitened circumstances, and it had worried her for some time, prior to Mr. Merrick's visit. I understand that Mr. Merrick welcomed the arrangement; she wrote, asking him to be your guardian, before he sailed for Australia."

"I wish she had consulted me! I could earn a living. Other young women in my position have done so! Have you met Mr. Merrick?"

"No," Arthur Jarley replied shortly. "I know nothing of him, but rest assured that I shall make enquiries. The whole business leaves me dissatisfied and disappointed."

He leaned forward and patted my arm.

"Perhaps I have been a lawyer so long that I have grown suspicious of people and their motives. We shall not lose touch. You must write to me. If, at any time, you are troubled, then you must tell me so. I am your friend."

Arthur Jarley paid Duffy six months' wages, as Aunt Vee had instructed him in her Will. We parted tearfully, and next day I went to stay with Anne. I cannot say I enjoyed Christmas; but youth is resilient, and I began to recover from the first grief and shock of Aunt Vee's death.

On New Year's Eve, at Anne's, I lifted my glass, wondering what the year ahead would hold for me; I shivered, as though a cold wind had blown over me; it was the feeling I had known the night before Aunt Vee had died.

Next day, I heard from Arthur. He wrote that Troy Merrick was back from his Australian visit and had called to see him, following the letter that Arthur had sent to Sandleford, informing him of Aunt Vee's death.

Troy was sending the coach for me, in three weeks' time, and trusted I would be ready to leave for Sandleford by then.

The three weeks passed quickly; preparing to leave the home in which I had spent so many happy years, was a sad business.

Arthur did not say so outright, but I knew that he was not reassured by his meeting with Troy, and considered him an arrogant, high-handed man.

"I would have expected his wife to have come with him; or at least, to have sent a message of condolence," he pointed out.

I pondered the remark, strapping my trunks, on the day the carriage was due; perhaps Selina Merrick did not want me at Sandleford. It was a depressing thought.

The maroon-coloured coach arrived promptly; the horses drew up with a clattering of hooves, to shouted commands from the coachman. The sight of such an opulent coach caused a stir in our quiet village.

I was scared and miserable; Arthur, who had come to see me off, spoke consolingly, but I wasn't listening.

The coachman swung himself down from his box, with great agility, for he was not young and, to my surprise, as he opened the door, a man stepped down from inside the coach.

The man was young, slenderly built. He had a crest of reddish hair and bright hazel eyes. He was elegantly dressed, and had none of Troy's cold, forbidding air.

Chapter Two

He smiled and held out his hand to me. I noticed small things about him: the golden lights in his hair, the even whiteness of his teeth, the firmness of the handshake.

"I am Rufus Herries," he told me, "as I am staying at Sandleford, Mr. Merrick thought it would be as well if I accompanied you on your journey." His smile was edged with humour, as he added drily:

"He does not think that young ladies should travel alone. Here is his letter of introduction."

I opened the envelope he gave me. Troy's heavy black handwriting covered a sheet of thick cream notepaper, stating that the bearer of the letter was Rufus Herries. It added what Rufus had already told me, and ended with a signature that flowed right across the page.

I handed the letter to Arthur. I think Troy's gesture of sending an escort won grudging approval from him though I didn't think it allayed any of his fears and suspicions.

Rufus handed me into the coach, and my luggage was strapped on the back. Arthur's face was separated from mine by a sheet of glass, then the coachman cracked his whip and the horses' hooves rang hollowly on the cobbles. I lifted my hand in a farewell wave which Arthur acknowledged with a nod; then we swept down the hill, out of the village, and away from a life that had been safe, warm and happy.

I felt tears in my eyes. The man opposite me smiled reassuringly.

"We are all looking forward to having you at

Sandleford," he said charmingly. "Selina is eagerly waiting to meet you."

"Why did she not come when Troy came to see me, last Spring?" I asked.

"She has not been well. She is delicate. No, perhaps that is not the right word. Highly-strung, and of a nervous disposition; she does not often leave Sandleford."

I sat back and looked at my companion. I was suddenly glad that I was wearing my best green velvet—for Aunt Vee had indicated clearly in her Will that she did not wish me to wear mourning for her. I also wore her sealskin cape, and my hands were folded into a muff of the same fur.

"Tell me about—my family," I said.

"Selina's mother and mine were first cousins. My parents lived at Kilstock Manor, until my father died, and then my mother moved away to Bath, where she has since remarriedd. Kilstock is quite near Sandleford. Last year, the Manor was burned down, whilst I was away from home."

"Burned down?" I echoed, astonished.

"The house caught fire. No one knew the cause. The damage was the greater as there were only a couple of servants there at the time. I am having it rebuilt, and in the meantime, Troy has kindly offered me the hospitality of Sandleford."

"Do you like my cousin's husband?" I asked slowly.

His answer was evasive.

"He has been kind enough to give me a temporary home," he pointed out. "He is not an easy man to know. He enjoys telling people that he is not a gentleman. He began life in the back streets of Portsmouth, born into desperate poverty; *now* he owns a fleet of cargo ships and is immensely rich."

"How did he meet my grandfather?"

"I don't know. Selina was staying with friends when Troy first arrived, out of the blue; I must say he seemed firmly established in the house, when she returned."

"Who else lives at Sandleford?"

"There is Alannah," he replied. "Has Troy not mentioned her to you?"

I shook my head.

"We have only met briefly," I pointed out.

"Troy brought Alannah back from his last visit to Australia." Rufus looked uncomfortable, as he added:

"You will find out soon enough, Catherine, that she is Troy's illegitimate daughter. Her mother was his mistress in Sydney, and has recently died; however, I don't think he should have brought the child to Sandleford. Her presence can only remind Selina that she and Troy have no family of their own."

"How old is Alannah?"

"About nine, I imagine. There is a further complication: the child is unable to speak, though she is no deaf-mute—she hears and understands all that is said to her."

"How strange!" I murmured.

"She is a rather wilful child. She needs a governess or someone in authority who will be responsible for her," Rufus added wrily.

"Did you know my grandfather well?" I asked.

"Yes. He was always a hermit. In his later years, he was very eccentric and became a complete recluse. He had a fine library of books on the Occult and the Supernatural, which he studied constantly." He smiled ruefully. "It was all above my head; and I believe that such reading only encouraged him in his belief that Sandleford was cursed."

"Troy said that Selina will tell me the legend," I said.

"There are twin legends; of Good and of Evil," he replied.

"Do *you* believe in them?"

"No, indeed! I am not fanciful, as Selina is; *she* believes whole-heartedly, which, no doubt, is why she tells the story so well!"

"Does *your* house have such a legend?" I asked.

He shook his head; he began to speak of his childhood; how he and Selina had played together. He mentioned a man called Seton Blair.

"Seton lives at Ashmead Grange, whose grounds run parallel with those of Sandleford. Seton's godparents, Emma and Geoffrey Creighton, owned Ashmead, and left it to him when they died, together with a handsome sum of money. As a child, Seton often stayed at the Grange and made a threesome with Selina and myself. Then there is Agnes."

"Who is she—his sister?"

"No. The Creightons accepted Agnes Oakes into their home when she was fifteen. Her mother was Mrs. Creighton's spinster sister, who had brought disgrace on the family, I understand, by producing a daughter. When Agnes' mother died, Mrs. Creighton took the child, and made her useful at Ashmead. It wasn't much of a life for her, and she was left penniless on the death of the Creightons. However, Seton made it his business to look after her, insisting that she should stay at Ashmead to run the place for him. Some months ago, she met with an accident that has left her confined to a wheelchair. Shortly after this accident, she and Seton became betrothed. I admit we were all greatly surprised, though it is obviously a very suitable match. Agnes has a deep affection for Seton and he is a man with a deep sense of responsibility."

"You sound as though he became betrothed to her because he felt sorry for her," I said. "That would not seem to be a good basis for marriage. Was he responsible for the accident that crippled her?"

"Good gracious, no!" Rufus looked startled. "No date has yet been set for the wedding, but I am sure they are well-suited and will be happy together."

I listened to him, thinking that I was lucky. I travelled in state, in warmth and a degree of splendour such as I had never known, being borne away to a splendid country house that belonged to my family.

We passed from Wiltshire into Hampshire. The scattered villages, folded in the lee of the downlands, were pretty enough; a few snowflakes whirled aimlessly past the window, and muffled children ran, shouting, beside the carriage, as long as they had breath to do so.

The motion of the coach made me sleepy and I dozed, whilst Rufus fell silent, lost in his own thoughts. My head was nodding when suddenly the coach came to an abrupt halt.

We both looked out of the window; we were outside an ancient Inn, with swinging sign that said: 'The Packhorse'.

"What's wrong?" Rufus demanded sharply, as the coachman climbed down from the box.

"One of the horses has shed a shoe, sir."

"How long will it take to get another?"

"Just as long as it takes me to find the blacksmith, sir. They'll give you tea in the parlour of 'The Packhorse' while you wait."

"Some hot tea would be welcome," I murmured.

Rufus helped me down from the coach. My limbs were cramped and the cold air was like a sword-thrust.

"How far are we from Sandleford?" I asked.

"Not more than an hour's journey."

The Inn-keeper's wife was a sharp-faced woman, muffled into a great many wraps. She glanced at the Sandleford coach and a look of mingled anger and astonishment crossed her face. She greeted Rufus's request for tea with great reluctance; he seemed ill-at-ease.

"Who is she?" I whispered, as we were shown in to the parlour, where a fire burned brightly.

He shook his head, frowning, and put a finger to his lips.

"Mrs. Armond; her niece once worked at Sandleford," was all he said.

We sat there in silence. I stretched chilled fingers to the blaze, until Mrs. Armond brought in a tray of tea and toasted muffins.

Her hard little eyes raked over me.

"So you're going to Sandleford?" she said. "Are you the governess for Mr. Merrick's child?"

"No," I replied coolly; and Rufus's voice was several degrees colder.

"Miss Fairfax is Mrs. Merrick's cousin, Mrs. Armond."

"Oh indeed?" The look of curiosity deepened. "Well, I wouldn't let anyone of mine go *there*, that's a fact! No fit place for any young woman! My Lallie worked there; a decent girl, properly brought up. They said she jumped from a window because she was expecting Mr. Merrick's child and couldn't face the disgrace. Rubbish! Not our Lallie! All hushed up, quick …"

"Thank you for the tea. If we need anything more, we will ring for you," Rufus said curtly.

She shrugged and left the room.

I poured tea for us both.

"Is it true?" I asked Rufus.

"I don't know whether Lallie took her life or whether it was an accident; she fell from one of the upstairs windows."

He didn't want to talk about it; that was obvious. I felt uneasy, remembering Mrs. Armond's words: I wouldn't let anyone of mine go *there*!

Mrs. Armond collected the tea-tray, without a word, though her face stated that she could say a great deal if she chose. I was glad enough to leave 'The Packhorse' and rejoin the coach.

I thought a great deal about what she had said, as I rode through the quiet lanes. The Meon Valley was gently landscaped, with rolling downland, pretty villages, snug-looking cottages. I saw a stream beside a mill, and Inns that looked older than 'The Packhorse'. People, passing along the road, turned to stare after the coach.

Finally, we rounded a bend, and I saw a high, flint wall beyond the grass verge; I guessed that this was the boundary wall of Sandleford Park.

The wall continued for some distance, then we came around another gentle curve to face a pair of tall, wrought iron gates, which were wide open.

Ahead of me lay Sandleford.

Like a Castle, Aunt Vee had said; she had been right. I saw a long, grey facade, its many windows deep-set into stone arches with pointed tops. At each end of the house were square towers, with battlements, and I could imagine the splendour of the view from there.

In the centre of the house was a huge stone canopy over a massive front door, flanked by stone lions, like sphinxes on either side of it. The area immediately around the house was paved, and I saw the rim of a great circular stone basin; I realised it was a lily pond.

Smoke curled lazily from the chimneys of the house, and from those of the Lodge, just inside the gates. The Lodge keeper and his wife stood to let us pass, a tow-headed boy between them. The man bobbed his head, the woman gave a quick curtsey; and I saw the curiosity on their faces.

I remembered nothing of my childhood visit, with Aunt Vee holding me up to look through the gates. The area drive was long and winding, and ran through open parkland, with grassy knolls and several trees scattered over a wide area. A wide stream flowed right across the grounds, the centre of it spanned by a hump-backed bridge over which we passed.

The water flowed fast and noisily; it curved away towards a belt of trees in the distance on my right, and I saw that it was joined by other, much smaller streams, like silver threads.

To my left, just over the bridge, I saw a small stone Chapel; it had crooked gravestones clustered around it; and the ground was thickly patched with white; it looked as though it had snowed, and then begun to thaw.

As we drew near, I saw that I was looking, not at snow, but at thousands of snowdrops.

They grew only around the Chapel; nowhere else. It seemed as though the snow itself had flowered, and I was entranced.

There were several large stone vaults beside the Chapel, ribboned with dark-green ivy, in contrast to the small, pale flowers. Some of the vaults were sinking, their walls cracked and green-stained with damp. A broken marble urn lay on its side near a slanting headstone. The Chapel door with its great iron hinges, was closed; the place had a strange desolation about it—and yet, there was a sense of quietness and piece also, as though no turbulence of any sort ever came near it.

I heard a sudden shout from the coachman as he reined so hard that I was almost flung from my seat.

"What is it?" I cried, opening the window.

"*There!*" He pointed with his whip. "Miss Alannah! nearly under the horses' hooves! Never *do* look *nor* care where she's going!"

I had a brief glimpse of a blue coat, boots, long, dark hair streaming from beneath a blue bonnet, as a child ran towards the Chapel, with incredible swiftness. I watched her weave in and out of the tombstones; I saw her stand on tiptoe and struggle to lift the heavy iron latch. It was a tremendous effort, but she managed it, and disappeared inside like a fugitive seeking sanctuary.

"Alannah!" Rufus cried angrily; but she went on running as though the Devil himself was after her.

He sat back in his seat as the coachman urged the horses forward again.

"Exasperating child!" he said, angrily. "She might have gone under the wheels, or caused the horses to bolt. I suppose half of the staff are out looking for her again!"

"Why? Does she often behave so?" I asked, puzzled.

"You saw for yourself. She is like quicksilver. Never to be found in the right place. The Chapel is her favourite haunt."

"I shouldn't think that was such a bad thing," I pointed out.

He shrugged.

"Well, here we are. This is Sandleford. Selina will be waiting to welcome you," he said.

The horses were wheeled smartly to make a turn that brought the coach door exactly opposite the door of the house; a feat of skill of which the coachman was obviously very proud.

So, in the dying light of a bitter afternoon, I, Catherine Fairfax, came to the house in which my father had spent his boyhood, and in which my ancestors had lived for so long.

It was a day when the world seemed to have died, and the snowdrops were winter's shroud rather than the first outriders of Spring.

There was no sound, save the snorting and breathing of the horses, the jingling of harnesses, the restless scrape of hooves on stone.

The door of the coach was held open for me. Rufus stepped down and handed me out with great ceremony, watched by the coachman; for a few seconds, I stood, nervous and lonely, under the sullen sky.

Then the huge oak door was swung back, as though our arrival had been noted, and the opening of the door timed precisely to coincide with it. A footman came out, bowed to me, and indicated that I should enter.

I stood and looked at the scene before me; the opening door had been like a curtain lifted on a tableau. Before me, was a great hall, its walls hung with rich tapestries; there were silk rugs on the floor, chairs and coffers of intricately carved wood everywhere.

On either side of the great, curving staircase, twin lamps

burned in silver holders; other lamps, set in the walls, gave light enough for me to see clearly the two women waiting for me.

One woman was beautiful; the other, standing a few paces behind her, and obviously a servant, was very plain.

"I am your Cousin Selina," said the first woman, in a soft, pretty voice. "Welcome to Sandleford, Catherine. I am sorry that Troy is not here. He has had to go to Portsmouth on urgent business."

She came towards me and kissed my cheek. She smelled of clove carnations, a scent both warm and spicy. Her hair was pale gold, dressed in a high, old-fashioned style that suited her lively face.

I had never seen anyone so beautiful as Selina; any woman would have seemed dull and ordinary beside her. She had eyes of a deep violet colour, a creamy skin, a soft, rosy mouth. Her dress, in a delicate shade of blue, was both fashionable and expensive, and suited her small, slender figure perfectly.

I murmured a greeting, and looked past her at the servant.

She was tall and thin, sallow-complexioned, her black hair going grey and scraped back in a hard knot from her bony face. She was tall and strongly built; the plain black dress with its buttoned bodice showed the flatness of her breasts, the narrowness of her hips.

Selina saw my glance, and said:

"That is Marie, Catherine. She has been with me since I was a child."

I smiled, as best I could, at the woman; she acknowledged me with a brief bob that was, somehow, more an insult than a courtesy. Her black eyes were small, bright and hard.

"You must be cold and famished," Selina murmured. "Did Rufus look after you?"

"Excellently," I said.

She smiled at Rufus, and then turned to me, her eyes bright with excitement.

"We shall have so much to talk about, Catherine. I did not know, until just before Grandfather died, that my Uncle Daniel had a daughter. I imagined I had no relations living."

"As I did," I told her.

"Now I have a cousin; so have *you*!" She squeezed my arm affectionately, and called over her shoulder to Marie.

"Ask Milly to come here, Marie."

Selina turned again to me.

"Milly will show you to your rooms, and see that you have all you need. When you are ready, she will bring you to the drawing-room, and we will have tea. Milly will look after you all the time you are here; she is your servant."

It sounded very grand; I was over-awed at the thought of having a servant to myself.

"Seton and Agnes will join us for tea," Selina explained. "Rufus has told you about them?"

I nodded, and she told me:

"Seton is kindness itself to Agnes, and has devoted himself to her welfare since her accident. He brings her over to see me every day. It is good for her to get out of the house and I enjoy her company."

"We have seen Alannah," Rufus told her; and he recounted the incident in detail. She sighed and looked exasperated. At that moment, Milly arrived.

"Take Miss Fairfax to her room, Milly. Thompson will bring up the heavy luggage, later."

Milly took my hand-luggage from me. She was a tall, thin girl, with a permanently-worried look and a frizz of sandy hair half-hidden by her cap.

I followed her up the shallow-stepped staircase; at the top was a big gallery, with settles ranged around the walls, and, above them, a great many portraits in heavy gilt frames; severe-looking men, plump women and solemn children stared down at me, dressed in the fashions of previous centuries.

To left and right, were long wide corridors, with here and there a flight of stairs leading to upper floors. The carpet beneath my feet was thick and soft; we passed small niches in which stood statuettes and ornaments. I saw a squat, grinning Buddha carved from alabaster, a jade figure of the Chinese Goddess of Mercy, Kuan-Yin. There were porcelain bowls and jars, their surfaces painted with brilliant designs of birds, trees, flowers and butterflies.

At intervals along the walls, were pairs of lamps, wrought

in chased silver, with shades of rosy silk. Each pair of lamps had a matching mirror between it, the frame wreathed in fruit and flowers of silver.

The evidence of so much wealth completely subdued me; Sandleford was a magnificent place; almost a palace.

At the end of the corridor, we stopped at a door on our right. Milly opened it and stood aside for me to enter.

Delighted, I realised I had been given a tower room.

"This is the bedroom, Miss ..." Milly said.

A vast bed, with a crimson brocade coverlet, embroidered with flowers, dominated the room. The headboard was of rich black lacquer, painted with Oriental scenes in crimson and gold. The furniture was of the same lacquer, some of it inlaid with mother of pearl, and the curtains matched the brocade of the bedspread. On either side of the ornately carved fireplace were silver gas-brackets, similar to those in the hall outside.

The curtains were not yet drawn; I walked over to the window and looked at the parkland spread below me, blurred in the chill mist of early evening.

"This is a splendid room," I said.

"Mr. Merrick had this one specially furnished for you, miss," she told me. "Here's your dressing-room."

She opened a door and led me into a small room; cupboards lined the walls, and there was a sewing box on a table, nearby, together with a high-backed chair.

I looked at a pair of magnificent fans on the dressing-room wall.

Each fan was a peacock's tail, spread open to display its exquisite colouring. The base of the fan was carved and enamelled to represent a peacock's head, with tiny jewels for eyes, and small stones outlined each cruel, curved veak.

"They are *beautiful*!" I breathed, entranced. "What a pity to hide them away in here."

"Some say peacocks is unlucky, miss," Milly pointed out solemnly.

"I'm not superstitious!" I told her.

I discovered that I had a sitting-room of my own; Milly led me back into the bedroom and pulled aside a heavy velvet curtain; behind it, carpeted steps led downwards.

I followed her down the stairs. There was no door at the bottom, only an archway leading into a very masculine-looking room.

It had the bland impersonality of a room that has not been used for a long time, and so has lost the imprint of its owner's personality. It was much less luxurious than my bedroom; but the walls were lined with books, there was a big writing desk, several armchairs, and a chaise-longue that had obviously been an afterthought.

The windows of all my rooms looked out over the front of the house; this room was immediately below my bedroom, and there was no way in and out, save through the arch and up to the bedroom; it made the place very cosy and self-contained.

"You have your own bathroom, too, miss," Milly explained. "Just across the corridor from your bedroom, but *quite* private, for no one comes this far unless it's to the tower rooms, and they are *your* rooms now."

"How old are you, Milly?" I asked her.

"Nearly eighteen, Miss."

"Have you been here long?"

"No, miss, only since Lallie ..." she bit her lip. "That is, six months. I came last July."

"What became of Lallie?" I asked casually.

"Drowned in the lily pool," Milly whispered, swallowing nervously. "Fell from the window, I was told. It was a hot day, and they was all open. I expect she leaned out too far."

"*Which* window?" I asked slowly, remembering the lily pool far below me.

"Your bedroom, miss. I'm not supposed to tell you."

I managed a smile.

"That's all right! I won't give you away. After all, *I* asked."

Milly breathed a sigh of relief.

"It was an accident. Accidents DO happen, miss."

"Yes, I know. Now, may I have some hot water?"

After I had washed, she helped me to change into an afternoon dress, and brushed my hair. I dabbed eau-de-cologne on my wrists, and followed her down to the drawing-room, feeling refreshed and trying not to remember how Mrs. Armond had poured scorn on the suggestion that her niece had taken her life.

Selina was seated by the fire. It was a large room, full of exquisite porcelain and silver; there was a table covered with a fine lace cloth, in front of my cousin, and a trolley set with an elaborate silver tea-service and spirit kettle.

She smiled and held out her hand to me; then turned towards a man standing by the fireplace, who came forward to greet me.

"Catherine come and meet my very good friends: Seton Blair and Agnes Oakes."

Seton Blair was tall and slim. He had a fine head of thick, wheat-coloured hair, and blue eyes. They were almost turquoise-coloured, and, with his fair hair, produced an attractive and unusual combination of good looks. His features were clear-cut; his look was penetrating, his smile slow in coming.

"I am delighted to make your acquaintance, Miss Fairfax," he said conventionally.

Agnes Oakes, in her wheel chair, was a small woman, the same build as Selina. There, the resemblance ended. Agnes had dull brown hair, dead-leaf in colour, smoothly dressed over her ears, and fastened in a loose bun on her neck. Her skin was pale, as though she spent most of her life indoors, her mouth looked tight as if she disciplined it against too much smiling. Her eyes were deep and dark and secretive.

The drab grey dress did nothing for her; it was fastened at the throat with a small gold brooch and she wore no other jewellery, save a pearl and garnet engagement ring on the third finger of her left hand.

She gave me a long, cool, thoughtful look; her smile was pleasant but cautious. Yet I sensed that though the Creightons had probably subdued her spirit, they had certainly not broken it.

"Miss Fairfax," she said, offering me a cool, dry hand that held my fingertips with surprising firmness.

"Oh, we mustn't be formal!" Selina cried. "It is 'Catherine' my brand-new cousin. Come and sit by me, Catherine."

"Where is Alannah?" Agnes enquired.

Selina shrugged, looking exasperated.

"Still hiding in the Chapel, presumably. She almost ran under the coach wheels, Rufus says. Troy is the only one of whom she takes notice."

"Naturally, my dear Selina," Seton retorted, with raised eyebrows.

Selina glanced quickly at me, and then bent her head over the teapot.

"Alannah is Troy's daughter, Catherine," she said unhappily. "Not mine."

"I understand. Rufus has told me."

"Troy's business takes him to the far corners of the earth, and means that he is absent from home a great deal," she explained, as though apologising for Troy's misdemeanours.

"I would not have said it was in keeping with Troy's character to bring his illegitimate child here," Agnes said unexpectedly.

I thought I saw disapproval in Seton's face for her remark. He merely said:

"My dear Agnes, we all know that Troy is a law unto himself; and an unpredictable man."

"Troy is a man who enjoys the pleasures of the flesh," Rufus added, so quietly that only I heard him.

"I should like to hear the Sandleford legends," I said quickly.

Selina nodded. Then her hands dropped into her lap and her face grew still, as the door opened.

Troy stood there, one arm around Alannah's shoulders.

He had the same effect on me that I had experienced the first time we met; he radiated a very powerful magnetism that was so positive everyone stopped talking and the room was as still as though no one breathed.

His eyes met mine; cold, clear green eyes. I looked away uneasily from that powerful glance and smiled nervously at Alannah.

She was small for her age, with straight dark hair brushed back from her face and held in place by a velvet band. Her eyes were dark, her face pale. She shrank closer to Troy, and I saw her small fists clenched and then unclench in the folds of her skirt.

I wondered under what circumstances she had been conceived. Had he satisfied a moment's hunger, carelessly? Had Alannah's mother yielded out of fear or generosity? Or had their coming together to create a child been a mating of tenderness and mutual longing?

"I did not expect you back so soon," Selina said, in a small, colourless voice. "Will you have tea?"

"Yes. Alannah will also have tea with us."

It was a command. Selina looked subdued. Seton and Rufus were trying to seem unconcerned. Agnes was watching Alannah intently. For some reason, the presence of Troy made everyone ill at ease.

Troy himself was evidently quite unaware of the impact he had created. He brought Alannah across to me.

"Alannah, this is Catherine Fairfax. She has come here to live with us. You will have someone to walk in the grounds with you, and be company for you. There was no need for you to be afraid of her; she has not come to take you away."

His voice was reassuring; the child looked half-defiantly, half-timidly at me.

"Alannah does not speak," Troy added, for my benefit.

"Rufus has already explained that to me."

He turned to the child.

"Sit beside Catherine. You may have some milk and some cake."

She sat stiffly on the small brocaded chair beside me. Her feet didn't reach the floor. She looked so pathetic that I felt a deep compassion for her. It was not right that she should have been thrust so unceremoniously into such a strange household of adults.

To Selina, I thought, she can only be a flagrant reminder of her husband's unfaithfulness.

Troy took a shallow, flowered teacup from his wife. Their fingers touched, but their eyes did not meet. He walked across to the window, and stood surveying us all; his masterful air annoyed me. Why could he not sit down, as anyone else would have done? He was like an Emperor surveying his kingdom.

"Selina was about to tell Catherine the legends," Seton said, breaking the silence.

Selina's face took on a dreamy quality; excitement danced in her eyes.

"Everyone enjoys hearing about the Sandleford Legend, Catherine. It goes back to the eighteenth century. There was a shoemaker living in the village of North Meon, near here. His name was Tom Gringle; everyone said how talented he was, what beautiful shoes he made.

"They say the Devil heard about Tom Gringle's cleverness. He was on his way to a Ball at Sandleford, to be given by my ancestor, Argus Fairfax. The local people were afraid of Argus; they said he was in league with the powers of Darkness. He had a daughter, Anna, who had been lame from birth.

"Tom Gringle and Anna were in love. Secretly, because Argus Fairfax would never have let his only daughter marry the village shoemaker.

"The Devil rode into the village, stopped at Tom Gringle's shop and demanded that Tom make him a pair of shoes to wear to the Ball, without delay. He could name his own fee, Tom was told. So Tom, recognising the Devil, was bold enough to say that his fee was a cure for Anna's lameness.

"The Devil agreed. He told Tom to make a second pair of shoes to fit Anna. He was very precise in his instructions for Anna's shoes, as well as for his own dancing shoes: both were to be of scarlet leather, very soft and supple. Anna's shoes were to have golden heels.

"So Tom Gringle worked all day and night and had the shoes ready in time for the Ball next evening. The Devil was pleased with the shoes. Tom didn't go to the Ball, of course, but he heard that Anna danced exquisitely, all night through, and that the Devil fell in love with her, and tried, by every means in his power, to persuade her to go away with him; he was angry when she refused.

"The legend says that at dawn next morning, the Devil took the shoes from Anna and hid them in this house; he swore he would one day return and dance with her again, in the ballroom, and this time she would *not* refuse him.

"They say Anna was completely changed, after that night. She didn't see Tom Gringle again, and he was heartbroken. She was silent and withdrawn, she never danced, and spent her days searching for the shoes. In the end, she was completely unbalanced. The Devil didn't return, but people said he had left ill-luck in the house. Anna's brother, the heir to Sandleford, married and had two sons, one of whom was an idiot. His daughter, Sibella, died in infancy. His surviving son, who inherited Sandleford, had an accident that crippled him. Night after night, Anna stood at the window, watching for the Devil to return. One night, she was found drowned in the lily-pond. The window was wide open; there was a violent thunderstorm that night. People say the Devil came to claim her."

I thought about Lallie. The room was very hot; the heat of the fire was too great, and I was tired after my journey.

The faintness passed away. Selina brought her tale to a dramatic conclusion.

"To this day, no one has ever found the shoes!"

"We have certainly looked for them!" Rufus retorted, laughing. "Do you remember the times we searched the house, when we were children, Selina?"

I saw Alannah's wide eyes, her fixed expression; it didn't seem to me to be a particularly suitable tale to be told in front of a child.

"Rufus said there were two legends," I said to Selina.

She nodded.

"After the misfortunes," Selina said, "a strange visitor came here, in the middle of winter. Some say she was a novitiate. Argus told her she could have food and shelter for as long as she pleased. It was bitterly cold, that winter; he looked from his window, one day, and saw her walking barefoot, where the Chapel now stands. He was horrified, until he saw that she didn't seem to be affected by the intense cold. She was wearing a long white robe and a blue cloak, and she appeared to be praying as she walked.

"Soon afterwards, she left as suddenly as she had come and was never seen again. Argus Fairfax, thinking to destroy or minimise the Devil's curse, had the ground consecrated and a Chapel built where the woman had walked. The following winter, the snowdrops appeared, like footprints. They have grown there more thickly each winter, since then; the house has had more than its share of ill-luck and disaster, still, but they say whoever shelters in the Chapel is safe from the powers of Darkness."

There was a moment's silence; Rufus said lightly:

"Of course, such a thing was not really possible!"

"As possible as lameness cured for a night!" Troy argued.

I thought of the scarlet shoes, with the twinkling heels, in all their impudent beauty. Red was the Devil's own colour.

I thought of the white flowers growing around the Chapel; white had always represented purity. Evil and good were forever at war here. One woman had danced with the Devil; one had walked barefooted in midwinter.

"They say Anna can sometimes be heard dancing at night," Rufus told me. "For the Devil punished her more than by a return to lameness. He said that, after her death, she would be compelled to dance forever, wearing the shoes that were his gift to her. They say the sound of her dancing was first heard on the night she died!"

I laughed.

"On Hallowe'en, Lammas, Walpurgis Night and Midsummer Eve, also?" I teased.

"Grandfather declared he heard it," Selina insisted. "Some say it is always heard on the anniversary of the Ball; or in the rooms she occupied."

"Which rooms were those?" I asked.

"The ones you are in; are you nervous, Catherine?" Rufus teased.

"No," I replied calmly.

"It was Troy's idea that you should have those rooms," Selina told me.

His eyebrows rose.

"I made a sensible choice. Catherine is obviously not easily scared."

"I forgot to tell you," Selina added, "you must never NEVER pick the snowdrops and bring them indoors. It is considered to bring ill-luck to the household."

Troy turned to Alannah, and ruffled her hair; her eyes were huge.

"That is an end to fairytales for today. Go to the nursery, now. Catherine will come and talk to you, later."

Looking relieved; she walked out of the room, a small,

lonely figure; perhaps she was missing her mother.

With Alannah's departure, the others left. Seton wheeled Agnes from the room, saying it was time they returned to Ashmead. Rufus took his leave of us, saying that he had business to attend to and Troy asked me, rather belatedly, I thought, if my journey had been a pleasant one.

"Very pleasant," I told him coolly. "I was in good company. Rufus was an entertaining companion."

Troy stood, tall, splendid-looking, his head thrown back; his back to the window, hands clasped behind him. Dominating the scene, as always. Dwarfing us all by the power of his personality.

"You are not dismayed at the thought of sleeping in the tower rooms?" he asked.

"Not at all." If I had been scared half out of my wits, I would not have said so.

"The haunted rooms," Selina murmured, her eyes huge and brilliant.

"Nonsense. There is no truth in the tale of Anna and the Devil," he retorted.

Selina tossed her head, pink colour in her cheeks. It was obvious that Troy and his wife were estranged. Whether permanently or temporarily, I did not know.

"This is your home, now," Troy told me. "You also are a Fairfax, Catherine."

I lifted my head and looked back at him, meeting those cold green eyes with an inward shiver.

"I shall not live here permanently; I must set about earning a living," I retorted.

"At what?" he demanded, the corners of his lips twitching into a sardonic smile that infuriated me.

"A governess."

"The last resort of the impecunious young miss! Not *you*, Catherine! A governess must conduct herself with due humility, and be subservient. YOU could never be at the beck and call of a pack of snivelling little brats!"

"You know nothing about me!" I replied, infuriated by his high-handedness.

"After only a short acquaintance, I know a great deal about you!"

"That is an arrogant statement!"

"I am an arrogant man. I am also your guardian until you are twenty-one."

"My Aunt decided the matter, not me!" I pointed out.

"You do not approve?" he asked, his eyes bright with malicious amusement.

"No," I replied shortly.

"How sad, Catherine! You have no alternative but to accept your Aunt's choice. How that must gall you! However, in a little over a year, you will be twenty-one and may then do as you please. Until then, you will remain under my roof, and be obedient to my wishes concerning your welfare."

Obedient? I all but choked on the word!

I hated Troy Merrick. I stared angrily at him, and he returned my glance with a look that was quite unperturbed. Selina said nothing, but her face looked strained and anxious as she glanced from one to the other of us.

"If you wish to make yourself useful," Troy added, "then you can be a companion to Alannah. That may ease the discomfort of your tight-pinching pride."

His sudden, devil-may-care look was as fascinating as his deep voice; but I reminded myself that it was all part of his magician's sleight-of-hand, performed to trick me into believing I saw a person who did not really exist.

When I did not reply, he added softly:

"Pride, like conscience, is a most uncomfortable companion, Catherine!"

"Not if one treats both with the respect they deserve."

"Is that an original observation? Or do you quote from some sage I have not had the pleasure of reading?" he mocked.

"The observation is my own," I replied coolly.

I thought I might enjoy looking after the strange child who was this man's daughter; the idea attracted me. It would give me something constructive to do, and I hated being idle.

Troy took my silence for doubt.

"God give me patience!" he cried furiously. "Any other young woman of your age, and in your situation, would welcome the prospect before her, especially when the alternatives are so much less attractive. Be damned to you, Catherine Fairfax, you may please yourself what you do! I wash my hands of you!"

With that, he strode from the room, wrenching open the door, and crashing it resoundingly behind him.

After his departure, the silence seemed infinite, deep as a bottomless pit. Selina broke it, her voice troubled.

"Troy has a violent temper, Catherine. It is wiser not to cross him in any way. He demands absolute subjection to his wishes, in all things."

"Then I shall be a great disappointment to him!" I retorted, with a show of bravado. "He cannot *force* me to stay here, even until I come of age."

"If you tried to leave, he would have you brought back; if he was challenged, he would say that you are incapable of earning your living in the world outside. He would produce whatever reasons he thought fit to keep you here."

"Why should he wish for such an unwilling captive?"

"He enjoys having power over people. He is wily as well as strong."

I stared down at the woman who was as beautiful and fragile-looking as a piece of valuable porcelain.

"Are you happy in your marriage?" I asked bluntly.

She stared down at the hands folded in her lap, so that I could not see her face; her voice was low and tremulous.

"He has been generous to me; the house was in a sorry state because Grandfather refused to spend money on it. He said the place was cursed. Troy had the whole house completely restored, filled it with treasures, made a handsome settlement upon me. He gave me jewels and fine things, and a position as his wife that I did not have before. I am grateful to him; also, as I am his wife, I must obey him."

I felt so sorry for her, that I could have knelt and put my arms around her, but shyness prevented me from doing so. For the first time I realised why Aunt Vee had never married; to be shackled for life to a man like Troy Merrick would be a terrible punishment.

Selina obviously regretted the choice she had made; but there could have been no other for HER, I thought. Unlike me, she was not fitted to battle with the world.

"I was lonely here, as a child," she told me. "Grandfather shunned company. He would not even tolerate servants around him, save only Kellatt, the head groom, Mrs. Treville, who first came here when Grandfather was a young man; and my faithful Marie, who has always looked after me. When Troy arrived, he was like a splendid being from another world. I was completely swept from my feet."

I could well understand that.

She looked at me, as though there was something else she would have told me; she seemed to change her mind, grasping my hand, suddenly, with surprising strength, her eyes full of tears.

"I am so glad that you are here, Catherine! When I knew that you were to come to Sandleford, I was overjoyed. I am lonelier, now, than before I was married, for I believed I would have a husband whom I could lean upon, who would give, and wish to receive, affection from me; but Troy does not need the kind of affection I would give. There is much you do not know about the Master of Sandleford, Catherine. Much that it is better you should *never* know."

I thought about her words, as I went upstairs, past the portraits of dead and gone Fairfaxes, along the silent corridor to my room.

I had never thought of myself as imaginative. Yet I had a feeling that I was being watched and followed. An awareness of something wholly evil clung persistently to the edges of my mind; twice, I scolded myself for looking over my shoulder.

I was glad to reach the door of my own rooms in the West Tower. The toe of my shoe touched something soft, and I drew my skirts back instinctively.

Lying at my feet was what appeared to be a crumpled white handkerchief.

I went and looked closely. It was a posy of snowdrops.

I remembered Selina's words, as I picked them up.

"You must never pick any snowdrops and bring them indoors. It is said that a death will follow if snowdrops brought into this house."

Who had left them there—for me—I wondered?

Chapter Three

They looked so innocent, so soft, as I held them in my trembling hand; the bunch had been tightly tied with a piece of thread.

I opened the door and went into my bedroom; someone was moving about in the dressing-room.

"Who is there?" I called; and Milly appeared in the doorway, looking guilty and flustered.

"You didn't 'arf give me a start, miss!" she protested.

Then she saw what I was holding and looked horrified.

"You NEVER went and picked them snowdrops, miss?"

"No, Milly, I did *not*. I found these outside my door, a moment ago."

"Who would have done such a thing?" she said sceptically. "It's unlucky to pick the snowdrops. Didn't nobody tell you?"

"Yes. Mrs. Merrick told me. *Someone* must have picked them."

"Well, it wasn't me," she muttered, aggrieved.

"How long have you been in here?"

"About ten minutes." Her manner was both nervous and defiant. "I was drawing the curtains, then I was going to turn down your bed. I know I'm not supposed to do it until you've gone down to dinner, but Mrs. Treville said I might go early if I was finished."

"You didn't hear or see anyone?"

"No, miss."

I stared down at the bunch of snowdrops I held. Milly's pale blue eyes were apprehensive.

"Best let me throw them away, miss."

"No," I said shortly. "I shall put them in a vase. They look very pretty. I don't see how these flowers can bring ill-luck, especially considering the legend that surrounds them. If someone meant to play a practical joke on me, then I'm not going to give them any satisfaction."

"Don't keep 'em," she pleaded earnestly. " 'Tis unlucky, whatever you may say, miss."

"How do you know that? Has anyone ever brought them into the house before?"

"Miss Alannah picked some, last week. The mistress was very upset."

"Well? Has anything happened?" I persisted. "Anything bad or strange, that is?"

"Not yet, miss."

There was a significance in the word 'yet' that made my lips twitch. I refused to be intimidated. I did not believe in bad luck, signs and omens; not even though there was an atmosphere about this house that I did not like.

"Well, then!" I said briskly, "that proves the tale is nonsense. Nothing is going to happen."

Milly looked at me as though I was mad.

"What shall I put out for you to wear for dinner, miss?" she asked.

"You needn't stay to help me dress for dinner, Milly; I've always done it for myself," I told her drily.

Her face flushed with pleasure, as she stammered her thanks; obviously she had a follower waiting outside the high walls of Sandleford.

I lifted the small watch pinned to my bodice; it was more than an hour to dinner time.

"Will you show me the way to Miss Alannah's room, please?" I asked her.

As we walked along the corridor, I asked Milly if she had ever heard the sound of Anna dancing.

Her eyes were round; she shook her head.

"Never miss! Nor would I wish to!" she declared vehemently.

I asked who looked after Alannah.

"Well, there's Julia keeps her room clean, Betty does her

washing, me or Katy sees to her meals. Poor little thing, not being able to speak! She just looks at us all with those great eyes of hers."

We went up a short flight of stairs to the Nursery, and Milly tapped at a door.

"Come in!" called a woman's voice.

"This is Mrs. Treville," Milly said to me, ushering me in. The woman who had been sitting by the fire near Alannah had a round face, guileless eyes and a bun of white hair. She looked hard at me.

"Are you Miss Catherine Fairfax?" she asked.

"I am," I said.

"You're not much like your father in looks," she told me.

Milly left the room, closing the door behind her; Alannah sat with a picture book on her lap, watching us gravely.

"Did you know my father well?" I asked Mrs. Treville.

"Indeed I did! I was here before your father was born. He was a right handful as a boy, too. He and his brother did their lessons in this room. Look, there's his name!"

I looked at the initials scratched on the scarred desk. 'D.F.' Damon Fairfax, Daniel Fairfax. I felt a moment's sadness that I had never known either of them.

"*Fight*?" Mrs. Treville was laughing. "I never saw two boys fight like they did. The times I've separated them and sent them to old Mr. Damon for a dressing-down. The Mistress—your grandmother—couldn't manage either of her lads."

"Do you know what became of my father?" I asked curiously.

"No, Miss Catherine. He and his father never got on, and Mr. Daniel up and went one day. We never saw him again. We'd heard he married, and that there was a child; that was all we knew, until Mr. Merrick said that *you* were Mr. Daniel's daughter and would be coming here to live."

"So my father never came back here, after the quarrel?"

"No," she said positively.

I sighed.

"I'll sit with Alannah awhile, Mrs. Treville," I said.

At the door, she paused.

"Mr. Daniel wasn't much more than a boy when he left.

He was so full of ideas, planning all the things he was going to do in the great world outside. It upset the old man dreadful; he'd set his heart on Mr. Daniel following in his footsteps, and helping his brother to look after the place.''

She closed the door, with a great sigh. It was no use sighing over lost yesterdays, I thought. My father was dead; otherwise he would have come back, long ago.

I pulled up a chair beside Alannah, and gently took the book from her.

"I see you're reading 'The Red Shoes'? It's very like the tale you heard downstairs, isn't it? They are only fairy-tales, you know. I liked the story of the Lady of the Snows."

She nodded and put a hand timidly on my arm. It was a small victory, I felt.

"So you like the Lady of the Snows? Is that why you go to the Chapel?" I asked.

Again she nodded, more vigorously this time. I took her small, cold hand in mine.

"Did you go and hide there today because you didn't want to meet me?" I asked.

She shook her head and shivered; her eyes troubled me, they were so big and scared.

"What frightened you?" I asked gently; but she shook her head stubbornly.

Anxious to change the direction of her thoughts, I picked up a pad and a pencil.

"Write your name for me. We shall have to learn to get along with pencil and paper as you cannot talk to me," I said.

She printed her name in large, clear letters, but made no attempt to add her second name. I thought it would be imprudent to press the matter.

She drew a ship, with a small, matchstick figure standing on the deck. She pointed to the figure, then to herself, and then added a much taller figure.

"That's the ship you came to England in, and that's Mr. Merrick beside you. You sailed from Australia, didn't you?"

She nodded gravely. I looked at the face upturned to mine and could see nothing of her father in her.

Slowly, she turned the pages of the book. I looked at the

flames flickering behind the wire guard, the two desks and chairs and rows of books, the ancient Globe, the counting frame and blackboard. It must seem very strange to Alannah, after life in Australia, I thought.

Alannah held up the book; it was open at the Story of the Ugly Duckling. Unselfconsciously, she climbed on my lap and I held her close to me, feeling strangely contented. It was the first time I had ever held a child.

I didn't care—as Selina must obviously care—that she was Troy's illegitimate daughter. It was no fault of the child's that she was in such an unenviable position.

I read the story to her; when I had finished, she smiled her thanks.

"Are you happy here, Alannah?" I asked her.

To my dismay, she shook her head vehemently, and clung to me with a fierceness that made me uneasy.

"What is it?" I whispered, forgetting that she could not speak.

She shook her head again; no child should look so desolate, I thought, angry and perplexed.

"Alannah, is anyone here unkind to you?"

She stared at me, without answering, as though she was afraid to deny or confirm the fact.

"Not—Mrs. Merrick?" I faltered.

To my relief, she shook her head. At that moment, there was a knock at the door; a maid came in, with two slices of bread and butter and a glass of milk on a tray.

"Your supper, miss," she said to Alannah.

"Who are you?" I asked.

"I'm Katy, miss."

The girl spoke pleasantly enough and Alannah did not seem afraid of her.

This child is alone with servants far too much, I reflected. I agreed with Rufus that she needed someone to be responsible for her. The thought of being a companion for her, as Troy had suggested, seemed a good idea. I bent and kissed her goodnight.

"Tomorrow," I told her, "we will go for a walk, and you shall show me the Chapel."

She clung to me for a second; Katy's look expressed

disapproval at such a display of emotion, but I thought that the child was missing her mother badly.

Rufus escorted me into dinner; he saw that I was nervous.

"You look as fresh and cool as a waterlily," he told me. "You are altogether charming, Catherine, and a delightful addition to the household. I, for one, thoroughly approve of your being here and intend to become better acquainted with you without delay. Ah! Your look says you think I am a flirt. It will be pleasant to flirt with you, and if my words—though they are the truth and no less—give you confidence tonight, I'm well pleased!"

The dining-room at Sandleford was a vast, splendid room; the table appointments would have graced a royal banquet; at the head of the table, Troy looked like some splendid, remote Emperor; evening dress suited him.

Selina looked exquisite in rich oyster-coloured satin that had a mother-of-pearl sheen; there were emeralds at her throat and in her ears. Her face looked strained, and her eyes were watchful.

Troy acknowledged our entrance with a curt nod. The meal was served by a footman and a maid. Selina scarcely touched the courses put before her.

"What ails you?" Troy demanded sharply.

"Nothing," she said quietly.

"Then why do you not eat?"

"Because I am not hungry. Don't remind me, once again, Troy, that a starving family would live for weeks on the food we eat—and leave—at one meal!" she added, with an unexpected flash of spirit.

Her cheeks were pink, her blue eyes were brilliant, as they met his cold ones defiantly.

The servants were well-trained, their faces impassive. Troy looked away from Selina, and his glance met mine. His powerful eyes were the colour of Selina's emeralds, and I could not unlock my glance from his, no matter how hard I tried.

Nervously I said the first thing that came into my head.

"Why is Alannah dumb?"

"She suffered a severe shock," he replied calmly; and still that piercing glance held mine.

"What kind of shock?" I asked.

"She saw her mother raped," Troy replied, without any emotion in his voice.

There was a moment's silence; Selina gave him an angry glance.

"You should not say such things in front of the servants!" she whispered vehemently.

"Our servants are not blind and deaf," Troy retorted. "They must wonder why Alannah does not speak. What happens above stairs is of the greatest interest to those who live below stairs. Is that not true, Hoskins?"

The footman blushed deep red, but the hand holding the dish towards Troy remained steady.

"Sir? We do not gossip below stairs," he replied.

"You are a liar," Troy said amiably.

"My father would never have behaved as you do!" Selina told him angrily.

"Your father was a gentleman. I have often reminded you that I am not one. Nor do I pretend to be one. I enjoy the fruits of success: fine clothes, good food, good wine; but I do not forget I was once the barefoot boy, living in a hovel. A boy who left the rat-infested alleys of Portsea to sail away and make a fortune. Surely a man is to be congratulated on such an achievement?"

His glance challenged Selina, who looked away, and shrugged, tight-lipped.

"IS it not a matter for congratulation, Catherine?" Troy asked me.

"That depends."

"On what?"

"Whether or not success has given you happiness as well as material comforts."

His look was angry; deliberately, and in silence, he went on with his meal. Selina sat up very straight, staring ahead of her, signalling to the footman to remove her untouched plate.

As for me, I had lost my appetite and didn't dare show the fact. I ate half-heartedly.

At the end of the meal, Troy dismissed the servants, selected a peach, and peeled it with a small silver knife, as though he had all the time in the world. I looked at the strong, well-kept hands and wondered how he had obtained such wealth. By work alone? Or had he reached his pinnacle by other routes, as well?

"Have you no shame?" Selina demanded suddenly.

"I'm not aware that I should be ashamed of anything I have said," he retorted.

"Alannah is the child of one of your many mistresses!"

"Many? How you flatter me! I have had only a few."

Selina rose to her feet, looking over his head.

"I am going to my room," she announced.

Troy and Rufus both stood up. Rufus looked uncomfortable. Troy crossed the room and held the door open for Selina, with exquisite courtesy; she swept past him without a word or a glance, her head held high; but I thought I saw the glimmer of tears on her long lashes.

"Who raped the child's mother?" Rufus asked bluntly, as Troy took his place at the table, again.

"A drunken miner. He broke into the small house in Sydney where Alannah was alone with her mother. He was notorious for his violence and his appetite, and he had been drinking heavily. Alannah's mother died some time afterwards; she never really recovered from the incident."

"Was the man caught?" I asked.

"Yes; and lynched," Troy replied, with great satisfaction.

"Australia seems to be a rough country," I commented.

"It is raw, tough and vigorous, my dear Catherine. If the justice is rough, then it is only to be expected. It is a tremendous place; vast, full of wealth which only a few have as yet discovered. It is a land of opportunity, that will break a man's heart and his back or give him riches and power."

"It made YOU powerful," Rufus said.

"I took the opportunities offered to me. I was ready to grasp them, and I was not afraid to work until my hands were raw," Troy retorted arrogantly. "I helped to build roads, tend sheep, clear land, pan for gold. The gold I found bought me sheep and land of my own; more important——it bought me the first of my ships, when I returned to this country. The Golden Princess."

"A very fanciful name for a ship," Rufus murmured, with a lift of his eyebrows.

Troy's look was hostile. I wondered if the ship had been named after a woman.

"I can recommend Australia to you, Rufus," Troy commented, with a hint of sarcasm.

Rufus smiled lazily.

"I'll play you a game of chess instead," he offered.

"Not this evening."

Troy's voice was curt. Rufus shrugged, looked ruefully at me, and announced his intention of going for a walk in the fresh air, if I would excuse him.

That left me alone with Troy in the big dining-room; I was ill-at-ease.

"Someone left a posy of snowdrops outside my door," I told him.

His eyebrows rose; his face was amused, a hint of devilishness lay behind his smile.

"Not a well-wisher, surely? The rule against picking snowdrops is strictly observed in this house."

His amusement stung me to anger.

"Hardly the way to greet a guest," I replied. "Whoever did it has not succeeded in frightening me!" I looked closely at him. "The flowers were too pretty to discard. I have told Milly to find a vase for them."

He laughed delightedly.

"Are you brave or foolhardy, Catherine?"

"Many people think the two attributes are one and the same. Did *you* place the snowdrops outside my door?"

"I am not in the habit of wandering around Sandleford clutching posies of flowers as anonymous gifts for young ladies!" he mocked.

He gave me a wicked, sideways glance; he generated in me an extraordinary combination of fear and excitement. I felt as breathless as if I was running uphill; exposed and naked, as though he could read my mind.

I searched for a new topic of conversation; anything was better than enduring that cold, penetrating glance.

"How does Rufus entertain himself in the evenings?" I asked.

"How on earth should I know? I daresay he and Selina find a great deal to talk about; perhaps he follows other, more interesting, pursuits."

I tried again.

"How long will Alannah be staying with you?"

His eyes narrowed; he was like a tiger ready to pounce.

"As long as I choose; why?"

"I merely wished to know how long I shall be looking after her."

"What does that matter? This is your home, now."

"You cannot keep me here if I do not wish to stay!"

"I can, Catherine, and I will. I am your guardian until you come of age."

"This is little over a year, thank goodness!" I cried.

"Why do you dislike me so much?"

I could not answer him. I couldn't say: I don't understand you, and people always fear what they do not understand.

He leant across the table, his eyes dancing.

"I swear that you have a passionate heart under that very proper exterior of yours!" he said.

"An indelicate remark," I retorted, tossing my head, and trying to look dignified.

Abruptly, Troy pushed back his chair, got to his feet and held out his hand.

"Come with me," he ordered.

He caught hold of my hand; carelessly, as though he was leading a child. His fingers were warm and firm. I trembled, without knowing why. I did not want to come too close to this man; he was dangerous, I thought.

Troy led me from the room, across the great hall and upstairs to the picture gallery.

He pointed out a portrait that had pride of place, in the centre.

Inside the ornate gilt frame, was a picture of a plump, olive-skinned woman with masses of heavy dark hair. She had a full, sensuous mouth, and rather close-set dark eyes. Her nose was too long, her mouth too wide; her hands, folded in her lap, were heavy with rings.

"Anna," he said.

"She is not beautiful," I commented, disappointed.

"Perhaps the artist didn't do her justice." He looked at me, unsmiling. "Perhaps her beauty was the intangible kind that cannot easily be repeated on canvas."

He moved along the gallery.

"Come and look at your father, as a young man."

There had been nothing of Troy in Alannah's face. In the face I studied now, I could see nothing of myself.

My father did not look like a man with sufficient strength of character to turn his back on such an inheritance as Sandleford. Nevertheless, his blue eyes gazed steadily at me. There was kindness as well as good-humour in his face; my mother had loved him enough to leave her home and family for him.

Beside my father's portrait was one of a heavy-jowled, unsmiling man, whose piercing eyes seemed intent on searching out my most secret thoughts.

"That is your grandfather," Troy told me.

Beside Damon Fairfax was a portrait of Selina, magnificent in a ball-gown, with bare shoulders, long diamond drops swinging from her ears, and diamonds at her throat.

"The painting was commissioned by your grandfather to celebrate her coming of age," Troy told me carelessly. "I cannot tell you the identity of the other Fairfax women; you will have to ask Selina about them. I have no portraits of *my* ancestors to show you. They were the people who built such houses as these, long ago, stone by stone; sweating, ill-paid; who sailed the seas, not in command of ships, but spending half their lives below decks; who tilled the soil for other men to grow rich, and then, no doubt, died paupers in the poor house!"

"You will never be numbered amongst them," I pointed out.

"No," he agreed, a strange light in his eyes. "Though I have no regrets for the years I ran the dark alleys and slept on a straw pallet with six older brothers and sisters. YOU have never seen the kind of hovel in which *I* grew up, Catherine; the walls and floors ran with water and we shared a privy that drained into a cesspit whose contents seeped back under the floor! My father deserted my mother when I was born, and she eked out a doubtful living by taking in linen to wash. We went barefooted, and often hungry; but we lived in a place that teemed with life, raw, rowdy, rumbustious."

"Where?" I asked, interested.

"Down by the Point, within sight of ships that came and went from Portsmouth Harbour, out across the seven seas, and back again!" he replied. "In a welter of common lodging houses and cheap music halls, where prostitutes, thieves and beggars rubbed shoulders and scratched out a living as best they could; in Matrimony Row and Jacob's Ladder, and Paradise Street and Bonfire Corner! Things are a great deal better, now, than when I was born there; the smells of rotting garbage and unwashed bodies and linen have been traded for the sweet scent of sea-breezes blowing up the Channel; but *I* remember, Catherine! My eyes—my ears—my nose—*they* bring back memories of those days that I do not *want* to forget!"

He stood there, arms folded, staring over my head; and it seemed, we were not in the Picture Gallery of Sandleford House; the walls melted into a great surging sea that lifted a ship eagerly and thrust it forwards, with a wind behind it to speed it on its way; he was no longer Troy Merrick, Master of Sandleford, in the expensive elegance of evening dress; he stood in the ship's prow, arms folded; he was smiling and his emerald eyes were fixed on distant horizons; a dark giant of a man, a pirate who had sailed all over the world and taken his treasures as he chose ...

The vision was gone as swiftly as it had come.

"How did you escape poverty?" I asked.

"By hard work, as I told you: I learned to read and write. I learned about injustice, when I was nine years old. I came first in a race organised by the Governors of the local Sunday School. I won the race because I so badly wanted the first prize, which was a book. I was given a wooden doll, instead, because the little golden-haired daughter of one of the Governors wanted the book."

"That was unjust!" I protested.

He shrugged. "I still have the doll. When I was old enough, I walked to London and found work; I was eighteen when I sailed to Australia with a crowd of other emigrants. We had all paid our passage money to be packed to suffocation in hot, dark, stinking hell-holds of a ship, to eat food that was not fit for animals, and to be allowed on deck for one hour at night to breathe a little fresh air. In rough weather, many were sick, and a great many passengers died on the voyage. The Captain put out the ship's lights each night in order to save oil. When I told him he was jeopardising the safety of crew and passengers, he had me put in irons until we reached Sydney, as a lesson, he said, to other intending trouble-makers."

I tried to imagine this man, with his fierce, wild pride, in irons; the thought was intolerable. I could sense his agony of spirit.

"Today, Catherine, I own a fleet of ships and those who sail in them do so in decent conditions. When I became rich, I bought the ship in which I had first sailed to Australia. I celebrated my ownership by flinging the Captain into the harbour and watching him swim ashore!" he told me.

"What became of your family?"

"My mother and four of her children died of a fever, long before I became rich," he said shortly. "One sister still lives."

"You have *this*!" I murmured. I was moved to pity though every word and glance rejected comfort.

"Yes," he agreed. "I have my fine house, my treasures from all over the world; but I am not a gentleman, Catherine! Nor ever shall be! And I do not regret it!"

As though to prove his point, he suddenly drew me roughly to him, his fingers gripping my shoulders, as he bent and kissed me full on my startled, unresisting mouth.

It was a kiss that mocked me, and lit a raging fire in all my limbs; a devil-may-care kiss, such as he might have given to any woman who had given him her favours.

"Goodnight, Cousin!" he murmured. "Sleep well—if you can!"

I turned and fled; his laughter followed me, and I could still feel the imprint of his lips against mine.

I reached my room and locked the door behind me. The

silence was absolute. Outside, the darkness pressed thickly against the walls. This was the room that had belonged to Anna, the woman who had danced with the Devil.

The room Troy had chosen for me.

I slept fitfully; when I put out the lights, the dark seemed to wrap itself, fold upon fold around me, muffling me until I could not see nor speak. I awoke, gasping for breath, comforted by the faint red glow of the dying fire.

Once, when I awoke, I heard the soft sound of the door opening.

"Who is there?" I cried.

There was no reply. Someone passed close by my bed. I heard the sound of breathing; when I put out my hand, I touched a fold of material, but it was whisked out of my grasp as my fingers found it. The door opened and closed again; the carpets were thick, and I did not hear who walked away.

Trembling, I lit my bedside candle, pulled on my wrapper, and opened the door.

The corridor was empty. I peered into the shadowy alcove on my right, but no one was there.

I walked to the top of the stairs; I could hear a voice. Every other light had been left burning, and I had no difficulty in finding my way.

I went downstairs, one at a time, determined that I would not be afraid. Somewhere a clock struck one, a single, mournful note.

I made my way in the direction of the voice, which I recognised as Troy's. I was walking away from my own apartments, towards the opposite tower, at the other end of the house.

Someone was beating furiously, on a closed door; I rounded a slight bend, and came suddenly upon Troy, alternately hammering, and rattling the door-knob; his face was dark with fury. From a distance, Marie watched him, naked loathing and hatred on her face.

"Let me in Selina!" Troy insisted, with a savagery the more terrible because he spoke quietly. "Let me in! You shall NOT bar your door to me, do you hear? *I* am your husband!"

"Leave her in peace!" Marie whispered furiously, in a thick, accented voice. "She cannot bear your touch! She does not want you. You are *le Diable* himself, and you shame us all with your passions!"

Le Diable. The Devil; and in a towering rage, too.

"Do you want to be sent away from here?" Troy demanded savagely, still hammering at the door.

"That is not for YOU to say; it is for Madame. I serve her and no one else!" Marie cried.

At that moment, they both saw me standing uncertainly there.

"Go back to bed!" Troy said angrily.

"I heard a noise … I thought … I came to see …" I faltered.

They both looked at me and said nothing; I turned and almost ran back to my room.

I could not sleep; I lay and thought about what I had seen and heard. Perhaps I had only imagined someone coming into my room, standing by the bed; but I had certainly not imagined the scene outside Selina's room.

Just before dawn, I fell into a deep, troubled sleep; when I awoke, Milly was pulling back the curtains.

" 'Morning, miss; did you sleep well?"

"Yes," I lied.

There was no sign of Troy at breakfast, for which I was thankful. I sat alone in the morning-room, where a fire had been lighted. Alannah had her breakfast in the nursery, and I had almost finished mine when Marie came to tell me that her mistress wished to see me.

"Catherine," Selina said softly, "Marie tells me that you witnessed last night's distasteful scene. I am sorry you did so. *I* am used to these scenes—Troy has strange moods and sudden, insatiable appetites that I cannot satisfy. I am sure you know what I mean."

"Yes," I said, thankful that Aunt Vee had taught me not to be embarrassed about such things.

She put a cool, soft hand on my arm.

"You should take a walk in the grounds this morning," she said.

"Alannah is going to show me the Chapel," I explained.

"You will make better progress with her than I have done, because *you* will not be trying to forget that she is your husband's child by another woman. *I* shall never bear Troy a child."

"Why not?" I stammered.

She did not reply; there was a veiled expression on her face, and she seemed to be lost in unhappy thoughts.

Marie signed to me to leave the room. Outside the door, she thrust her plain bony face so close to mine that I could smell the scent of faded pot-pourri about her.

"Men are animals!" she whispered venomously. "If a woman takes a man's fancy, he will lust after her until he has seduced her. Remember that, miss!"

With which parting shot, she went back into Selina's rooms and closed the door in my face.

I walked across the hall on my way to collect Alannah. Seton had just arrived with Agnes. He was well-wrapped against the cold; Agnes sat sedately in her chair, thick rugs over her knees.

"I am going for a walk with Alannah," I told them.

"Once, *I* enjoyed walking," Agnes said harshly.

"You will do so again, my dear," Seton said gently, patting her shoulder reassuringly. "You know that it is only a matter of time and patience."

Agnes gave me an unsmiling look and said slowly:

"I was riding in Sandleford Park when I was thrown. The horse was not a skittish animal, difficult to control; yet he was frightened suddenly. I do not know how or why. He bolted and was caught with some difficulty. Perhaps he saw the ghost of Anna." Her smile was thin. "My spine was injured, Catherine. Seton was kind. He engaged an excellent man, a specialist in his field."

"So you must have faith in what he says," I pointed out.

"You see? Exactly what *I* have told you, my love," Seton murmured, his face close to hers.

I saw her love for him, shining clearly in her eyes. For a moment, she looked like a young girl, instead of the twenty-five years or so which I judged her age to be. Yet, the light died too quickly from her face. I saw something else there; was it doubt, uncertainty?

It seemed to be; perhaps she did not believe in the good fortune of being engaged to a man like Seton, of becoming the future mistress of Ashmead. Could it be that she believed he was marrying her from motives of pity?

He did not seem to notice her sudden withdrawal; he smiled at me and said:

"Catherine, if I can help you in any way, whilst you are here, you must not hesitate to call upon my services. Selina has always made me most welcome here, and looks upon Agnes as a friend. I want to repay such kindness, if it is possible."

"I am sure it is not expected of you!" Agnes retorted, sharply.

I felt uncomfortable. Seton gave me a look of resignation, as though silently apologising for Agnes. He was a grave, dignified man, extremely courteous and somewhat reserved. How unlike the light-hearted Rufus he was, I thought.

As I went up the stairs to the Nursery, I felt that Agnes' eyes followed every step of my progress. I heard her call out to me.

"You must remember not to pick the snowdrops, Catherine!"

I stared down at her, nonplussed; her smile was still friendly.

Alannah was pleased to see me; she was warmly clad, for the day was raw, with a fierce bite to the air, and the lifeless trees looked like half-opened fans against the colourless sky.

The grounds immediately surrounding the house had been laid out in a formal, but not unpleasing pattern, with stone urns and dark, pointed cypress trees giving on to the less ordered planning of the parkland, with its winding stream and bridge, and the paths that led away in all directions.

At the back of the house, running its entire length, was a long, flagged terrace, with a carved stone balustrade. In the centre of the terrace, a flight of several steps led down between grassy banks to another garden, on a much lower level than that at the front.

In the centre of the terrace, and at the back of it, was a wrought iron summerhouse, open at the front, and so commanding a beautiful view of the rear gardens. At each end of the terrace, the balustrade curved into a semi-circle, with stone seats. It would be a pleasant place on a hot day, I reflected.

I thought I heard the sound of water; Alannah, aware of my listening attitude, tugged eagerly at my hand, and led me to the far end of the terrace, towards the woods.

The sound of water grew louder as we approached; surprised, I looked over the back of the stone seat, and saw a waterfall, breaking out from under a tangle of ivy and twisted trees. It fell, in a white veil of foam, between deep-cut banks, and over boulders until it lost itself in the garden below. Halfway down and over the waterfall, was a small rustic bridge.

It was pretty, even on such a colourless day. The force of water was quite fierce, and the waterfall was probably fed from small tributaries of the main stream that ran through the park. The banks were slippery and the soft ground was broken in places, near the bridge; it would not be a very safe place after dark, I thought.

"It will be a lovely place in which to sit on a summer afternoon," I told Alannah.

We walked in the gardens by the waterfall, and came upon a maze of clipped yew; I pretended I could not find my way out again, much to Alannah's amusement, and she escorted me to the exit, with a very superior air. I saw the colour in her cheeks, the sparkle in her eyes and I felt happier than I had done since coming to Sandleford.

Afterwards, we went through a small archway to the kitchen garden; I named some of the vegetables and herbs growing there, and she looked interested. Beyond the kitchen garden were the stables.

The hands of the stable clock stood at half-past eleven as we passed underneath it. I saw a couple of grooms, hard at work on the horses in their loose-boxes, and a man cleaning the carriage that had brought me to Sandleford.

I lifted Alannah up to stroke the nose of one of the horses, a beautiful creature, with a coat like black velvet. The head groom came up to me; he was a small, silver-haired man with a face like a wrinkled brown nut.

"Is it Miss Fairfax?" he asked diffidently.

"Yes. I am Catherine Fairfax."

"It's a pleasure to see you here, miss. I served your grandfather. I taught your father to ride," he said simply.

"I am delighted to make your acquaintance," I told him gravely.

"My name is Kellatt," he said. "Do *you* ride, miss?"

"Yes." I was glad that Aunt Vee had taught me, declaring there was nothing like a good canter whilst the day was still fresh. Though we had not been able to afford our own horses, Aunt Vee had been friendly with the local squire, who had kindly placed two of his at our disposal.

I looked at the child.

"Can *you* ride?" I asked her.

She shook her head, stroking the velvet nose; gently I set her down.

"We will ask Mr. Merrick if you may have lessons; would you like that?" I asked.

She nodded slowly, as though not sure my request would be granted.

"Is there a suitable mount?" I asked Kellatt.

"It could be arranged, miss, I'm sure. A nice quiet pony, to get her used to the feel of it—oh yes, Mr. Merrick would agree."

Alannah looked pleased at the prospect of riding lessons; it would be something for her to do, I thought, besides giving her fresh air and exercise.

We said goodbye to Kellatt and walked out into the parkland that surrounded Sandleford. The lands seemed to stretch for miles. We climbed a small, grassy knoll and I saw the wood that I had glimpsed from my bedroom window.

I thought the wood looked dark and sinister, its trees growing close together; to my surprise, Alannah tugged at my hand and looked imploringly at me. Her eyes were large and full of fear; she shook her head vehemently in the direction of the trees.

"There is nothing in the woods to hurt us!" I protested.

She nodded, her mouth set obstinately; I was uneasy.

When I walked towards the dark firs, very tall against the sky, she stood back against the bole of a tree, shaking her head as though to tell me I would have to explore the wood alone.

There was a path under the trees; apparently well-used, and carpeted with pine needles.

A short way along the path, I came suddenly upon a small building.

It was a Folly, built on two floors, in the shape of a grey stone tower, complete with battlements; a perfect replica of one of the towers at Sandleford; but the windows of this one had shutters tightly fastened over them.

A green shawl of ivy hid much of the lower part of the Folly, and was wreathed around the heavy oak door. The whole building was enclosed in tall, spiked iron railings, which gave it a tomb-like appearance, and there was an elaborate wrought iron gate, facing the front door of the Folly.

Both gate and door were securely locked. Yet the path leading through the gate and up to the door, had been cleared of nettles and brambles and undergrowth, and was obviously used regularly.

I felt a strange premonition of evil. It was all about me, a tangible thing that I felt I wanted to fend off. I turned quickly away, and as I began to walk from the place, I thought I heard a faint rustling of leaves breaking the unnatural stillness.

I looked sharply over my shoulder. Long ago, I had been given a book of fairytales that had an illustration of a bewitched wood, where trees were half-human, and had contorted faces and grotesque limbs. Even the brambles were thin, whip-like fingers, ready to catch at an unwary traveller; the picture had impressed me vividly with its air of menace.

I pulled my skirt free of a clinging bramble. Not for all the world would I walk in this place after dark, I told myself.

As I freed my skirt, I saw a trap, half-hidden in the long grass; its jaws were primed.

I found a lump of rotting wood and inserted it on the trap. The teeth fastened on it, with a splintering sound. I shivered, thinking of a small, furry creature, caught fast, screaming in agony as steel bit deep into flesh and bone.

The leaves rustled again. A man stepped out from behind a concealing tree.

He had bright, sly eyes set deep in a coarse face with weatherbeaten cheeks. His tow-coloured hair was greying, his mouth was cruel. I looked at his greasy leather jacket, his stained corduroys, the thick hands with their broken nails, and fleshy fingers. The dirt of years seemed to have been grimed into him, and he gave off a rank, unwashed smell.

"Tha' shouldna' ha' done that," he said sourly.

It was not a South country voice; his broad vowels belonged to the Yorkshire dales.

"Who are you?" I demanded, hoping he would not see how I trembled.

"Joseph Smeech."

"What are you doing here? This is Sandleford land!"

"Ah knows that." He cleared his throat and spat his contempt of me.

"Then you are a trespasser!"

"Nay. Game-keeper to Mr. Merrick."

"I'm sure he doesn't allow gin-traps on his land."

"He knows on it," Smeech retorted, his voice surly. " 'Tain't nowt to do wi' thee. Best mind tha' own business."

"You have no right to speak to me so," I told him shortly. "I am Miss Fairfax, Mrs. Merrick's cousin."

"Aye?" He sounded disinterested. His slow, humourless grin showed yellow teeth.

Suddenly I could not endure his presence. I turned and walked away, willing myself not to run.

His laughter followed me, rasping as harshly as a file. Not until I was clear of the wood did I breathe freely of air that felt clean and sweet to my lungs.

Alannah was standing where I had left her, her back still clamped rigidly against the tree. She was like someone clinging to a lifeline.

Her expressive eyes regarded me gravely.

"I met a horrible man called Smeech," I told her.

If she could have spoken, she would have said: *I tried to tell you. I tried to warn you not to go there.*

Chapter Four

"We will go and look at the Chapel," I said.

We walked down the slope together, and went over the bridge that spanned the stream; a few flakes of snow drifted mournfully against my cheek.

Something about Sandleford troubled and frightened me; I felt that evil still existed as a living entity within its walls.

Was Troy part of the corruption I could feel? Did it stem from him?

I could not forget Smeech; his careless impudence suggested that what he did was with Troy's approval.

I watched Alannah tread carefully amongst the snowdrops, so as not to bruise them, and I followed suit. I looked at the damp and sunken headstones; even the broken urn, lying on its side in the earth, seemed as though it had been placed there to make the whole scene more effective.

I paused to read Fairfax names, cut into the marble. There was Julia Fairfax, who had died in 1780, aged seventeen: 'a chaste, sober and obedient young woman'. William Rohan Fairfax, who had died in 1789 aged 81, after living, according to the tribute, 'a long and goodly life.' I read my own name with a feeling of unreality: 'Catherine Fairfax, died in 1793, at the tender age of 21 months, infant daughter of Richard and Grace, deeply mourned; and a sad epitaph to one Mede Fairfax, a gallant young Captain, who had died of injuries sustained at the Battle of Waterloo.

I found my grandfather's tomb, newer than the rest, surmounted by an elaborately carved, weeping angel. I thought how sad it was that he had died without an heir, penniless, with so little money that it had taken a stranger to restore Sandleford to its former glory.

Alannah reached up and lifted the heavy latch; the door swung inwards with a soft, protesting squeak. Inside was the musty smell of decay that belongs to old places of worship.

I saw a dozen carved pews, a tiny Altar; an impressive tomb to Argus Fairfax, his children and weeping wife carved around the base. He lay in state on the top, wrought in the same marble, a grave, cold man with a dog at his feet.

Here, there was only peace. I could feel it, breathe it in like cleansing fresh air, feel its strength, know that it shielded me from harm. Here, the tale of a woman dancing the night away, in scarlet, golden-heeled shoes, was nonsense.

Above the small Altar was the stained glass window. It depicted a tall woman, with strongly-marked features, reminiscent of Aunt Vee. Her dark hair flowed over her shoulders, confined only by a narrow white band about her forehead. She wore a long white dress and a blue robe, and carried a silver Cross in her clasped hands; her feet were half-hidden in the flowering snowdrops.

She was tranquil, beautiful, timeless; my eyes filled with tears. The face above me had compassion, strength, humour. No power could prevail against her and all that she represented.

I looked at the worn flagstones beneath my feet, the thick hassocks of blue velvet, rubbed in places; at the carved lectern and stone pulpit, with the heads of cherubs carved around its base. On an impulse, I knelt in one of the pews; my prayer was muddled and confused, a request for strength against the witchcraft charm of Troy, a miracle cure for Alannah; the prayers that most people make, put together piecemeal, haltingly whispered.

When I opened my eyes, Alannah was standing beside me, grave and watchful; impulsively, I put out an arm and drew her close.

"Listen," I said, loudly and firmly, "here you will always be safe. You remember that good is stronger than evil, and will always win in the end. *Never* be afraid of anything in life."

She did not give any sign that she understood; her eyes

were fathomless, too old for a child. I remembered the terrible thing she had looked upon: the rape of her mother.

The faint scrape of a footfall made me turn my head sharply.

Troy stood in the aisle, sombre in his long dark cloak, his silver-black head bare. His face was unreadable. If he had heard what I had said to his child, he gave no sign.

I looked at the deeply-etched lines in the hawk-like face, the sardonic expression he wore so arrogantly, the brilliant eyes. He had no right here, I thought; not a man who hammered on his wife's bedroom door, who tolerated cruelty, brought his illegitimate child to his home as a reminder of his liking for the sins of the flesh.

If I was honest I would admit that I needed to pray most earnestly for strength to fight the terrible fascination he had for me; it was an obsession, a magnetism that would draw me within the orbit of his power, against my will.

I got to my feet, with as much dignity as I could. Alannah went to his side and stood there, as though rejecting everyone else as soon as he appeared on the scene.

"Lunch is ready," Troy said briefly to me. "No one knew where you could be found until I saw you from my study window."

I felt like an erring schoolgirl. Stiffly, I followed him from the Chapel.

As he walked, he lifted his arm in a sweeping gesture, so that his cloak fell back, showing the scarlet lining. "My lands stretch as far as you can see, in every direction."

"Land that once belonged to the Fairfaxes?" I asked coolly.

"Yes. Farms, cottages, hamlets; the villages of North and South Meon. I know every tenant by name. I see my people, go out and talk to them."

I refused to be impressed.

"I have spoken to Kellatt," I said. "He knew my grandfather."

"He was one of the few servants left here, when I came. Kellatt. Everything was rotting away for want of time, money and attention."

I thought of Selina, blooming like a golden rose against

the decay of the old house. She must have seemed very desirable to the man who had taken her and made her another beautiful possession.

"Grandfather must have been grateful to you," I said.

"On the contrary, he said it was better that the house should be left to fall into ruin; that way the old curse might be lifted."

"How odd! Was he very superstitious?"

"He was old; he had lost son, daughter, son-in-law, early in life. He believed it was all part of the curse. His wife—your grandmother—also died when he was still only a young man."

"The loss of his son—my father—was no part of the curse," I retorted. "It was his own fault. People bring a lot of their own misery down on their heads, though they may wish to blame Fate!"

"Don't be pious, Catherine! You have to be much older than you are to make a remark like that and get away with it."

"Don't you think I am right?"

He lifted his head proudly, looking fierce.

"Life moulds us a little, shapes us a little, pares away here, adds something there, Catherine Fairfax. Underneath it all, we are essentially ourselves, living with our failures and sorrows."

"I wish I had known my grandfather," I said.

"Also your father, perhaps?" Troy suggested. "Do you not wish you had known HIM?"

I considered his question, and answered as honestly as I could.

"My father chose his own path; it led him away from my grandfather and it may be that the fact contributed to my grandfather's strangeness. My father left my mother; he walked away out of her life, and told her to forget him. How could she, when she was expecting his child? He just left a note for mama; he said if he stayed, he faced a prison sentence."

"Perhaps he felt that no husband at all was better than one in jail!" Troy commented drily.

"He was wrong; he should have stayed with her. She

needed him; she died of a broken heart. Well, HE believed that what he had done was right; and he did not know that mama was expecting me. I know nothing of where he went, what happened to him. He must be dead, now, or I am sure he would have contacted Aunt Vee; or tried to find mama, when he was older and wiser."

Troy walked beside me in silence for a while. Then he said abruptly:

"What had your father done that merited a prison sentence?"

"He had borrowed a great deal of money that he could not repay; or else that he had no right to borrow. I only know what Aunt Vee told me."

"Your judgement is harsh, Catherine! He was bedevilled by money, then, and behaved foolishly; many men have behaved as he did. He left your mother, believing she would be better cared for by her family; perhaps his conscience tormented him for the rest of his life."

"How can I say? I know nothing of him," I replied indifferently. "Perhaps he became strange, like grandfather."

"Your grandfather was suspicious of everyone," Troy told me. "He would hide away, in order not to meet people. He sat for hours, writing, in his room and no one knew what he wrote. He believed in Anna, as a presence in the house."

"Certainly there is evil here," I said bitterly.

His laugh was mocking.

"You look as though you smell corruption in the very air!"

I thought of dank woods, the foul smell of Smeech, the sinister air of the locked Folly.

"Why do you allow keepers to set gin-traps on your land?" I demanded.

His eyebrows rose enquiringly. I told him of my encounter with Smeech.

"I was not aware of the existence of such traps," he said curtly. "I will look into the matter."

I looked at him thoughtfully, and murmured:

"I would like to see the inside of the Folly."

"That you will never do." His voice made me shiver. "I, alone, possess a key, and the place is out of bounds!"

Seton and Agnes joined us for lunch. Troy was very agreeable to Seton, and the two men discussed a new farming project in which Seton was interested.

"Ashmead land is not as productive as it might be," Seton told Troy. "I wish to develop it to its fullest capacity, to enhance my inheritance."

"A laudable sentiment," Troy said drily, his face expressionless. "A man with a wife may reasonably expect to have sons to follow him, and it is for them, as much as for his wife, that he desires to be rich."

I saw naked challenge in the look he gave Selina; the air was charged with emotion, raw and fierce, until Agnes turned to me, and asked me composedly if I had enjoyed my walk with Alannah.

"Very much," I replied. "The grounds are vast. One could easily be lost."

"There are many dark corners," she said softly.

"Smeech will set no more traps," Troy told me curtly.

In response to Selina's enquiring look, I was forced to explain what had happened.

"Smeech has been here for years; *I* did not know he set traps," she said.

Adroitly, Seton guided the conversation into other channels; Agnes spoke softly to me.

"Have you seen the Folly, Catherine? The place where Troy entertains the women he brings from London and Portsmouth? There is a small gate, near the Folly, giving access to the road. Most convenient for the arrival and departure of—conveyances of all kinds."

I looked at her suspiciously.

"How do you know all this?"

"I listen to gossip. It passes the time. I have little else to do; Ashmead almost runs itself," she said, without any expression in her voice.

"IS it gossip—or is it true?" I asked, in a voice too low for anyone else to hear.

"About the Folly? You must ask Troy, my dear!" she whispered back, "no one else can answer you!"

Her eyes sparkled; whether with innocent amusement or malice, I did not know.

I did not trust her; she was not open and pleasant as Seton was.

I looked across the table; Selina was certainly not picking listlessly at her food today; she was listening to something that Rufus was saying, her head thrown back, her face alive with laughter.

Troy looked at his wife; a slow, smouldering, angry look. Only Seton seemed completely at ease.

Suddenly, Selina turned towards me.

"I *must* give a Ball for you, Catherine! So that you can meet all our friends and neighbours!"

"A fancy dress Ball," Seton suggested.

Selina turned to her husband.

"Well, Troy? What do you say?"

"As you wish," he agreed smoothly.

"You would make a splendid buccaneer, Troy," Agnes told him.

"We will dress you as Anna, Cousin Catherine!" Selina told me wickedly. "A red dress would suit your colouring!"

"After hearing the legend, I'm not sure that I want to be Anna!" I said.

"You don't believe that nonsense, surely?" Rufus protested, still amused.

"*I* believe it!" Selina whispered, her eyes huge, her face excited.

I looked at Seton.

"Do *you*?" I asked.

He gave me that slow smile of his; his greatest charm lay in the fact that he gave his entire attention to whoever was speaking to him, as though the words he listened to were the only ones he wanted to hear.

"Yes," he said calmly.

I looked questioningly at Troy; but he stared sombrely at me and said nothing. His dark, brooding glance held mine for a moment, his green eyes ice-cold. Then, with his usual abruptness, he rose from the table and strode from the room.

Selina looked after him, her face puckered with embarrassment and distress. Agnes leaned towards me and whispered in my ear:

"He is very handsome, isn't he, Catherine? Do you fancy yourself to be a little in love with him?"

"I hardly know him!" I replied coldly.

"What does that matter? He has a powerful personality. Have you not heard of a rabbit mesmerised by a snake?"

"Do you compare me to a rabbit?" I asked, annoyed.

"Of course not, but have you never considered that it might be exciting to be one of the women Troy entertains at the Folly?"

She was teasing; her teasing had too sharp an edge for my liking, but I felt sorry for her, confined to her wheelchair.

"Have you and Seton set a date for your wedding?" I asked her.

"Not yet. Seton says there is no need to hurry the matter; he wishes to wait until I am well again. I SHALL be well, Catherine."

There was a fierce intensity in her expression; I said soothingly:

"Of course you will. In the meantime, you can plan."

"I have planned so much," she whispered. "My dress, my trousseau. We shall honeymoon in Venice, he says, for a whole month; and then a month in Paris, before we return here. Oh, the joy it will be to be mistress of Ashmead!"

There was triumph in her voice, as well as pleasure.

That afternoon, at dusk, I took a walk in the grounds. Inevitably, my footsteps led to the Folly; the ivy-shrouded building in the dark woods drew me with a fascination that repelled even while it beckoned me onwards.

I thought I saw a thin streak of light between one of the upper shutters—which appeared to be slightly open. I went slowly forwards; and something closed with a vicious snap on my stout leather walking-boot.

There was an agonising pain across my instep as rusty teeth tore through the leather, gripping my foot fast.

I cried out as the prongs bit deep and warm blood oozed through the broken flesh; this was probably the trap I had seen only that morning.

In trying, frantically, to free my trapped foot, I fell forward full-length. I lay, winded and gasping, tears of pain running down my cheek. Automatically, I lifted my head and looked at the sliver of light between the shutters; but the lamp had been extinguished.

I cried out for help, trying to sit up, and ease off my boot, but it was hopeless. As I paused for breath, I heard the sound of heavy breathing, and someone moved along the path behind me.

It was almost dark; as I tried to twist around, I felt a savage blow between my shoulders. Two hands pressed hard against the back of my head, forcing my face cruelly down into the damp earth.

The path was muddy; the pressure upon me was inexorable. My mouth, my nose were filled with earth, and I was smothering, feeling blackness pour over me in great waves.

I was nearly unconscious; I was going to die, under the shadow of the Folly, and I should never know who had killed me ...

Then I heard the sound of running feet; abruptly the hold upon me was released and whoever had held me so viciously, let me go, violently, racing away in the direction of the Folly.

I lifted my head. Air poured into my lungs. Air that had never tasted so sweet; I lay there, gasping and crying.

A small figure came up and knelt beside me, peering into my face in the last of the light.

"Alannah!" I whispered, thankfully. "Go and get help ..."

She ran back along the path. Faint and sick, I struggled into a sitting position. I wondered why Alannah was out of doors. She wore no coat nor hat.

It seemed a very long time before help came. A lantern, held high, bobbed between the trees. Troy and Rufus stood staring down at me, Alannah in front of them.

"What, in God's name, has happened?" Troy demanded furiously.

I realised how I must look: my hair awry, my face smothered in mud. Alannah tugged at Troy's sleeve, and showed him my foot. I heard his oath; Rufus's sharp, indrawn breath.

Together, they released the trap and eased off the boot. Troy picked me up in his arms, as though I was a child, and I marvelled at the massive strength of him.

"Go ahead," he said to Rufus. "Take Alannah with you. Send one of the servants for Doctor Garrod."

"You'll need a light—" Rufus began.

"I know every inch of these woods," Troy retorted. "I have eyes that can see in the dark."

Rufus and Alannah hurried back to the house. Troy carried me so easily, and I was a full-grown woman, no delicate little creature like Selina. My head lay against his shoulder, and I began to cry.

"What were you doing there?" he demanded, striding out along the path, as though he did, indeed, have eyes that could see in the dark.

"Walking," I whispered.

"Near the Folly? Were you not told to stay away from there?"

"*You* said that Smeech would set no more traps! I was attacked! As I lay there someone tried to kill me."

"How?"

"By smothering me. Pushing my face down into the earth."

He made no reply; whether or not he believed me, I could not tell.

For all his strength, he was out of breath when we reached the house. His face was close to mine as we walked. I felt the warmth that came from his body, the tremendous inner power of the man, and I was afraid.

It was wonderful to be cared for; fussed over, scolded, by Milly and Selina. My foot was bathed with antiseptic; the puncture wounds were quite deep and my instep had been badly bruised, as well as other bruises I had sustained, in falling. The loathsome, clinging mud was washed from my face and mouth, and a clean nightdress put over my head.

I lay in bed, shivering, sipping hot milk laced with brandy, trying to stammer out an explanation of what had happened. I was still very shocked.

"Hush!" Selina whispered. "Don't talk. Rest."

"You should never have picked them snowdrops, miss; what did I tell you?" Milly murmured, big-eyed; but Selina told her, sharply, to be quiet.

Dr. Garrod looked at my foot and bandaged it; he said I was to stay in bed, for at least a day, and if there was any swelling, he was to be called at once. One couldn't be too careful, he said; those traps were always rusty.

Selina drew him aside, and I heard them murmuring together, though I could not hear what was said; once or twice he glanced towards me, frowned thoughtfully, and stroked his chin. Something about the whispered conversation made me uneasy; it was reaction, I told myself.

Dr. Garrod prescribed a sedative; when I had taken it, Selina sent Milly away and sat beside me. She put a cool hand across my forehead, looking worriedly at me.

"Catherine, are you CERTAIN that you were attacked?" she asked.

"How else do you account for the mud in my nose and mouth?"

"You fell heavily. It is possible you were badly winded, or only half-conscious."

"*Someone* was there. I felt hands on me, pressing me down. I would have suffocated, had not Alannah appeared just in time."

"Who would attack you?" she asked.

"Smeech, perhaps; because I was near the Folly."

"Smeech would never do such a thing."

"He sets traps."

"That is different. He is a countryman and they don't look at these things as we do. As Troy's gamekeeper, he knows it is his duty to keep down vermin, as well as be alert for poachers."

"He could use a gun. That would be quick and clean," I argued. "Trapped animals die slowly and in agony."

"You heard Troy say that Smeech will set no more traps. Are you not satisfied?" she asked sharply.

"Satisfied? I don't know what you mean," I said. For a moment she seemed alien and unfriendly.

Her voice was contrite; she patted my hand.

"I am sorry, Catherine. Yes, of course, Smeech is wrong

to trap animals as he does. I wasn't aware of what was happening, you know; and Troy is difficult. You have seen for yourself the situation between my husband and myself. He is hard and impatient, arrogant and tyrannical. I am guilty of grave disloyalty to him in telling you this; but you don't *know* how much I need someone to confide in. I cannot talk to Agnes; she would not understand. Besides ..."

She paused and bit her lip, looking at me with troubled eyes.

"I do not think Agnes likes me," she added reluctantly.

"I am sure you are wrong, Selina. Agnes has a sharp tongue, she chafes at her inability to walk, and it makes her seem intolerant, perhaps."

"She was always strange. The Creightons made her a drudge. They were harsh people. She never played with us, you know. Rufus was the only one who ever made her laugh with his nonsense. Well, I hope she will be happier in her marriage to Seton than I have been in mine to Troy."

"Were you and Troy not happy when you were first married?"

"I had a very deep affection for Troy, and I was grateful that he restored this house in all its splendour, as his wedding-gift to me."

"Affection? Gratitude? Are such things firm enough foundation stones for a marriage?" I wondered aloud.

"Ah, Catherine, you have too romantic a heart! I did not really know Troy; few women ever know the man they marry—until it is too late. I believe ours would be a happy marriage; Troy's demands terrified me, and then he tired of me, now he has little need of a wife, except when he has an overmastering desire to possess a woman, any woman within reach. Do I shock you by such revelations?"

"No; my Aunt was a broad-minded woman who told me things that mothers seldom tell their daughters—out of modesty or embarrassment, I suppose. She said that facts should never be embarrassing, and to be armed with knowledge was the best defence against all life's ills and sorrows."

"She sounds a wise woman. If only I had met her!"

I thought of the bleakness of Selina's marriage and felt

sorry for her; when she left me, I was almost asleep. Vaguely, I felt the touch of her lips as she kissed my forehead. The fire crackled pleasantly; drowsily, I was aware that Milly looked in, once or twice …

When I awoke, much later, the fire had burned low, and a rising wind prowled restlessly outside the windows. I shivered, burrowing under the blankets.

Then, above the cry of the wind, I heard the sound; a rhythmic tapping that seemed to come from the dressing-room.

I sat upright, every nerve pricking with fear. My hands were clammy and my heart raced.

Someone was dancing a lively jig, keeping good time to music I could not hear.

I forced myself to get out of bed. I did not want to; but Aunt Vee had said that no one should run away from fear.

It was not the easiest advice to follow. My foot throbbed as soon as I put it to the ground; but I could not rest whilst that tap-tap-tap of dancing feet went on, near at hand.

I groped for the matches, and lit my bedside candle.

Then I limped painfully across the room, and lit the two gas burners, above the mantelshelf. They hissed into life and filled the room with a comforting yellow glow.

I found my dressing-gown and pulled it around me; but it was not cold that made me shiver, as I opened the door leading to the dressing-room.

The sound was much louder, in this room. It seemed to be coming from the cupboards lining the far wall.

"Who is it?" I cried.

I jerked open one of the doors, and abruptly, the sound ceased. I put down the candle I was carrying and reached to the back of the cupboard, past my clothes hanging there.

I prodded the wall. I poked it, beat on it with my fists, in vain; the wall of the cupboard was solid, and smooth, with no kind of opening in it.

Old houses played tricks with one's hearing. Perhaps it was a sound carried from another part of the house; something without any sinister overtones.

Determinedly, I made my way to the door of my bedroom that led, out into the long passageway from the gallery.

Putting my injured foot to the ground made me wince with pain, but I went stubbornly on my way.

I opened the bedroom door slowly; it was very late and the household had gone to bed, but every other lamp along the corridor was always left burning. I was glad.

I heard a clock strike one, somewhere, as I was opening the door.

Then I saw the child standing a few feet from me, and the shock was so great that I almost fainted.

In her long white night-gown, with her hair flowing over her shoulders, she looked like a ghost. Her face was pale, her eyes large and brilliant. At first I thought she was sleep-walking; but when she saw me, she put out a hand in a gesture, half-timid, half-reassuring, that I could not understand.

I put my finger to my lips.

"Come into my room, Alannah."

Her small, bare feet peeped out from under her night-gown as she walked. She caught hold of my hand, and looked up into my face, as though to assure herself that I was really there.

I sat on the edge of the bed, and put the eiderdown around her. She was shivering; her long, grave look worried me.

"You shouldn't be out of bed," I scolded gently. "Who sleeps in the night-nursery with you? Katy? No. Betty? No. Julia?"

Alannah nodded.

"She must be a sound sleeper," I said.

Again she nodded. I thought of Julia, young, healthy, and probably tired-out from her day's exertions.

"What were you doing near my door?" I asked.

She just looked searchingly at me, and I sighed, daunted by the difficulty of being able to communicate with her.

"Let me think." I did so, concentrating as best I could. Not easy, for part of my brain still seemed hazed with sleep.

"You were awake," I guessed. "You were worried about something?"

She nodded vigorously, and jabbed a finger at me.

"You thought *I* was in some kind of—danger?" I said, astonished.

Again she nodded vigorously. I felt goose-pimples on my arms and thought: does she have some kind of second-sight?

"So you came to see for yourself?" I asked.

Again the nod.

Carefully, I questioned. No, she hadn't known what kind of danger I was in. It was something she could not explain: a need to come and satisfy herself that all was well. Had she felt it when I had lain in the woods, my foot caught in the trap, I asked.

I was both troubled and astonished when she nodded. I discovered that she had been sitting in the Nursery and had suddenly run out, without a coat or hat, to Julia's anger and alarm. She had run straight to the woods. No, she had not seen anyone except me. She had just known that I was in the woods and that she must find me.

"Perhaps the Lady of the Snows sent you," I whispered, puzzled.

She nodded slowly, and in perfect agreement. She believed implicitly in such miracles; why should *I* look for coldly practical explanations? I was certain she had saved my life in the woods. Had I been in similar danger tonight?

I thanked her and kissed her, and sent her back to bed, hoping that Julia would still be asleep—as she obviously was, for I heard nothing about the episode, afterwards.

When she had gone, the room seemed very still. I turned out all the lights and the blackness was intense. I felt as though I was drowning in a black velvet sea. I thought about Good—and Evil. They lived in this house, side by side. Evil, at least, was active; I did not know about the force for Good, nor how strong it was.

In the dark, I put out my fingers and touched the snowdrops I had insisted on keeping. Already, the petals were brown and shrivelled.

I was in danger; and only Alannah was aware of that fact, it seemed.

I did not know from whom the danger came; but to someone, my presence here was a threat, for I did not really believe it was Smeech who had attacked me, out of petty revenge.

What possible threat was *I* to anyone, I wondered?

I stayed in bed for a day, and was made much of; Selina visited me, and brought messages of sympathy from everyone. Troy, she said, had told Smeech that if ever he set another trap, he would whip him from here to the village ...

It sounded melodramatic; it also sounded like Troy, and I had no doubt he would carry out the threat if required.

When I insisted that someone had tried to smother me as I lay on the ground, Selina patted my shoulder, smiled, and was evasive.

Alannah came, and I taught her to play draughts. I thought how small and defenceless she looked, and suddenly I put my arms around her, hugging her fiercely.

She responded by putting her arms around my neck, and smiling trustfully at me. I marvelled, thinking of the horrible thing she had seen; perhaps she had been too young to understand the full depths of her mother's agony and humiliation. Yet, sometimes, her eyes looked old, wise and unchildlike.

I had a growing affection for Troy's love-child.

I was young and healthy; the injured flesh healed well. Next day I dressed and went downstairs; there was no more than a slight stiffness in my foot, and all my bruises would soon fade.

In his usual high-handed manner, Troy summoned me to his study. It was a sombre, book-lined room, with deep leather chairs.

He stood with his back to the fire; a man to dwarf any room. I resisted the strong pull of the attraction I felt for him, knowing he exerted a powerful animal magnetism that he used for his own ends.

Behind him, the winter sky was grey and cold. I could not see his face clearly.

"Sit down, Catherine," he said.

I sat primly on the edge of a chair.

"Are you feeling better?" His voice was formal.

"Yes, thank you."

"I would like you to explain exactly what you think happened to you, two nights ago."

Think? I stared defiantly at him.

"I will explain what I *know* happened to me. I caught my foot in one of Smeech's traps and fell. As I lay winded, face down, someone pressed my face into the earth. The path is soft and muddy there. I couldn't see, I could not breathe; nor could I escape because my foot was still caught in the trap. Whoever attacked me was physically very powerful. I could have been smothered."

I looked straight into his cold green eyes; his smile was sardonic.

"Do you imagine that *I* was your attacker?"

"If you were, I cannot imagine what motive you have," I retorted.

I was furiously angry—I had been near death, and he seemed quite unperturbed about that.

"As my guardian, I would have expected you to show some concern," I said bitterly.

"You met with an accident; you fell, you were dazed and confused, as a result," he pronounced calmly.

"I was not too dazed to know what happened to me!"

"You were in a state of shock, and your imagination played tricks!"

"You are WRONG!" I cried furiously. "Why will you not believe me?"

"Because I do not accept that someone here would wish you harm. It certainly was not Smeech; I have made extensive enquiries—he was nowhere near the Folly at that time. Neither should you have been. You have an exceptionally vivid imagination, my dear Catherine!"

"I am not your dear Catherine!" I stormed. "I KNOW what happened! It is not pleasant to be disbelieved! I do not wish to stay in this house, and I prefer to return to Dorset as soon as possible."

"No!" he thundered. "You belong here; you are a Fairfax! Your grandfather had no wish to see you subjected to the indignity of having to earn a living."

"My Aunt appointed you to be my guardian. It was foolish of her!"

He glared at me, his eyes cold, his mouth bitter.

"There was no one else. She presumed your father to be dead ..."

"As indeed he must be! If he HAD been alive, he would be as much a stranger to me as *you* are!" I retorted.

I knew that I had hurt him by those last words; had pierced his defences in some way. I wished I could have recalled the words; I shook my head and said wearily:

"Can you not see that earning my own living is preferable to charity, in my eyes?"

He came across, towering above me, and bent his head until his face was only inches above mine. His eyes were like green glass.

" 'Charity' is the most abused word in the English language. You do not know its true meaning. You WILL stay here; because you have no alternative. Because I am responsible for you. I, Troy Merrick—and *no one else*! Understand that. The sooner you do so, the better we shall get along."

He paused. His eyes were no longer like glass.

"*I* want you to stay here," he finished quietly.

His expression was quizzical; it invited a cessation of hostilities, but I dared not surrender; I turned and limped from the room with as much dignity as I could muster, under the circumstances.

Outside, I leant, trembling, against the wall. I was no longer in control of myself. All my emotions were slipping out of my grasp.

Troy was a man who could make a fool of any woman; and he did not lack experience in that particular skill.

As I stood there, two women came along the wide hall, deep in conversation; one was Mrs. Treville. When she saw me, she smiled brightly, wished me good-day, and hoped that I had recovered from my accident.

"I am feeling better, thank you," I assured her.

The round, kind face expressed only benevolence. Not so Marie, walking with her. The expression on the face of Selina's maid was as sour as a quince, her sharp eyes raked over me as though they could read my thoughts and dissect my emotions.

"Ma'mselle should not walk alone, in the woods, at such an hour," she said, in her gruff, accented voice.

With an effort I smiled back at her.

"I will remember that," I assured her.

Seton, Rufus and Selina were much more sympathetic. Selina fussed over me, showing great concern, though I knew she shared Troy's belief that I had imagined the attack that followed my fall.

Agnes said little; I could not tell what she thought.

"You must take me with you next time you go walking in the woods," Rufus insisted.

"I didn't imagine myself to be in danger; after all, I was on Sandleford land."

"Oh, there are strange people about!" he replied enigmatically.

I looked up into the bright, hazel eyes; they were very shrewd. His face had the bright, alert look of a fox, I thought.

"Strange, Rufus? How? And who are these people?" I asked.

"Well, there's Smeech. The man has always given me the creeps, and he's probably furious because you've stopped him using traps. Not that I approve of them. There's Marie. A very odd creature, I've always thought. I can't think Selina enjoys having her around. She was as fierce as a watchdog over Selina when we were kids. Then there's Troy?"

"Don't you like him?"

"You asked me that question once before. I don't KNOW him. He's unapproachable. I imagine he'd use less stealthy methods than sneaking up behind you."

I shivered uncontrollably.

"I haven't been here very long, Rufus. Troy is my guardian and I'm dependent on him, unfortunately. I am no threat to anyone. Why should someone wish to harm me?"

"Oh, people have many motives," he said lightly. "Fear; sheer hatred. Jealousy. A desire for gain."

"No one would gain from my death. Grandfather had only the house to leave and that is Selina's."

He nodded.

"*I* don't understand, any more than you do. Selina believes you were overwrought, and imagined it." He tucked his hand under my arm, in a friendly manner. "Come along. Let's take a stroll on the terrace. You look as though you need fresh air."

We walked along the terrace and he talked of his impatience to see his house restored.

"I swear the workmen sleep half the day, whilst I kick my heels here. Nothing to do except play Chess with Troy. "He gave a vast sigh, belied by the laughter in his eyes.

"I am a great disappointment to Troy. Seton, you see, applies himself seriously to the business of managing his estate."

"Unless you are a good landlord, you cannot hope to get the best from your land or the people who look after it, for you," I said, with a straight face.

He looked sharply at me, then roared with laughter.

"Now you are quoting Troy. So be it, I acknowledge the truth of that; but I wish it would look after itself and leave me free to do the things I like best."

"What are those?"

"To travel. To paint. To enjoy life, dear Catherine, without too much effort. Don't waste your time giving me a lecture. Roots, land, the things that matter to Troy and to Seton have no charm for me."

He moved closer to me as we walked, his voice teasing me gently.

"I have had very little opportunity of getting to know you better, Catherine. There are too many people around you. I shall carry you off, to Kilstock, make you my prisoner."

"The house has neither doors nor windows; I should easily escape," I retorted, falling in with his mood.

"Perhaps you will not want to return, once you are away from here!"

"Selina likes this house well enough!" I said wrily.

"Sandleford and its legends are her life. She married Troy to keep the place perfect, as she wanted it," he retorted carelessly. "YOU aren't like that, Catherine. No pile of stones would claim YOUR soul!"

Deliberately, he made his voice sound deep and ghostly; I laughed at him, beginning to feel the nightmare move away from me.

"Oh, Rufus, you're full of nonsense! I wonder what you would say if you came face to face with the ghost of Anna Fairfax?"

"The Lady of the Red Shoes?" His smile was quizzical. "Judging by her portrait, she was no beauty. I don't know what the Devil saw in her. Perhaps she had hidden charms; still, she would probably not be willing to stay long enough for me to discover them!"

"Selina would be outraged to hear you making fun of the legend!"

"Selina is not here; and *you* are, Catherine. I have made you laugh and you have forgotten that you were so unhappy last night. Is that a bad thing?"

"It is a very good thing."

He stopped suddenly, lifted an imaginary hat from his head and doffed it, bowing low.

"Am I appointed Court Jester, then, Your Majesty?"

I extended a hand graciously.

"By all means; your credentials are excellent."

"Thank you, Your Majesty. I can promise to make you smile at least once every day and to make you laugh as often as possible."

The ridiculous, silly little speech delighted me. Rufus was like sunlight dancing on the water. He did not possess the deeps that Troy and Seton possessed; nor the complexities, the ruggedness of character, that was Troy's. He did not pretend to be other than what he was: a light-hearted young man, bent on finding pleasure where he could, frankly acknowledging his dislike of responsibility; nevertheless, he brought to Sandleford a light-heartedness that I needed very badly.

Later that day, I asked Seton if he believed in the legend. He considered the question carefully, giving it the serious attention that he always gave to such questions.

"Yes, I do believe in it, Catherine. I have read much that has contributed to that belief. In his sitting-room, your Grandfather has a small library of books on Occult matters: Black Magic, Witchcraft, Supernatural Happenings. He was passionately interested in studying these things; he had little else to occupy his mind. Eventually, he came to believe that

Sandleford was an unlucky house and that the Fairfax happiness and good fortune could only be restored when the place was burned to the ground."

"How fortunate that he didn't put his theory to the test. Do YOU believe in the powers of Darkness?"

There was a moment's stillness about him, as though the question was one he could not answer without prolonged thought. His eyes seemed almost luminous. I was startled by the strange beauty of his countenance. How CAN one call a MAN beautiful? Yet, Seton Blair seemed to be at that moment, staring into the distance, his hair like a golden crest above his quiet face, with its good bones and long, firm mouth.

The moment passed; he came back from whatever distant place his thoughts had led him.

"I believe in such powers," he told me. "If we believe in good, then we must accept that there is evil, also. It is but the other side of the coin, so we are told."

As they days passed, I tried to forget about the incident in the wood. No one mentioned it; but one outcome had been the awareness of a loving bond between Alannah and myself; it was something that gave me great pleasure.

I saw little of Troy. He was extremely busy, I heard, and had sailed across to France on one of his ships. When he came back, he tossed a great armful of rich red silk in front of me.

"To make you a dress," he told me, his eyes challenging. "You are going to the Ball as Anna, are you not?"

"I hadn't decided—" I murmured.

"I should think you would fit the part very well," he replied.

Selina was delighted with Troy's gift to me. She looked out some old drawings of eighteenth century costume, and sent for the village dressmaker. Miss Preston was extremely skilled with needle and scissors, Selina assured me; and I was to have a pair of red shoes, my hair was to be dressed so ...

It was good to see Selina so happy. I thought Miss Preston eyed me askance, as though she diapproved of the choice of costume, but I endured the fittings as patiently as I could.

I walked to the two villages with Alannah. North Meon was the prettiest, with its thatched cottages and the little stream running beside the main street.

There was only one shop, crammed from floor to ceiling with everything under the sun. I bought sweets and a hair-ribbon for Alannah; on an impulse, one day, I bought a cheap, but pretty little box for Agnes.

I had very little money; there would be no more when I had spent it, for I was determined not to ask Troy for anything.

The next afternoon I went to Ashmead to have tea with Agnes.

I liked Ashmead. It was very much smaller than Sandleford, but less intimidating, too; more like an English country house than an exotic museum for trophies from every corner of the world, and that was how Sandleford seemed to be.

I gave Agnes the little box.

"For *me*?" she murmured, surprised, fingering the lacquer lid with its tiny mother-of-pearl motif.

"Yes. It was pretty; I thought you would like it."

"Because I have had few pretty things in life?" she asked bitterly.

I sighed.

"Agnes, you are like a hedgehog. I only ever tried to pick one up, once in my life."

She looked at me with narrowed eyes; as usual, I could not tell what she was thinking. When she spoke, her voice was colourless.

"Thank you for the gift, Catherine. It is most kind of you to think of me."

Selina took me out driving, showing me the local beauty spots. Alannah rarely came; neither of them seemed at ease in the other's company, which was perfectly understandable, in the circumstances.

My cousin often expressed her delight in having me at Sandleford.

"You are splendid company, Catherine! You make me

laugh! It was too bad of grandfather to have kept you from me, all these years!"

"Family quarrels are sad," I agreed. "So pointless, too. Were you lonely at Sandleford, when you were young?"

"Not really," she answered frankly. "There was Marie, to look after me, and Mrs. Treville. I had Rufus to play with. He is like you, Catherine—he can make people laugh. Sometimes Seton came to stay at Ashmead, and it was such fun. We scarcely ever quarrelled. I *was* happy, though I knew we had no money to buy things, to keep the house as it should have been kept."

She leaned towards me, as the coach swung along the quiet country road.

"I was just a little girl when I first met Troy, Catherine. I was playing in the drive, when I saw this boy on the other side of the gates. He was about fourteen. He had no shoes on his feet and his clothes were patched and dreadfully shabby. He asked me my name, and when I told him, he said he would come back to marry me, one day, when he had made his fortune. I asked him *his* name. Troy, he said. Then Marie ran forward and snatched me up and scolded me for talking to a stranger outside the gate; she shouted at him to go at once, or she would set the dogs on him."

"It sounds very romantic," I said.

"I thought so, once. Now it is just sad," she told me tiredly.

Selina declared that the details of my costume must be kept a secret. No one was to see me in it until the night of the Ball. She found some pearl and tortoiseshell combs, and told Marie exactly how she wanted my hair to be dressed.

Marie was not enthusiastic. She was fiercely possessive with anyone who claimed Selina's attention; however, Selina's word was law, and I think Marie would have jumped from the tower battlements if Selina had commanded her to do so.

Selina produced a pair of scarlet satin shoes.

"There! Aren't they pretty? I am sorry I could not find shoes with golden heels for you." She glanced at Marie who looked sardonically at me and shrugged.

"Perhaps it is as well the shoes are not exactly the same," I said lightly. "I do not want to tempt fate."

"Why, what could possibly happen to you?" She laughed. "I told Troy he should go dressed as the Devil. He refused because he has no sense of humour. The Devil tried to seduce Anna, in the old legend!"

She looked at me through laughing, slanted eyes and I blushed; she pinched my cheek affectionately.

"Silly Catherine! I was *teasing*. Anna was faithful to her shoemaker, even though the Devil tempted her. Troy might try to tempt *you* but I don't think he would succeed."

"You should not say such things," I protested.

Marie's sloe-black eyes were bright with malice. I looked at the strong, bony hands. I smelled the faded scent of pot-pourri about her, and decided I did not like nor trust her.

"I'm not sure I shall like being Anna," I said. "She jumped out of the window, didn't she? She was drowned in the lily pond. Like poor Lallie."

Selina's eyebrows rose.

"Who told you about Lallie?" she asked sharply.

I mentioned the incident at the Packhorse Inn. Marie was busy mending a tear in one of Selina's house-gowns. She did not look up, but I sensed that she was listening intently.

"It is quite true," Selina said quietly. "I felt sorry for Lallie. I told her I would do what I could for her, but ..."

She shrugged, and I saw bitterness in her face. The Master of the House was always reckoned to have a right to his pleasures, I thought; the best that the maid could hope for was that her family would look after her when she bore his child.

The Ballroom at Sandleford was magnificent. The footman folded back the ornate doors and Selina led me inside.

The long windows overlooked the terrace and the waterfall. Between each window the walls were panelled in white and gold and hung with mirrors. Gilt cherubs and nymphs holding golden cornucopias looked down from the ceiling at the four corners of the room. The chandeliers were waterfalls of frozen raindrops, and above them, the ceiling was magnificently painted, with scenes from Greek mythology.

"Isn't it magnificent?" Selina said proudly. "There is not a finer ballroom in all the County. This room was always closed when I was a child. I scarcely ever came in here, but one day I saw it, with all the shutters open. It looked so neglected, that I cried. I vowed that one day it would be restored to all its beauty."

"Your dream came true."

"Yes. When I was betrothed to Troy, we had a magnificent Ball here. *Everyone* came."

She walked across to the window and stared down at the rolling parklands, the white foam of water, the elegance of the long terrace with its summerhouse.

I could not tell what she was thinking. I went across and stood beside her. I saw a small figure in a blue coat bowling a hoop along one of the paths, with Katy walking just behind her.

"I wish Troy had not brought Alannah to this house," Selina said bitterly.

"It is not her fault—" I began.

"I did not say it was, Catherine. It's just that she's such a strange creature. The way she stares at us all with those secretive eyes of hers. The way she runs away and hides. There's something about her that troubles me."

I almost forgot the incident in the woods. We were all caught up in preparations for the Ball. Selina told me she had ordered a band from London to play for the dancing, and the Ballroom was to be filled with dozens of her favourite pink carnations. A firm of caterers had been hired and a great number of people were invited.

I talked to Alannah about it.

"Perhaps they will let you stay up and look down from the gallery when everyone arrives. The ladies will wear beautiful dresses and jewels, I expect. The day after the Ball, I will tell you all about it."

She looked pleased, smiling and squeezing my hand.

I went for a walk with her every day. I was able to teach her the names of the trees, and to point out different birds to her, telling her about their habits, how they reared their young, where they had come from.

Sometimes, we were joined by Rufus, who teased me about being a walking encyclopaedia.

"Aunt Vee taught me all the country lore I know," I said to him. "I hope I don't sound too governessy."

"I am sure there are very few governesses like you," he said, with the solemnity that I had learned to distrust, for it invariably hid some nonsense that I enjoyed, or some flirtatious remark.

"Now what is that supposed to mean?" I asked him.

"All the governesses I have met have been very prim and proper, Catherine."

"Am I not prim and proper?"

"No, thank goodness. You are a delightful creature, Your Majesty. Isn't that so, Alannah? Catherine is delightful!"

Alannah nodded so vigorously that her tam-o'-shanter almost jerked itself from her head. Touched, I squeezed her hand.

"I fear you are a flirt, Rufus," I said, with a mock sigh.

"Nothing to fear. I shall behave like a gentleman, at all times," he said, so piously, that I was reduced to laughter.

"Flirting is a very pleasant pastime," he added, unabashed. "Much more entertaining than playing chess with Troy."

"Alannah does not know what you mean by 'flirting'," I told him, seeing the child's puzzled face.

He addressed himself gravely to her.

" 'Flirting', my dear Alannah, means paying compliments to a lady of whom one is very fond. It means making a charming little package of words and phrases to hide deeper thoughts and emotions that would probably alarm the object of one's affection, if she knew of their existence. There! You have not understood one word of that, have you, little Alannah? Never mind! When you are grown up, some nice young gentleman will flirt with you, and then you will not only find it enjoyable, you will understand what I mean."

His glance rested on me; I looked away, my cheeks pink.

I enjoyed our daily walks. I could have been happy at Sandleford, but for the shadows that seemed to gather about me. Rufus was good company; Seton was charming and kind. I was deeply attached to Allannah, and believed that I might become friends with Agnes, given time. Only with Troy was I ill at ease; and he was seldom in evidence.

The house itself I could not like; it might have been different if I had grown up in it, with Selina. To me, it would always be dark and forbidding.

Sometimes, at night, when I awoke suddenly, and without apparent reason, I touched the Bible on my bedside table. Aunt Vee had given me the Bible on my sixteenth birthday. Touching it, calmed me; the feeling of terror, of something wrong in this house, would recede, leaving me at peace.

There were times when I had strange dreams. Once, I was dancing in the Ballroom; I wore white shoes, not red, and a white veil floated out behind me. I could not see the face of the man who held me in his arms, but we whirled faster and faster, until I felt sick and giddy and awoke with a racing heart.

One night, the dreams were particularly vivid. I awoke, fumbled for matches, and lit my bedside candle.

The deep shadows made a mockery of the pitiful candle-flame. There was no sound. Yet I knew I was not alone.

Chapter Five

I sat up in bed, for a moment, shivering, not knowing what to do. I wished I had courage enough to investigate the darkness, and see what it hid. Aunt Vee would have done so, I reflected …

Determinedly, I thrust back the bedclothes, put on my wrapper and a pair of slippers.

I picked up the candle, and moved towards the dressing room. My hand was trembling violently, making the flame dip and soar, so that the shadows on the wall grew grotesque and danced wildly.

Red shoes. An old curse, or a fairytale for children, depending on one's imagination. I was *not* going to let my imagination get out of control, I assured myself.

The door of the dressing-room was half-open. I pushed it wide, and called:

"Who is there?"

The answering silence was deep and soft like black velvet. It was a ridiculous question, I thought, and smiled faintly, in spite of my fear. I forced myself to examine the entire room, but I saw nothing and heard not a sound.

Back in my bedroom, I looked at the thick curtain that hid the staircase down to the study. It was not possible for anyone to enter the house that way, I reminded myself; only yesterday, I had examined the window catches and knew for certain that the windows had not been opened for years.

Still, I was not satisfied. Slowly, I went down the stairs, still holding the candle high.

This room, unlike the other two, was not empty. I could

not have said how I knew that fact, for, at first, there was no sound; but I sensed that someone—or something—was near me, even though I could not hear it move or breathe.

The curtains were drawn over the windows; Milly did this every night, as a matter of course, though I seldom used my father's old study.

The candlelight glistened on the gold-lettered spines of books. I knew some of the titles of those books: witchcraft, black magic, tales of the strange twilight world of the supernatural.

Something moved, near my feet; as I glanced sharply downwards, my heart thundering in my ears, I felt a softness, a sinuous gliding motion along the bare flesh of my ankles.

I looked down into a pair of brilliant green eyes, a grave, curious face turned up to mine. It was a black cat, and fear turned to a terrible panic-stricken hysteria that made my skin clammy.

I fought down panic. A harmless cat! It wound itself sinuously around my ankles, giving a throaty purr of pleasure.

It was not the presence of the cat that so terrified me; it was the knowledge that someone must have let it into the room, for it certainly could not have been there when I went to bed. There was no way it could have got in.

The cat, probably affronted by my unresponsiveness, moved away, though I could still hear it purring. I heard another sound, also; someone breathing, close to me.

I thought I was going to faint. I almost dropped the candle, trying to flatten myself against the wall. Carefully, I began to edge along the wall towards the stair entrance.

I was holding grimly to my slithering self-control. I heard the cat close to me again, and suddenly it made a playful leap for the cord of my wrapper; as it sprang, I was so startled that I screamed and dropped the candle, stumbling backwards as I did so.

Now I was in utter darkness; my flailing hands encountered an obstacle; even as I touched it, it jerked away and I heard the sound of breathing very close to me.

I reached out again; but there was nothing in front of me.

Whoever had been so close had moved out of range.

As I moved, I stumbled against the cat. It swore at me, and in my confusion, I fell heavily. My one instinct was to reach the stair opening, to find my way up to my bedroom, where I could summon help.

The acrid smell of candle-grease stung my throat; my frantically groping hands flailed at empty air. Nearby, I heard the cat, spitting and snarling furiously. No doubt it was as frightened as I was.

Vainly, I groped for the candle. I felt movement beside me. The cat was very close to me; someone must have bent and picked it up, for I heard it swear wildly as it was held against my face. I felt the hands that held it; man's or woman's, I could not tell. Something leapt at me again. I smelt the faint dustiness of cat's fur and I was too terrified even to scream.

I was dimly aware of movements I could not place; it seemed as though a door opened, somewhere nearby. The cat growled loudly, then more faintly, in the distance. Someone had taken it away; and that someone was near me, more menacing than the cat, as I tried to crawl towards the stairs that led up to my room, and the bell-rope that would bring help to me.

My ankle throbbed. This second fall was more frightening than the first had been. Exhausted, remembering that the rooms at Sandleford were sound-proof, and no one would hear me, I lifted my head, and muttered:

"Whoever you are, what do you *want*? For God's sake, let me *go* ..."

The answer was in the sound of breaking glass. I smelled paraffin and remembered the ornate lamp that stood on my father's old desk. A match scraped into life, and a tongue of flame ran eagerly towards me.

The desk was quite near the bottom of the stairs. I tried to get up on to my feet, but two strong hands pinned me down. I fought and struggled and tried to see my assailant; but the figure that crouched over me was swathed from head to feet in a dark cloak.

My clawing fingers found something hard and slippery on the cloak; desperately, I wrenched it off, holding it tightly in my closed fist. The flames were beginning to move greedily towards the thin material of my wrapper. Deliberately, I was pushed towards them and I felt a searing pain against the bare flesh of my leg.

I screamed as loudly as I could again and again, as I tried to struggle to my feet.

I felt a blow on my mouth that stopped my screams. I rolled away from the flames, so managing to extinguish them, for they had only just caught the hem of my wrapper. I could see more clearly, for the flames had reached the candle lying on the floor; they crackled with joyous fury, as I pulled myself, step by step, up the stairs, with a strength of will I did not know I possessed.

I know that I prayed; a muddled, foolish prayer. To the Lady of the Snows and whatever active good still lived in this house. Someone had tried to suffocate me, to frighten me out of my wits and then burn me to death. That someone had now vanished as stealthily as they had appeared.

I doubted that I had the strength to find the bell-rope; and as I lay there, only half-conscious, the door of my bedroom opened, letting in a thin stream of light from the corridor.

Alannah peered uncertainly into the room, as though she had been summoned to come, and did not know why or by whom. She looked like a small ghost, as she had done on the previous occasion when she had come to me.

"Get help, Alannah!" I whispered urgently. "*Please! Anyone!* Go quickly!"

She stared down at me, as though trying to locate me in the darkness. Then she nodded and sped away. I lay there, thinking: I wish I had died in the flames.

I thought about Troy. *I have eyes that can see in the dark*, he had said to Rufus. Cat's eyes, green and brilliant. He would make it his business to know every inch of this house. Every entrance, every exit.

The room suddenly seemed to be full of people.

"Dear life!" Mrs. Treville was saying helplessly. "What *have* we here?"

"I can smell fire!" That was Rufus, surprisingly sharp and authoritative. "My God, the study is on fire!"

"Oh, Catherine!" That was Selina, sobbing bitterly, her

arms about me as I was lifted on to the bed. "Whatever has happened to you?"

I drifted between consciousness and complete detachment of all that was happening around me. It was like being supported on a frail cloud of awareness that might break at any moment.

I heard Troy giving orders to the servants. An acrid smell stung my throat.

"I'll take her!" said Rufus; and he lifted me in his arms. How strong he was, though he seemed slightly built. He was wiry, and his strength was steely, like Troy's.

A small hand fluttered against mine.

"Go to your room, Alannah!" Troy commanded. "This is no place for you!"

"Let her stay!" I cried. "I want her near me."

I felt the second's silence. My eyes met Troy's; his had never seemed so hard and so bright. He turned away without another word and I grasped Alannah's hand. As I did so, I dropped the small object I was holding.

I saw her pick it up. I was too weary to analyze the importance or otherwise of her action. I only knew I desperately needed her beside me, and she trotted along the corridor in the wake of Rufus, who put me down on a bed in one of the guest rooms.

I shall not have to sleep in the tower room again, I reflected thankfully.

It was a night of activity. I refused the sedative Dr. Garrod wanted to give me, and his face flushed with annoyance. He put a soothing lotion on the angry red burn on my leg. Selina sat shivering, traces of tears on her cheeks as she looked at me. I thought her look was uneasy, and I could not blame her. My lips were swollen from the vicious blow.

Rufus bent over me, pushing back the hair from my forehead.

"We shall have to put you in a glass case to keep you safe!" he murmured softly.

Mrs. Treville brought brandy and milk, Milly fussed and wept and was scolded angrily by her mistress. Troy came into the room.

"The fire is under control," he told Selina.

"Is there much damage?"

"The carpet and curtains are most affected. A few of the books suffered; the wood of the desk is marked. Nothing that is irreplaceable." His voice held dry irony. "What *is* certain is that Catherine cannot sleep there again."

"There was a cat," I murmured foolishly. "I had a candle, and I had gone down to the study because I thought someone was there. I felt the cat rub against me."

"Hush!" said Troy curtly. "You are talking nonsense."

"There is only one cat," Selina told me gently. "In the stables. Kellatt looks after it. It does not come into the house."

Troy's face was weary, as he turned to me.

"Try to sleep, Catherine. We will talk about this tomorrow."

I knew what he would say. I knew that he would never believe there had been a cat downstairs, as well as someone who had tried to kill me.

Throughout all the commotion, Alannah remained serene. She sat holding my hand and would not move from my side; the fact displeased Selina. I could tell, by the frown on her face, and the way she ignored the presence of her husband's illegitimate daughter.

In the morning, I felt better; shaken and spent, my leg hurting, my mouth still swollen but completely in control of myself again.

Milly helped me to dress. Her look said a great deal. She took me down to Troy and Selina.

I told them what had happened. Selina listened with downbent head, her hands folded quietly in her lap. Troy stood with his back to the window, looking unapproachable. Rufus sat a little way from them both, watching me intently.

"Why do you persist in this belief that someone in this house wishes to kill you?" he demanded sceptically.

I bit back an angry retort. In daylight, it seemed incredible enough. My thoughts scurried like mice: *in this house*. Not necessarily. There was Seton, at Ashmead; Agnes. Both of them, in their ways, unknown and reserved people. Nothing was too fantastic, when I looked back at the events of the previous evening.

Rufus said:

"Does it not strike you as strange that Alannah has this premonition of disaster where Catherine is concerned?"

The fierce, hawk-like face revealed nothing. Troy's voice was expressionless.

"Children and animals sense danger, where adults often do not know it exists."

"I would scarcely have expected such sentiments from you," Rufus answered, surprised.

The thick eyebrows rose; I was more than ever reminded of the Devil when Troy wore such a sardonic expression.

"You think me incapable of depth of thought? A materialistic man who knows only how to amass money and possessions?"

Rufus flushed angrily.

"I did not say that, Troy. I merely remarked that such sentiments do not seem to be in keeping with such a practical outlook as yours."

Selina looked up and flung out her hands helplessly.

"It is ridiculous to quarrel! Like Rufus, I find Alannah's behaviour very curious." She tossed her head as she looked at her husband.

He shrugged.

"I have certain beliefs. I believe that strange bonds can exist between people, where there is affection and understanding between them."

He was looking directly at me. I could not bear the brightness of those eyes that missed nothing, and seemed to look right into me. I stared beyond him at the milky-blue sky of Spring, framed in the window. The day was gentle; there would be dusty catkins swinging on hazel boughs, and perhaps a patch of creamy-yellow primroses hiding in the woods. The wind would feel clean and sweet on my face, the turf spring back easily beneath my feet; I longed to be out of doors, alone with my thoughts, far from this man and his extraordinary power over me.

Selina's blue eyes were enormous and very bright. There was colour in her cheeks, her soft red mouth trembled, whether with pain or anger I did not know. She was beautiful, I thought sadly, in a way that *I* would never be beautiful. She possessed a strange incandescence, as though a lamp had been lit inside her, and when she spoke, her voice was high and excited.

"You should not have given Catherine the rooms in the West Tower, Troy! From those windows, both Anna and Lallie fell to their deaths. It happened because something still lives there, the dark power that is stronger than anything in the world …"

"You talk like a feverish child," Troy said contemptuously.

The words were like a douche of cold water. Selina looked deflated. Her remark had been foolish, and she had been over-excited; but he need not have been so cruel, in front of Rufus and myself.

He told me, curtly, that the servants would move my belongings to another suite of rooms, and added that he trusted there would be no more such disturbances.

With that, he strode from the room, as though we no longer existed for him. I looked at Selina, seeing anger in her face.

"One day," she said softly, "he will regret all the unhappiness he has caused me."

I was astonished at the vehemence of her words. She seemed a soft, defenceless woman; I had not thought her capable of such strength of feeling.

Rufus spoke softly.

"You should not have married Troy, you know. He is a man of granite. Too hard, too strange for you. I wanted to marry you, years ago. *You* only wanted a house."

She lifted her lovely blue eyes to his, and I saw that there was no expression in them; they were as blank as the eyes of a sleepwalker.

"I have my house," she said slowly.

"The price was high," he pointed out.

They seemed to have forgotten that I was in the room. Embarrassed, I murmured my excuses, and left the room.

I went up to the Nursery; Alannah was sitting pensively by the fire. The windows were all closed, and the room was too hot. In the room beyond, Katy bustled about, putting away clean linen.

The child was bored. No wonder. I held out my hand, touched by the smile she gave me.

"Come along!" I said. "Put on your coat and hat. We'll go for a walk, just you and me. Would you like that?"

She nodded eagerly, and jumped down from the chair; Katy came into the room, her face troubled.

"Are you well enough to go out, miss?"

"Quite well enough, thank you," I said briskly.

She hesitated, clearly out of her depth. Finally, she blurted out:

"You're not supposed to go out on your own, miss!"

"What on earth do you mean?"

She smoothed down her apron with bony red hands, very ill at ease.

"It was Mr. Merrick's orders," she murmured.

"I see. Well, there is no need for you to worry, Katy," I said briskly. "I will answer to him for my afternoon walk, if necessary."

Alannah came back wearing her best coat and a tam-o'-shanter. Sedately, she put on her gloves. Katy shrugged, folded her lips together, and went back to her task.

"Did you pick up what I dropped last night?" I asked Alannah softly.

She nodded, and went across to the little lacquered box with its mother-of-pearl inlay where she kept her treasures. From it she took a small object and brought it to me.

It was a button; a cheap wooden button hanging by a coarse black thread. Hardly the kind to have been found on the cloaks or coats of the members of this household, I reflected; this came from the sort of garment a servant would have worn.

We met Mrs. Treville on our way out; she stood aside, giving me a strange, nervous look as though not certain how I would behave towards her.

"We are going to the stables, Mrs. Treville," I said brightly. "To look at the horses; and see if we can find the stable cat."

She looked nonplussed; I knew that gossip travels like wildfire amongst servants. Everyone knew, by now, that I had insisted a cat had been smuggled into the house.

"I don't understand it, Miss Catherine," Mrs. Treville said bluntly. "That cat belongs to Kellatt, and has never been in the house that I can recollect. Besides how would he get into your grandfather's old study when there are no doors, and the windows have been fastened for years?"

"*I* would like answers to those questions," I told her drily.

"There's none here would harm you. You've had a sad time, Miss Catherine, what with your Aunt dying so suddenly, and then coming here and finding you had relations you didn't know of; it's been upsetting and strange for you. I had a niece used to have dreadful nightmares just like you …"

"Is that what you've been told?" I asked bitterly. "That I have bad dreams?"

"It's what Mr. and Mrs. Merrick believe," she declared stubbornly, "and who's to say it isn't so? You'll be your old self again, in time, you see."

I looked into the honest, plain face and knew the folly of argument.

We skirted the woods, carefully avoiding the Folly and the little hut, with its tarred roof, where Smeech lived. We did not find any primroses, but came upon a patch of damp, purple violets.

Alannah picked them and made them into a posy. She pointed towards the Chapel and tugged at my hand.

"All right. We'll take them to the Lady and put them beneath her picture," I said.

Unexpectedly, Alannah caught hold of my hand and held it to her cheek for a moment, as though expressing gratitude as well as affection.

I was deeply moved, almost to tears; I smiled down at her. She could not speak to me, yet we communicated in so many ways. She was the only person at Sandleford with whom I felt completely at ease. Had she been my own child, I could not have cared more for her, and that fact gave me comfort.

As we walked to the Chapel, I looked towards the gates of Sandleford. They were closed, and I had a moment's panic. I was a prisoner. I could not go out through those gates and away from this house, to freedom from fear, because Troy was my guardian and he would bring me back.

It was strange to think that Aunt Vee had innocently set a terrible trap for me, believing that she was safeguarding my future.

There was peace in the Chapel. I felt it, like a tangible thing; a coolness, a stillness that I badly needed. How wise Argus Fairfax had been, to build this place, I thought, as I knelt and prayed for strength, for courage to meet whatever awaited me, for wisdom and understanding.

Alannah found the small vase that was always kept in the Chapel, filled with water, ready for flowers. She arranged the violets, and smiled at the figure in the stained-glass window.

Afterwards, we went to see the horses. Kellatt was nowhere around; one of the grooms told me he had gone to the farrier's. In a sunny corner of the yard, sat a black cat, grooming itself fastidiously. It looked up, staring at me with sleepy green eyes. When Alannah bent and stroked it, the cat purred and began to weave sinuously around her, much to her delight.

When she was tired of playing with the cat, she ran back to me, and put her hand trustfully in mine. Looking down at her, I thought: the things that happen in this house do not seem to affect her, thank God! How normal, how ordinary, she makes everything seem.

"Perhaps you will have a cat of your own, one day," I told her.

She nodded, pleased, and skipped beside me. I promised her a skipping rope with bells on the handles and told her the rhymes I had learned, as a child, whilst Duffy taught me how to hop, with great agility, the right side of the rope she held How happy, how faraway it seemed now!

As we walked back to the house, I was surprised to see Agnes, sitting in her wheelchair, on the terrace by the lily pond. There was a rug over her knees and she had removed her hat, letting the faint breeze lift strands of lustreless hair from her forehead. She did not wave to us; she waited until we approached before she greeted us in her light, rather colourless voice.

"It was too pleasant a day to be indoors! Seton has come to see Rufus on some private matter, and Selina has a migraine. I am not surprised, after what I have heard concerning last night's events!"

Her eyes were challenging. I saw that she was not wearing gloves. As she lifted her hand to push back a strand of hair, I noticed two or three small scratches near her wrist.

"I suffered an unpleasant experience," I replied lightly. "No one seems likely to believe my story. The general belief is that I dreamed it all."

"Perhaps you did," she murmured.

"The study caught fire. There is a burn on my leg," I retorted.

"Perhaps you fell down the stairs with the lighted candle, whilst walking in your sleep."

"Perhaps," I said cynically. Her answers were altogether too pat, I thought. "I was also frightened by a cat."

"The cat that nobody saw!" She laughed softly, and her eyes danced. "It couldn't be found, afterwards, I hear. Troy had everyone searching for it. Eventually, it was found in the stables, fast asleep."

"Who told you all this?"

"Rufus. He says Troy has given instructions that it shall not be discussed in front of you. He shows such concern for your peace of mind, Catherine!"

I fancied there was an element of spite in her teasing, yet I could not help but feel compassion for her, the wheelchair prisoner who should have been able to run over the grass on such a day, walk in the woods, dance for the sheer joy of living.

"You've scratched your hand," I said.

She examined the grazes dispassionately.

"Yes. Not through extending unwelcome caresses to a cat," she retorted drily. "I've been pruning the roses. I find gardening a great solace, even though I am hampered by my physical infirmity."

She spoke without bitterness. Agnes was a very deep,

very still pool, I thought. If there was tempest and passion, years of serving the Creightons had subdued it.

I glanced at Alannah. They say that children can always tell, about adults. They have an instinct that never fails them.

Alannah stood still and straight by my side. She looked gravely at Agnes, but made no move towards her. Agnes looked at the child and suddenly smiled. It was a smile of such sweetness that I thought despairingly: I give up. I shall never understand any of them.

"Did you enjoy your walk?" Agnes asked the child.

Alannah nodded vigorously. There was colour in her cheeks and the jaunty tam-o'-shanter had slipped back on her dark hair. She looked like any ordinary child who had been out in the fresh air for an afternoon. *I* knew that she was different from other children.

"Will you wheel me into the house?" Agnes asked me. "It will save Seton the trouble of coming out. How lucky you are to have the independence of being able to go wherever you choose!"

I was as much a prisoner as Agnes, I thought wrily, for I was compelled to stay within the boundaries of a house I disliked.

"In time you will be able to walk," I reminded her.

"In time, Alannah will be able to talk; is that not so?" She challenged the child; Alannah nodded, watching me as I turned the wheelchair and pushed it along the terrace.

"Seton is kind to you," I reminded her gently.

To my astonishment, she put a hand across her eyes; when she spoke her voice shook with emotion.

"Yes! He is very kind!" she whispered.

There was anguish in her voice and face; her hand was shaking. She seemed to be tormented by a sense of guilt.

It was gone in a moment. She began to talk to Alannah as we went indoors, leaving the thin Spring sunlight behind us. Nevertheless, I wondered greatly about that moment of betrayal. Selina had hinted that Agnes was in love with Troy; perhaps she had been wrong.

Troy came out of the house, as we walked towards the entrance; Seton was with him, and the two men made a splendid contrast: Troy, tall and powerfully-built, dark and rugged—a gypsy, a pirate, a buccaneer, a highwayman: all those titles would have fitted him easily. Beside him, Seton, his thick, wheat-coloured hair shining in the sun. Not so tall as Troy, but holding himself proudly, the look of a Viking warrior about him.

Seton fascinated me; not in the way that Troy did, for I knew there was nothing physical in my feelings towards Seton Blair.

"I hope you are feeling better," Seton said kindly, to me.

I looked into the finely-chiselled face, the turquoise eyes with their thick, short gold lashes.

"Much better," I told him.

Agnes was watching us both closely; it was a look that I could feel, burning through my skin.

"Do you believe I imagined what happened?" I asked Seton, as Troy bent to speak to Alannah.

"No," he said. "I believe that strange and terrible things can still happen in this house; that dark forces can be set in motion with powerful effect."

"Who would set such forces at work against me?" I asked, uneasy.

"Someone strong enough to command; someone possessing the will and the power to do so," he answered quietly.

I thought his words were obscure; he did not enlarge upon them, however.

Agnes still seemed to be in the grip of some deep emotion that had disturbed the depths of her being. She was watching Seton with a look of love, of yearning—and of despair; and then, as though she was aware of my interest in her, she lowered her eyes, her face assuming its usual expressionless calm, like a still sea on a summer evening.

I turned towards the house. Troy was teasing Alannah; I heard him laugh, saw him snatch the tam-o'-shanter from her head and ruffle her hair. She was obviously enjoying it, trying to leap up and snatch the blue velvet hat that he held just out of reach. It seemed so natural, so carefree; I had never seen Troy so relaxed. It could have been a happy domestic scene and was the nearest thing to normality that I had witnessed since coming to Sandleford.

Troy tossed the hat high in the air and Alannah caught it. I heard her gurgle with laughter as she raced indoors. Troy walked towards me; he came so close that I could have put up a hand and touched his cheek.

He towered over me; I avoided his eyes.

"Catherine," he said commandingly, forcing me to look at him; when, reluctantly, my eyes met his, he asked:

"How are you feeling?"

"Much better."

"*Should* you be walking on that ankle? With your leg injured, also?" he asked formally.

"The burn is only a superficial one, thank Heavens. The trap cut and bruised my instep, that's all. It's healing well."

"You're limping, though."

"You have sharp eyes, Cousin Troy. The exercise is good for me."

"Tonight, you shall have a different kind of exercise. I intend to begin teaching you to play Chess, after dinner. I think you will be a good pupil. You give your mind to whatever you are doing. Rufus lacks concentration."

Selina came to dinner looking pale and tired. Her eyebrows rose when Troy announced his intention of teaching me to play Chess.

"I trust you will not tire Catherine," she said coolly.

"Why should I? Learning to play will give her something to think about besides the legends and tales and the wild nonsense that seems to have infected everyone in this house."

"You don't like Sandleford!" she flared suddenly. "To you, it is just a pile of stones. For me, it is part of my life; a house in which strange things have happened. A place that keeps its secrets. *You* will never discover them, Troy."

"I have no wish to do so," he retorted blandly.

Selina had the strange, luminous look I had seen earlier in the day; the air of excitement, the brilliance in her eyes. She loved this house passionately, but I thought it was an obsessive love, for the place seemed to dominate her.

After dinner, Troy took me to his study. The cosy atmosphere of the booklined room disquieted me. In these surroundings, Troy's powerful animal magnetism came across more strongly than ever. I was so acutely aware of him that I wondered how I could concentrate on the game he was to teach me.

The chessmen were set out; they were exquisitely carved of onyx, set on a board of jet and ivory.

He saw my appraisal and smiled, standing so close that our shoulders touched.

"Beautiful, is it not, Catherine? It was once in the possession of an Indian prince who was taught the game by an Englishman."

"How did it come into YOUR possession?"

"I bought it. I paid handsomely for it, as I have done for everything I own," he replied arrogantly.

"Do you believe that money will purchase anything that one desires?" I asked.

"It is a fact, Catherine, whether you like it or not."

"I think you are wrong."

He smiled wickedly.

"There speaks a philanthropist. I am not a philanthropist, merely a man who has fought hard for his riches."

"Aunt Vee said that money is the cheapest thing of all."

"A profound remark," he agreed drily.

He was an excellent teacher. I enjoyed myself, but I could not be relaxed with him, for I was too intensely aware of his presence, and when his fingers accidentally brushed mine, the shock of the contact shivered all through me.

I thought of Alannah's mother, lying in his arms; of Selina, all grace and beauty and warmth. I imagined him making love to them both, passionate and demanding in his need of them. The thoughts brought colour to my cheeks that could not be blamed on the fire.

The clock struck a very late hour and Troy said abruptly that we had played enough for one night. He did not praise me, and I felt disappointed, for I thought I had begun to master the game quite well.

"Thank you!" I said sedately. "Good-night."

"Do I not warrant a cousinly kiss?" he mocked.

My heart floundered. It would be more than I could bear to feel the touch of his lips.

"You look as though I had suggested something improper!" He laughed, and bent his head, his face very close to mine, as he added softly:

"I find you attractive! Surely that pleases you?"

"It does not!" I replied briefly.

"*All* women love to be told they have the power to attract a man!" he retorted.

His face was so close I could see every line, every crisp curl springing back from his forehead; even a small scar on one cheek, and a tiny mole near his left eye.

"You are not pretty," Troy told me.

"I am aware of that. I have studied my mirror, over the years!" I retorted.

"You have more subtle qualities, Catherine. A feminine capriciousness, the dryness of a good sherry, a wilfulness. A fine spirit, a good, questing mind. They outlast prettiness."

Every bone in my body ached with longing. I clung frantically to shreds of reason, telling myself it was a clever prelude to seduction, and that he did not mean a word of what he said.

Reason shrivelled in the heat of the fiercer fires within me, and I could only listen.

"I wish you had been at my side in Australia. There are women like you, pioneers' wives, working beside their men to build a challenging new life. They travel great distances in rough conditions and never complain. They build their homes with their hands, out of unpromising materials; they have learned to do the tasks that men do, they have wit and courage and they are resourceful. Yet still they remain—*women*."

He spoke the last word so softly it was a caress. Slowly his head came down; with gentle deliberation he let his lips just touch mine. I closed my eyes and when he laughed, I flew into a rage.

"*You* think you can have any women you want!" I choked.

"You are angry because you thought I was going to kiss you and I disappointed you!" he taunted.

Scarlet colour flared into my face.

"What do you imagine I want of YOU?" I cried foolishly.

"Let me show you, Catherine."

His voice was as soft as silk. His arms went round me so fiercely that they hurt my flesh and I was exultant, knowing that I wanted the fierce touch more than anything in the world; I wanted to be held against him, completely at his mercy.

Still he tormented me by not kissing me. I hoped he would never know how much I longed for his mouth to be as demanding as his arms. His breath came slightly faster between his parted lips; his eyes were deep-green pools of water, as his fingers found the fastening at the back of my dress.

I held my breath, my heart racing; when I felt the dress come apart and his hands against bare flesh, I was totally unprepared for the wild surge of feeling that rolled over me in a huge wave. This was the passion Aunt Vee had spoken of; the danger of desire. I did not care that I was as shameless as any woman he had taken to the Folly. I had never before known what it really meant to be in love. The teasing, the touching of fingertips, the flirting with eyes and smiles; they were pale echoes of this rage in the blood.

One of his hands moved around me, and cradled my breast gently. Pain and ecstasy ripped at the last vestiges of my self-control. As I moved against him, I heard him sigh gently.

At that moment, there was a sharp tap at the door, and it was opened immediately to reveal the accusing figure of Marie.

Troy turned his head leisurely, as though he had all the time in the world.

"Well?" he said.

"Madame wishes to speak with you!" she replied icily.

"Madame has chosen a most inopportune moment," he replied, smoothly. "However, you may tell her that I shall join her in a moment."

I was speechless and embarrassed. I watched Marie close the door behind her with controlled violence.

"Go to bed, Catherine," Troy said absently, as though he had already forgotten I was there.

With trembling fingers, I rearranged my disordered dress.

I felt miserable and cheated, as I ran blindly up the stairs.

I did not expect to meet anyone at the top; but Rufus was there; he had a book beneath his arm and was wearing his dressing-gown.

"I could not sleep," he told me, "so I came down to fetch a book from the library and stopped on my return to admire the Fairfax portrait gallery."

His eyes missed no detail of my appearance. I was shivering, miserably conscious of my untidy hair and giveaway appearance. It must have been obvious, I thought. I felt soiled in some way. It had all been my fault for not having the will to say 'No' to Troy.

"Did you enjoy your game of Chess?" Rufus asked.

"Yes."

"My poor Catherine," he said wrily. "Don't look so unhappy. Troy has made a fool of you, hasn't he? Teased and tantalised and then laughed. He treats all women so— except those he takes to the Folly."

"How can you know that?" I asked sharply.

"I know more of life than you. Troy is a man of the world; skilful, experienced, ruthless. He is a generous host to me, and I admire all he has achieved; but morally, he is corrupt."

I thought, guiltily, of my own frightening desires; of the strange tumult within me, forever wounding peace, awakening me to a state of wild unrest and wonder.

I was silent, and Rufus looked at me quizzically.

"I ought to whisk you away from here, Catherine; take you to Kilstock, when the place is ready. Crown you with roses and make you my Summer Queen; does that please your Majesty?"

His eyes twinkled, and he was smiling; but there was something more—the gaiety hid a seriousness I had not suspected in him.

"I am proposing marriage, Catherine dear," he added. "I will go down upon bended knee, if you wish."

He put one hand upon his heart and I said suspiciously:

"You are making fun of me!"

"Indeed I am not. A proposal is no laughing matter. Though my Kingdom is not yet fit for your occupation, I offer it to you with all my heart. I have never proposed marriage to a woman, before." He considered that fact, head on one side. "When we were children, I asked Selina to marry me; it was first love, innocent as the daisies upon the grass and with no more substance. She refused me, of course, telling me that she would never leave Sandleford. She married in order to keep HER Kingdom."

"One should marry only for love," I said, with a sigh.

"You do not care for me?"

"Yes. I am very fond of you, but affection is not love. Besides, we know little of one another."

"On the contrary, I know a great deal about you; I have observed and delighted in many small things during our walks together," he replied, with a dignity that would have done credit to Seton.

"We can have a leisurely betrothal," he added. "A betrothal is a very pleasant prelude to matrimony, and a carefree time."

"Marriage brings responsibilities; you would not like that, Rufus."

"The pleasure of having you at my side would be compensation enough," he assured me disarmingly.

I looked searchingly at him. He was handsome, agreeable, sociable. If I married him, I would live in comfort. He would be kind and undemanding, he would be amusing and good company. What more did I need? As for love, that could come after marriage—people said that it was often the case. It was absurd to cherish romantic dreams; I should settle for reality and count myself fortunate that such a man as Rufus had asked me to be his wife.

It occurred to me that Troy might refuse to give his consent to my marriage; he could only do so until I was twenty-one; then I would be able to walk through the gates of Sandleford and never return.

I would be free. Free to forget Troy, to put away memories and thoughts that could only bring increasing anguish. In learning to love Rufus, would I not be able to subdue a passion that brought only sorrow in its wake?

"Rufus," I said gently. "I am honoured; and touched by your proposal. I need a little while in which to think it over carefully; it has been—so—unexpected, you see."

I put a hand pleadingly on his arm. He smiled and patted my fingertips; his hazel eyes were bright.

"Take your time, little Catherine; and whilst you are pondering your answer, be sure to keep the Master of the House at arm's length. He is as dangerous as a wolf."

"I promise to learn that lesson without delay," I assured him gravely.

"May I be allowed to accompany you upon your walks, still? And to flirt with you a little?"

I laughed.

"Of course! Are you NEVER serious, Rufus?"

"Yes," he said unexpectedly. "I was in earnest when I asked you to consider marrying me. Good-night, Catherine."

With that, he was gone. I went to my room, undressed and got into bed. The sheets felt blessedly cool against my hot limbs. My mind had never been in such a state of turmoil before.

If only, I thought bitterly, I could feel for Rufus, the longing I feel for Troy.

I tossed and turned, in the darkness. I will marry Rufus, I vowed. I will be a good wife to him. Then I shall be safe from torment.

In the morning, I was heavy-eyed. I was thankful that Rufus did not appear at breakfast; but Troy was there, which was worse. My hands trembled, and I could not look at him. When finally, he spoke directly to me, forcing me to meet his eyes, it needed all my self-control to answer him calmly.

"Tomorrow, I am going into Portsmouth. You and Alannah can come with me. You will both find it interesting." He turned to Selina.

"You will come as well?" he asked formally.

She shook her head.

"No thank you. I am busy with preparations for the Ball. Travelling by coach gives me a headache."

He shrugged and said to me:

"Be ready immediately after breakfast tomorrow morning."

It seemed impossible that this cold-eyed stranger could be the same man who had held me in his arms last night.

The morning's post had brought a letter from Arthur Jarley. He wrote that he was anxious to know how I was settling down at Sandleford.

I had an overwhelming longing to confide in someone. Arthur was the best possible person. I sat down at the desk in my room, and wrote a long letter to him, telling him all that had happened to me since I had left Dorset, and admitting that I was unhappy about Troy having the authority of a guardian over me.

I sealed and addressed the envelope. The feeling of being trapped was very strong, though I liked my new suite of rooms well enough. The rooms were lighter and airier than those in the West Tower, and I no longer heard the sound of dancing feet at night.

I thought about the person who had waited to attack me in my grandfather's study. I was curious. I put the letter into my jacket pocket and went to the West Tower rooms; in broad daylight, I argued, I was bound to be safe enough.

I was surprised to find Mrs. Treville there; she seemed equally astonished to see me. I thought her look was faintly disapproving.

"The room has been cleaned, as you can see, Miss Catherine. I'm here to check what's been done; you can't trust servants; they scamp the work unless you go round behind them and look at every little thing."

"Quite right," I agreed, gravely. "I came to look for a book to read."

"The library is downstairs," she pointed out.

"Something from my grandfather's personal collection, I thought."

"I don't think you'd care for his taste in books," she replied.

"I'll decide on that for myself, thank you, Mrs. Treville," I said pleasantly.

She seemed very reluctant to let me go to the study; however, I took a deep breath and pulled aside the curtain, deliberately shutting out my memories of the night when death by burning had been planned for me.

The evidence of the night's horror was apparent when I reached the bottom of the stairs. The burned curtains had been removed, the desk taken away for repair. There was still a trail of spilled candle-grease on the damaged carpet.

Mrs. Treville followed me, and stood on the bottom step. I was irritated and annoyed at the way her eyes followed my every movement; how could I search for a secret exit from this room under those curious eyes?

Idly, I picked at the contents of the bookcase. Eventually, I chose a book on Magic, deciding to return at a more opportune time. Mrs. Treville shook her head over my choice of reading matter.

"Those books will do you no good, Miss Catherine. 'Twill only stir up trouble in your mind. You want something to make you feel happy," she said.

I looked into the tired blue eyes; her concern seemed genuine enough. Like the other servants, she had been conditioned to believe that I was a silly, over-imaginative young woman, given to bouts of hysteria.

I returned later that day; to my relief, the door was unlocked, the rooms empty.

I worked quickly, praying that I would not be disturbed. I moved great quantities of books, in order to examine the walls behind them, and in the end, I was dusty, exhausted— and no nearer the truth; for the walls of grandfather's old room were solid and yielded nothing to my enquiring fingers.

I put all the books back again; as I wearily pushed the last few into place, something fluttered to my feet.

It was a small notebook with a shiny black cover and it had obviously been hidden between some large volumes on the Arts of Black Magic.

I opened it, without much interest; the pages were covered with fine handwriting. My grandfather's name leaped out at me, and my interest suddenly quickened.

I went back to my own room; there, I sat down and opened the notebook.

Chapter Six

On the inside of the cover, my grandfather had written his name: Damon Fairfax.

Beneath it, was the legend:

"Notes I have made from a study of many books on the subject of Superstition, Black Magic, and malign influences."

I felt a tremor of excitement and anticipation. As though I was about to discover something of tremendous importance.

I settled down to read the notes my grandfather had made so meticulously. It was not an easy task, for the ink had faded and the fine, close-packed writing was a severe test of one's eyesight.

Much of what I read had been copied, en bloc, from books in the library and contained appropriate references to the passages quoted. It was grandfather's own observations, from his reading, that aroused my interest and excited my curiosity.

Damon Fairfax had held the theory that evil lived on where once it had been active in a house; like a seed lying dormant in the soil, waiting the right conditions for germination.

"There are things I cannot dismiss as superstitious gossip," he wrote. "If one is to believe in the existence of good, then one must accept the presence of evil, also. When I find it difficult to believe that good *must*, eventually, triumph, I go to the Chapel and think of the young woman who caused flowers to grow where she walked on Sandleford land.

"I believe that, in this house, some peace has been forever

destroyed; perhaps it is true, then, that the Devil danced the night away under this roof and left the mark of his anger here. My dear wife insists that it is so. I thank God that the children seem untouched and are not chilled, as we are, by the long, cold shadows in this house.

"I cannot leave this house, as I would like to; to do so would be to turn my back upon my inheritance, upon the needs of my servants, my tenants, my people. Yet I would have no regrets if this building was burned to the ground; certainly I would not allow any other to be erected in its place."

His impassioned words were startling. Surely, I thought, if the house was so full of old evil, Damon's wife and children would have sensed it and been affected by it?

I read on, and was even more surprised.

"My father told me," Damon wrote, "that the Black Mass was often celebrated in the West Tower of this house."

The West Tower; the rooms I had occupied until recently.

"I never doubted that my father spoke truthfully. I am a practical man not given to hysterical fancies; but I know that, to this day, the West Tower rooms have a strange atmosphere, a sense of corruption and decay, originating from the acts of blasphemy committed there. Daniel occupies these rooms, and I have watched closely for any sign that he is affected by the atmosphere. I have found none, thank God."

There were more surprises, as I read on.

"Those who came to celebrate the Black Mass were—according to my father—very respectable local dignitaries and citizens who were afraid that their taste for perversion, their lust for titillation might be discovered. So they used the secret entrance to the West Tower. There is no other entrance—only by the window of my study which would have meant crossing the terrace and being observed. My father told me that HIS father knew about this entrance, but would never reveal its whereabouts. *I* have searched diligently, removing every book from the wall and tested every inch of the stonework, in vain. Yet I am sure the entrance exists, and that it connects with a passage running under the house, emerging near a gate or door in the grounds through which the visitors could come and go, unseen ...

"This house, like many old ones, is honeycombed with passages that were useful in the days of smuggling. Morgan Fairfax leased the passages to smugglers of contraband using the Portsmouth road to transport their illicit cargoes to London. It is said he charged an exorbitant fee for hiding men and goods, and then exacted a further fee for not betraying his guests to the Preventitive Men."

I put down the book, with shaking hands. I had almost reached the end of the writings and there was little else of interest.

My heartbeats were heavy and slow. A secret passage; not a figment of an old man's imagination, not a child's fairytale, but a means of entering and leaving the West Tower without trace.

Someone was still using it, today.

What should I do, I wondered ironically? Go to Troy, tell him that the existence of the passage was proof I had not imagined the sound of dancing feet, and the presence of an unseen attacker who had tried to kill me?

Would Troy believe, even if I showed him the book? Was it not Troy who had given me these rooms to use?

Someone was using the old tales to good account. Troy? Selina? Rufus, who had asked me to marry him? Someone from outside this house: Agnes was unable to walk. Seton, perhaps: the quiet, reserved man, whose thoughts were deep and encompassed many things to do with evil.

I thought about the wooden button I had torn from its cloth.

A fastening from a servant's cloak. Mrs. Treville? Why should she wish me ill? Marie? That was another matter. She disliked me; but that was not hatred ...

I decided to search the West Tower sitting-room again, as soon as I had an opportunity. Perhaps it was arrogant of me to think I could succeed where my grandfather and great-grandfather had failed; but I was determined to try.

I left the notebook on my bedside table, and went along to have tea with Alannah in the Nursery. Cook had made some gingerbread men, and a pile of hot, buttered toast. There was a jug of milk for Alannah, and a pot of tea for me.

It was cosy, and I was happy; Alannah came and leant her head against my arm, smiling up at me with her wide, candid eyes. I wondered what her thoughts were. Was she unhappy because she couldn't speak them aloud?

"When are you going to talk to me, Alannah?" I asked softly.

She looked away. She seemed troubled and uneasy. I had no right to ask her such questions, I felt.

I put an arm around her.

"Tomorrow we are going to Portsmouth," I reminded her. "Be ready, early. I'll tell Katy to put out your best coat and bonnet. I hope it will be a fine day."

She nodded and danced away, clapping her hands to express what she could not say.

After tea, I went back to my room. My Bible, my travelling clock, the candle in its silver holder and the box of matches were all there; but the black notebook had gone.

I rang for Milly; she came, after a pause, slightly out of breath.

"Yes, miss?"

"Have you been in here during the last hour, Milly?"

"No, miss." She was on the defensive.

"Has anyone else been here?"

"How would I know that, miss?" She looked faintly resentful. "I've been busy in the kitchen. Usually, none comes in here but me, speaking for the servants, that is. Have you missed something, then?"

"Nothing of value. Don't look so put out, Milly, I'm not suggesting you've taken anything. However, when I went to have tea in the Nursery, I left a small black notebook on my table, and now it has gone."

Milly went down on her knees and lifted the counterpane. She pulled the table away; searched all around the bed.

"You must've put it somewhere else, miss."

"No, I didn't." I sighed. "All right, thank you."

She went out, glancing back at me with a mystified look before she closed the door. I went across to the dressing-table and opened my hankerchief drawer; the button was still in its place.

To whom was the notebook important? And why?

There were four of us at dinner that evening. Troy was in a black mood; if Selina knew the reason, she hid the fact well. He spoke little and his face was sombre. I avoided meeting his eyes, for his compelling power frightened me, as always, with its intensity.

It was Rufus who brought up the subject of the Hellfire Club that had been founded nearly two hundred years ago, for young men of wild and depraved tastes.

"They held orgies in an old Cistercian Monastery; things too dreadful to mention. Once they dressed a baboon up as the Devil and endangered a man's sanity ..."

I looked at Selina. Her eyes were wide and brilliant with excitement, and her cheeks were flushed. She was enthralled with what Rufus was saying, but I thought it was wrong of him to discuss such things in front of her; she was too impressionable, I felt. Though she carried her role as Mistress of the House with charm and dignity, she seemed curiously young in many ways. She is bored, I thought; ready to listen to any nonsense to chase away that boredom.

Troy listened absently; once, I saw a faint, cynical smile on his lips which made his face seem even more saturnine.

I said, suddenly, to Rufus:

"Do you believe that evil can live on, through the centuries? To erupt again, given the right conditions?"

The hazel eyes narrowed; they were bright and speculative.

"What a fascinating theory!"

"You haven't answered my question, Rufus."

"I don't think evil has any power of itself; it needs a human hand and brain as instruments to execute its purpose!" he declared.

We had Troy's attention, at last; he was watching us both intently, waiting for my reply.

"I found a notebook in the West Tower sitting-room," I said. "Grandfather had written about such things inside it, and added some comments of his own. HE believed the house to be possessed."

"Houses cannot be possessed; only people," Rufus

replied. "Where is this book? I should like to see it."

"I left it in my room at teatime. When I went back, it had vanished."

"Oh well, what did you expect?" Selina said, with a delighted laugh. "Are you SURE, though, that it *has* vanished?"

"I rang for Milly. She searched everywhere, and couldn't find it."

Three pairs of eyes regarded me, all with differing expressions. Selina was amused, and didn't believe me. Troy's eyes were cold; Rufus's were bright and wary.

"You have simply mislaid it," Troy said coolly. "Why make such a mystery of it? That is how myths and superstitions are created."

"You don't believe in anything, Troy!" Selina cried, piqued. "Except, perhaps, your possessions! Those you can SEE and count!"

"I have earned the right to do so!" he retorted, with a flash of fire. "I have worked and fought to make and keep my wealth. It is much more satisfying than any ghost, any nebulous belief in the power of the unseen. You're too concerned with the past, with evil, with death. LIFE should be your concern; the things that will happen tomorrow, not the events of yesterday!"

I listened, fascinated, to the rich, resonant voice. How well he could speak on the subjects nearest to his heart, I thought. What a fine flow of words he had, what a splendid turn of phrase! He had taught himself to master words, just as he had taught himself to master everything else.

Selina shrugged, her mouth tight, all the light gone from her eyes. Troy seemed to take great pleasure in subduing her, I thought sadly.

Rufus changed the subject adroitly, and Troy took no more part in the conversation.

I had a moment alone with Rufus, on my way to my room that evening. He was standing outside the great white and gold ballroom doors.

"Are you looking for Anna and her unholy dancing partner?" I murmured.

He laughed.

"No. Selina asked me to check some of the work that has been done there for the Ball. She has set her heart on the event being a great success, poor girl! You see for yourself what her life here is like."

"Troy is not so materialistic as he pretends to be," I said. "Do you not remember that he said he believed strange bonds can exist between certain people?"

"I remember, Catherine. Troy says many odd things. The truth is, he believes only in power. What he wants, he takes."

I shivered. Rufus said softly:

"As Mistress of Kilstock, you would be someone in your own right, not an unwilling guest here in this house."

Selina married for similar reasons, I thought; it was like a warning.

"You will think it over, as you promised, won't you?" he urged. "I am tempted to carry you off to Kilstock as soon as my house is ready!"

"If you plan to kidnap me, I warn you I shall offer every possible resistance!" I retorted, laughing.

"That would produce an interesting situation, I fancy," he teased. "I should subdue you, of course; probably we should both enjoy the conquest."

"I am not easily subdued, Rufus!"

"Agreed. You are a young woman of spirit. You are not meek and compliant, like poor Agnes!"

"You are wrong to imagine that Agnes has no spirit. I think she hides a great deal of emotion behind that calm manner of hers," I told him.

"Oh well, I do not want to talk of Agnes, but of YOU. You are much more interesting. Do you know what you remind me of, at times, Catherine?"

"I have no idea!"

"An Egyptian Princess," he declared solemnly.

"How many Egyptian Princesses have you met?" I asked, equally solemn.

"Laugh if you like; oh yes, you ARE laughing, underneath. I have seen paintings. I think you must be a reincarnation of Queen Nefertiti."

"How strange that people who believe that they have

reincarnated were always rich and noble in their previous lives!" I mused. "Never a slave, never a hewer of wood or a drawer of water, you notice."

He laughed, and shrugged.

"True. Life as a servant or slave in such days must have been intolerable."

"What were YOU, in a previous life, Rufus?" I challenged.

He entered the spirit of the game, smiling wickedly.

"Ah, that's an easy one to answer. I was a Knight in the Middle Ages, and you were the lady in the moated Castle, awaiting my return. You wore a tall hat, like a cone turned upside down, and a gown with flowing sleeves."

"Life in a Castle was probably very draughty, Rufus!"

He laughed and shook his head in mock despair. I said goodnight to him and walked to my room; at the door, I paused and looked back. He was standing there, watching me, no longer smiling.

I awoke early, after a dreamless night, for which I was thankful. No sounds, no fears, no awareness that someone was in the dark, close by me. I was happy; the morning was already bright with pale-gold sunshine and Troy was taking us to Portsmouth.

I took great pains with my outfit. Milly scurried about, tidying up, helping me.

"It's my birthday, miss; so I've got the afternoon off," she said.

I went across to my jewel-case and took out a small brooch that I had bought myself years ago. It was not of great value, but pretty, a tiny cluster of mother-of-pearl flowers in a silver basket.

"A happy birthday, Milly. This is for you."

Her eyes grew round.

"I couldn't possibly, miss, thank you all the same. It's not that I wouldn't like it," she said longingly, "but the mistress would be annoyed."

"I promise you that she won't be, Milly. I shall tell her that I wanted to give it to you. The brooch is not valuable, and you have looked after me very well," I told her gently.

Satisfied, she took it from me, with great delight.

"Thank you ever so! It is *lovely*, miss. You're very kind."

She scuttled away, beaming joy at me. The pleasure I felt was out of all proportion to the value of the small gift, I thought. I hoped Milly would have a happy day.

I was ready ten minutes early. I went to the West Tower; the door was unlocked. I went in, leaving the door open. The dressing-room door was open; stripped of my possessions, it had lost its identity. Only the peacocks seemed to bring it alive, with their splendid colourful tails spread against the wall, and their eyes glittering.

I did not like them; there was something cruel and predatory about the birds, even though they were fastened to the wall, like butterflies imprisoned for ever, in death.

I shuddered, and went downstairs. There was no sign of anyone. I walked across to the gap in the bookcase from which I had taken the leather-bound book belonging to my grandfather.

The notebook had been replaced at the back of the gap.

Astonished, I took it out. What a pointless thing to do. Or was it? Was there some reason behind the action that I did not understand, a small, significant piece of a vast jigsaw puzzle?

I tucked the book into the pocket of the jacket. A slight sound behind me made me turn, my heart beating fast.

Marie stood at the bottom of the stairs. I looked at her felt slippers, and thought: no one ever moved so silently as this woman.

"What do you want?" I asked sharply.

"To tell you that the Master is waiting, ma'mselle," she replied shortly.

"It is not yet time—" I began.

"The Master is most punctual. If he says you will be here at this time, or that time, then you will be many minutes before then, for *that* is what he really means."

"How did you know I was here?"

"I follow," she said calmly. "At no time are you to come here alone. It is Madame's order. She fears for you."

The contemptuous face said that Marie considered I was not worth such protection.

"Perhaps it is only the Master of the house you should fear," she added, with unmistakable meaning.

I remembered that she had seen me in Troy's arms, and I coloured, infuriated by her insolence.

"I fear no man!" I retorted haughtily.

"Fine words, ma'mselle. I have not told the Mistress what I saw. Perhaps I shall do so, perhaps not."

"Do as you please," I said bitterly, hating myself; and, unjustly, hating Troy also.

"Men are liars and cheats. Do you not know that, or are you so innocent?" she jeered. "I was not yet your age when my parents died, in Paris. I came to England. I met a man who was kind to me and took me in; when he had seduced me, he left me, and returned to his wife. There was nothing then but the streets and the dance halls. You do not know the dance halls, ma'mselle? We wait, standing round the walls, ready like ripe fruit. In our pretty dresses and our red shoes."

"Red shoes?" I stared at her, uncomprehending.

"Yes, ma'mselle. Red satin with heels of brass." Her smile was cold and humourless. "The same as *le Diable* demanded of the village shoemaker! Is that not a joke? We *all* wore them! We were prostitutes. That is what we can do best: give a man pleasure. Give him excitement with our bodies; I know the many ways in which a man can be pleased. I could tempt the most jaded appetite ..."

I stared at her; she made no attempt to move aside for me to pass.

"What happened to you?" I asked, troubled.

"I had a child. It was born dead." She sounded prosaic. "I was rescued. Ha!" She threw back her head and laughed bitterly. "*Le Bon Dieu* preserve us all from good women who hope to find their own salvation in saving lost souls. The woman who found me in the gutter, took me home with her, and put me to work in her kitchen, scouring pots and pans, whilst she read the scriptures to me."

"Surely even THAT was better than the streets?"

"That is what SHE said, ma'mselle, when my hands were raw from scrubbing her kitchen, and I was so weary that I thought my head would topple from my neck with fatigue.

She believed that hard work purged the soul of all uncleanness. I slept in a bedroom as bare as a Nun's cell on a palliasse of straw; and by day, it was work, work, work, do this Marie, do that, Marie, do not stop, Marie, for Satan finds mischief for idle hands to do. In the end, I could endure no more. I ran away. I came to the village. I found work in this house, and I tell you, ma'mselle, it is Paradise to me—whilst I serve Madame. She is good to me. As for HIM—ask yourself, WHO is he? Poverty's child, running in dirty alleys without shoes to his feet. Thinking he is good enough for HER!"

She turned, with a contemptuous shrug of her shoulders and went soundlessly up the stairs, muttering sarcastically that the Master of Sandleford disliked being kept waiting.

Troy waited by the coach; he showed no sign of impatience. Alannah was already inside the coach, excitedly jigging up and down on the seat, much to the coachman's disapproval. She looked pleased and happy, as she waved to me.

Troy strode towards me as though he wore seven-leagued boots. I saw by his face that he was in a good mood, and I breathed a sigh of relief.

"Come, Catherine!" he said gaily. "We are not going to waste one second of such a day!"

I sat beside Alannah, her small, soft body close to mine. She leaned against me, smiling up through her long, dark lashes. How sweet, how innocent a child she was! I thought of Marie, and sighed. Once, *she* had been like Alannah, young and untouched and carefree.

Troy sat opposite us. I saw how his eyes searched us both, missing nothing. Trying to control my feelings about him was like trying to hold on to a runaway horse.

The sun played hide and seek with a few lambs'-fleece clouds; dusty catkins swung yellow, gypsy earrings from hazel boughs; the blackthorn flowers made a foam of white along the hedgerows, forerunners of the bitter, dark sloe; country people said that when the flower bloomed early, the weather became cold again, and heralded a 'blackthorn winter'.

We passed through villages, curled like sleeping cats in the sun. At first, Troy confined his remarks to Alannah, pointing out things of interest as the horses trotted briskly along the country lane.

We left the villages behind, and began the long climb up the hill on whose other side was Portsmouth. At the top, the carriage stopped; the horses were glad of a rest.

Troy turned to me and held out a hand.

"Come!" he said imperiously.

His fingers were hard and strong. I hoped he would not guess how mine, prisoned beneath them, were trembling, as he helped me down from the carriage. I wished with all my heart that I could hate him.

The three of us walked over springy turf to look at a town unrolled like a map at our feet.

The boundaries of the town were deeply indented by the gleaming tide of water that encircled it; Portsea Island, Troy explained, was the oldest part of the town, joined to the mainland by a bridge.

I saw the masts and funnels of ships at rest in the harbour; rows of little houses; fields, where cattle grazed. A splendid grey Church with a large square tower dominated the skyline, and beyond it was a strip of hazy blue water. In the farthest distance was a long purple smudge that Troy explained was the Isle of Wight.

"Look, both of you!" He pointed away suddenly to the right. "See the Castle? It is as old as history."

It was merely a ruin, a broken tower and four walls, balanced on the tip of a finger of land that jutted out into the upper reaches of the harbour. Like a battle-scarred old warrior, it slept in the sun, dreaming, no doubt, of past victories.

"Once, it was a prehistoric settlement. Are you listening, Alannah? I am a better teacher than your history books, for I had no schooling and learned these things because I had a thirst for them. The Romans came and built a fort there. It was the scene of many raids and battles. From that Castle, the First King Henry left for Normandy, and Richard the Lionheart set sail for the Crusades. What a splendid sight that must have been? Wouldn't you like to have seen it?"

Alannah nodded vigorously. Troy had the gift of

communicating enthusiasm; of making me feel that I heard the shouts, saw the shields and banners, and the lifted spears, the sun burnishing armour until it shone ...

He spread his arms wide, encompassing the town as though he loved it.

"The Tudors did much for Portsmouth," he told us. "Some of the money obtained from the dissolution of the Monasteries was spent on building fortifications around the town. Not, I imagine, with God's approval!" he added drily.

Alannah looked puzzled. I did not try to explain the meaning of his words. He was Troy Merrick, who said what he pleased, whose humour was dry and light and quick, who could be a starless night, or a summer day, as he chose.

In silence, we walked back to the coach, and drove down to the pleasant little village of Cosham; we passed over the bridge and so came to Portsea Island. Troy pointed out Inns to us; the Green Posts—from which more than one smuggler had been routed, he told us—the boundary stone of the town was placed nearby.

So we came to the Church with its high tower, and the marble headstones and crosses and weeping angels in the fields all around it. We came, at last, to streets of fine houses and elegant shops, close by the sea.

"I have business to do in Southsea; it will take no more than an hour. Amuse yourselves at the shops!" Troy said.

He handed a sovereign to Alannah, with great ceremony.

"Buy Catherine a present, and do what you please with the rest!" he told her.

Long afterwards, when the shadows grew thicker and darker around me, I remembered that day. Alannah and I walked hand-in-hand, in and out of the shops. She bought me a red velvet pincushion shaped like a heart, and a tiny picture, made of shells and feathers; she bought a tooled leather book-mark for Troy, and, for herself, a very grown-up box of bon-bons; I had not the heart to tell her it was unladylike to eat in the streets, and that she would have no appetite for lunch—because the first seemed to me a rule made to be broken on such a day, and the second was probably not true, anyway. She skipped happily beside me, her eyes shining, her face bright with happiness.

Troy took us to lunch in a fashionable hotel, where his presence commanded immediate and attentive service. I noticed how the women glanced with open admiration at the tall figure, with the silver-streaked hair and deeply-carved lines on his face. *I* knew too well the potency of his charm! He had but to smile or speak, for its magic to ripple through a whole room full of people.

It was Troy's idea that Alannah should see the house in which Mr. Charles Dickens had been born; so we drove there, and looked at its neat facade, fronting a busy main road.

"Have you read his novels?" Troy asked me.

"All of them; and enjoyed every one."

"He tells a good tale," Troy said, "and exposes the wounds of our society, as he does so; many must find him an uncomfortable story-teller, and no one can ignore the truths he delivers. Now I'll satisfy your curiosity as to my birth-place, though you will find it has been tamed, its dirty face washed clean, its hair combed!"

I do not remember when I enjoyed myself so much. It was more than the fugitive warmth of the sun, the fact of being in Troy's company, the pleasure of seeing Alannah looking as excited as any child on an outing.

We passed a splendid Guildhall with a pretty little park hidden behind it; I had never seen so many sailors, most of them walking arm-in-arm with girls who looked like Milly or Katy; nor such solemn young officers, very conscious of the dignity of their uniform.

Down by the harbour was the great main gate of the Dockyard and a harbour where small ships were tethered; a railway station ended at a jetty where paddle-steamers left for the Isle of Wight, and Alannah made Troy halt the coach so that she could watch the London train unload its luggage and passengers on to the platforms.

Troy looked at the shining tide flowing around the piles under the railway pier, and told me:

'It is not such a pretty sight when the tide is out; and reveals the mud, where urchins scrabble for the coins thrown by passers-by, diving down into the mud for them, and fighting over them when they have fished them up!"

"Did *you* ever do that?" I asked innocently.

"No!" He looked as fierce as an eagle. "*I* would not scramble for meagre offerings thrown to amuse a handful of people, who have nothing better to do than stand, dry and at a safe distance, to watch!"

The horses picked their way very disdainfully through meaner streets along to the Point; we passed several wharves, where ships were being loaded and unloaded.

I asked Troy if any of the ships were his.

"Most of them," he replied carelessly.

"What do they carry?"

"Wines and spirits from France; timber, tar and hemp from Baltic ports, grain and fruit and vegetables from the Channel Islands, and many other things. In return, they take back the finest goods that Britain makes, to countries all over the world. These are my workaday ships."

"Why, what others have you?"

"More powerful ships than these; they go across the world to bring back its treasures: silks and ivories, jade and alabaster, fine things of leather, silver and gold ..."

"All the things I have seen at Sandleford."

"All those things," he agreed.

"How you love beauty!"

"Beauty is timeless and unchanging," he replied.

The narrow street ended abruptly at the Point, where the sea slapped against the stones with great zest, and a curious, flat-bottomed contraption, like a wide bridge, loaded with grain and packages and people, made its way across to the little township on the far side of the harbour.

I stepped down from the coach, tasting the clean, salt breezes. I enjoyed the diversity of water-traffic in front of me: skimming ships with haughty sails, important tugs fussing on their way, rowing boats bobbing impudently, a superior looking ship making its way out of harbour, obviously bound for more exotic ports; behind it, the paddle-steamer, staid and comfortably built, her decks lined with people, churning the water into white foam.

Troy swung Alannah up on to his shoulder and pointed.

"Look well, Alannah. See the most famous ship of them all; home from the wars since before I was born!"

I followed his pointing finger; I saw a beautiful ship, with soaring masts, her giltwork shining, her paintwork gleaming in the sun. On her decks, one of history's greatest sea-battles had been fought, and England's most famous Admiral had died. I wished suddenly that I had seen the 'Victory' in her heyday, when she had sailed out, haughtily, to do battle with the French.

I shall not forget today, I thought. This place is part of Troy; and he is part of it still.

How could such a man be content to be Master of a great house in the country, attending to the affairs of estate and village? He belonged on the high seas, my dark buccaneer, my proud Troy, with his eyes turned seawards.

He led us through streets and alleys that I would not have cared to walk after dark. They were full of cramped little houses and shops selling pots and pans and old clothes; I saw wrinkled men outside beerhouses; sailors with their girls, old women shawled and stooping—and always the barefoot children, running, singing their rhymes and calling their jibes, being cursed at, and ducking away, laughing, as children have done all down the years; sticking out their tongues, playing hide-and-seek, running beside us, with hands held out to Troy.

I fancied Alannah looked wistfully at them, envying them their freedom; Troy sent a whole purse full of money tinkling amongst them, as though he remembered that, a long time ago, he had been one of them.

"You have come here years too late," he told me drily. "These are genteel days, when even the brothels have grown discreet, and there are fewer drunks to be seen reeling home on a Saturday night; though it is still not a wholesome place for a woman to walk alone after dark."

"You have great affection for it, Troy," I said.

"For its people; for the great mass of sweating, seething, brawling humanity, flowing like a muddy tide along its lanes and alleys. My grandfather talked about the days of the Press-gangs; HE was born two years before the battle of Waterloo and died when I was twelve. As a child, I sat with him on the Point, watching the ships sail away to the ends of the earth and home again; I vowed, then, that MY ships would one day sail up and down these waters!"

"It all came true," I reminded him.

His face was sombre.

"Aye. The boy dreamed; the man made the reality. I remember my grandfather telling me that the very stones of this place are soaked in blood and history. Over these cobbles, men have marched to board ships and sail away to fight in foreign countries; these stones were the first dry land they felt beneath their feet, when they returned. Prisoners of war, condemned men—all have walked here. Life at sea was hard; the homecoming sailor wanted only the comforts of life, and had the money to buy them!"

I though of Marie, and the girls like her, ranged around the walls of sleazy dance halls. I shivered: there but for the grace of God, I thought soberly ...

"Don't you hear it, Catherine?" Troy asked softly. "The echoes, haunting the streets and alleyways? Of men swearing, fighting, quarrelling, dying, loving and laughing? Don't you realise that the sea breaking against these stones is the same sea on which Roman galleys first sailed up the harbour to conquer Britain?"

Troy was like a diamond, turned this way and that to catch the light in all its different facets. This was a new facet; one I had not known existed.

We came to a narrow street, sunless and empty; on either side were small, four-roomed houses. Between the neatly-parted lace curtains in the windows, I saw curios from all over the world: carved ostrich eggs, painted shells, coral from the Philippines, stuffed humming birds beneath domes of glass.

Every doorstep was white; every knocker shone.

"Behold the street of the Little Daily Bread People!" Troy told me.

"I never heard such a name for a street!"

"That is not its real name. It is what *I* called it when I was a child. 'Give Us This Day Our Daily Bread' was a fitting prayer for the people who lived here. We are, in fact, in Plumtree Lane—a misnomer, for no plum tree ever bloomed within a mile of this place!"

I saw that the children followed him, even though all his

bounty was dispensed; he reminded me of the Pied Piper of Hamelin. The women came to their doorways to smile at him, and the men stood aside to let him pass. Alannah was clearly delighted by the importance of our royal progress.

"I was born *here*, Catherine!" Troy said suddenly, with sly amusement in his voice.

I looked at a neat little house with an aspidistra primly framed in looped-back curtains of Nottingham lace.

"Oh, *no*!" I said sadly.

"There's nothing wrong with the place—now; it was very different before it was rebuilt."

"It looks too self-effacing for YOU!" I murmured.

"I like that!" he said, delighted. "I like that *very* much! Self-effacing or not, it is a vast improvement on what was there before!"

"Who rebuilt all these houses?" I asked.

"I did," he replied arrogantly.

I should have known, of course.

"We have another call to make," he added.

Collins waited for us, with a ludicrous expression of disapproval on his face; the coach was attracting attention, and he was clearly of the opinion that his master should not have expected him to wait in such a low-class area.

I looked at Troy, sitting opposite me in the coach; a man who openly boasted that he indulged the sins of the flesh on every possible occasion, and found them enjoyable; a man, ruthless, generous, harsh and tender; an enigma, a pool with unfathomed depths.

A short drive brought us to a quiet, tree-lined square of old and gracious houses whose upper windows overlooked the sea wall to the tumbling waters beyond; near this square was a small green with seats upon it, where nursemaids pushed prams and children bowled their hoops.

The coach stopped outside a white-painted house with tubs of laurel on either side of its front door. A woman came out to greet us; tall, handsome, well-built, with dark hair.

Her clothes were good rather than fashionable; there was an air of solid prosperity about her.

Troy kept his mistress in great comfort, I reflected; I saw her put her arms around him, and he kissed her cheek, before he turned to me, a devil of mischief dancing in his green eyes.

"Catherine, come and meet my sister. Anne, will you assure Catherine that you ARE my sister and not my mistress?"

I blushed furiously as Troy introduced us both. On closer inspection, I realised that she *was* like him—the same tallness, the same proud carriage; but her face was not etched with such lines of bitterness as her brother's.

"I am sorry my husband is not here to greet you," she said to me, "nor my two grown sons; they are all on the high seas. My husband is Captain of 'Seawitch' somewhere in the Bay of Biscay, at this moment."

"Homeward bound from North Africa," Troy agreed. "That is my finest ship."

Anne took our wraps, and sent a maid for a tray of tea; the house was furnished with great taste and comfort.

I looked at Anne and Troy; what aristocratic ancestor had been mated with a dead and gone Merrick, to produce these two? A French prisoner-of-war? A Lady of high degree, fallen from grace?

After tea, Anne took me upstairs to look at the sea from the window of her favourite room; a little wind was blowing out of nowhere, tipping the waves with white.

"I like to sit here," she said, "and think of my husband and sons. They are away from me a great deal."

"That must make you sad."

"Only for myself. They love the sea."

"I would like to live in a house like this, by the sea!" I said.

She looked amused.

"It doesn't compare with Sandleford!"

"Sandleford is a strange, cold house. I think it rejects me."

"Yes. It rejects most people. I rarely go there. It would not be *my* choice of a home. Years ago, when he was walking to London to find work, Troy passed the house. He looked through the gates and saw a little girl, walking with her nursemaid."

Selina. It could not have been anyone else.

"Troy wrote to me, and described her. He said that she

was beautiful, with golden hair, and that he had promised her he would come back and marry her, one day, when he was rich. The nursemaid called him a fool, and told him to be on his way."

I looked at the clouds like white sails in the sky. Then Troy came in, and the spell was broken.

"It is time we were going," he told me.

At the door, Anne said to me:

"Come back again; whenever you wish."

She was much happier in her little white house by the sea than Troy would ever be as King of his splendid Castle.

Alannah was asleep before the horses reached the top of the hill; she lolled against my shoulder, and I supported her with my arm. It was dusk; lights twinkled below us, sea-mists unfurled ragged banners around us.

"I have enjoyed myself today," I told Troy.

"You did not find it dull? Its tumbledown buildings have long been swept away; but poverty is only picturesque to the man who views it from the comfort of affluence!"

"Perhaps there is no greater incentive to ambition, than comfortless surroundings?" I suggested.

"A man has a right to earn himself a fortune by hard work. To say that he should be content to continue in that station of life in which he was born is a rich man's platitude!" Troy replied.

"Now YOU are rich, Troy; and you enjoy the power it gives you."

"Certainly I do! The man who says he does not enjoy the power of wealth is a liar or a weakling!"

"Like wine, power is heady; a taste not to be over-indulged," I told him.

His lips twitched.

"How solemn we are! My wealth has brought comfort and security to a great many people. The lands and farms of the Sandleford estate are the best-kept in the County!"

"You say you are not a philanthropist; yet you swept away slums in the town, and built new houses," I told him.

"Commonsense, my dear Catherine, not philanthropy. The men who live in my houses are the crews of my ships, they load and unload my cargoes, and perform a multitude of tasks—for me. If they are decently housed and paid, they will work better."

My eyes, too, were heavy; the lids drooped. The motion of the carriage was like the ebb and flow of the sea. Troy stood at the helm of a great ship, his arm around my shoulders.

"Catherine. We are home. Must I carry you BOTH indoors?"

I roused myself, declaring hastily that I was wide awake. He helped me down from the carriage, and lifted the sleeping child in his arms. Above us, the night sky was frosted with stars, and the dark bulk of the house seemed to lean menacingly over me.

Chapter Seven

I dined alone; Selina and Rufus had accepted an invitation to dine with Seton and Agnes. Troy had unexpected visitors, a deputation from one of his largest farms, where there had been some trouble. Hayricks had been fired and a thatch set ablaze. I wondered about the culprit; it must surely be someone with a grievance against Troy.

After the excitement of the day, dining alone gave me a feeling of anti-climax. I could not even go and sit with Alannah; she had been put to bed, tired out by the outing.

I went early to my room. I undressed, put on a wrapper, and brushed out my hair. The night was unexpectedly warm, and I opened the window, looking up at the stars, thinking about the many sides to Troy's character. He had been generous to those who had shared his poverty, he was, by all accounts, a conscientious squire of Sandleford lands; but he did not love his wife, nor was he loved by her.

Perhaps he had seen her only as a possession, to be bought and proudly displayed. She had resented that; but she had married HIM for the ease and security he could give; if she had *not* married him, Sandleford would have crumbled into decay, and Selina would have been penniless. It must have been a difficult choice. Probably they had both tried to come to terms with their ill-founded marriage, and failed.

It was nothing to do with me, I reminded myself firmly. They had found their own solutions to their problems: Troy had his women, the power of authority. Selina had the house, and her position as mistress.

A light tap at the door startled me.

"Come in," I called.

Selina entered, still in evening dress. She looked flushed and happy, as though she had enjoyed spending time away from the house, in the company of other people.

She held out her hands and came across, kissing my cheek affectionately.

"Dear Catherine, have you been lonely? Troy is still shut in his study with some rather dull men. I have told Marie to bring us a nightcap and I will sit and talk to you."

She sat in one of the armchairs. How pretty she was, I thought yearningly! The thick, golden hair; the skin like fine porcelain, almost translucent, the soft, cherry-coloured mouth and bright eyes. Was she delicate, I wondered? The hands resting on the chair arms were small and thin, like a child's, the blue veins showing clearly.

"Tell me about your day," she said.

"It was—instructive. Troy told us much of the history of Portsmouth."

"He has studied it at great length. I admit I do not share his interest," she admitted frankly.

"He showed me the place where he was born. We shopped in Southsea, Alannah and I, before we lunched with Troy. We had tea with his sister."

"Anne?" Selina looked surprised. "She never comes here. I have invited her often, but she declares she finds this house too overpowering. I am glad that you enjoyed your day. Seton's invitation to dine was a pleasant surprise. It must be rather dull for him, at times, alone with Agnes."

I looked astonished.

"He is going to marry her! Surely a man does not find his future wife—dull?" I exclaimed.

She looked contrite.

"Poor Agnes. I should not have said that. She will make him an excellent wife; she is thrifty and painstaking and has been well schooled in the domestic arts. She is not lively nor entertaining; perhaps marriage will give her a new lustre. Let us hope so, for Seton's sake."

"You make it sound as though they are ill-matched."

"Indeed, I do not mean to imply any such thing," she answered wrily.

"Do you believe that Seton feels—sorry for her?" I asked curiously.

"One should not ask even oneself that question," she replied. "No doubt he sees in Agnes qualities that we do not see, and is well satisfied with his choice."

I was silent, thinking about the Master of Ashmead and his strange bride-to-be. Selina watched me for several seconds, before she said reminiscently:

"Seton is a splendid person, Catherine. We played together as children, and I was desolate, at first, when he went away. When he came back, he was quite grown up into a handsome young man."

"Did you not have Rufus for company?" I asked.

"Yes. Rufus is not in the least like Seton. He is so light-hearted."

"Surely that is a good thing to be?"

She glanced at me with sly amusement.

"I think you like Rufus very much, don't you, Catherine? Your championship of him proves me right! Rufus is a will-o'-the-wisp, a man who does not like to be too long in one place, who finds the inheritance of land a great burden on his shoulders. He studies carefully all that Troy tells him, and makes most impressive plans for Kilstock. He accompanies Troy on his rounds of the Sandleford Estate, and I am sure he does his best to understand all that Troy shows him. It is not easy for him. He, more than Seton, needs a wife with Agnes's qualities, I am sure."

At that moment, Marie brought in a tray with cups upon it and a silver jug filled with hot milk; she did not trouble to glance at me, as she set the tray on the table by my bed.

When Marie had gone, Selina sat back in her chair, her smile warm.

"I am so happy to have you here, Catherine," she declared. "You cannot know what a difference it has made to me to have a kinswoman of my own. I have felt so lonely without parents, Aunts, Uncles, Cousins. I hope that you will stay for a long time."

"I have no choice but to stay. Troy has made that clear," I said grimly.

She looked distressed. I had never seen her so troubled;

she made two or three attempts to speak, before she finally got the words out.

"I am deeply concerned on your account, Catherine. To such an extent that I have today written to your lawyer, Mr. Jarley, and asked him to visit me."

"Why?" I stared at her in astonishment, my heartbeats painful.

"There is something I wish him to know. Something I should have told him before, but I did not guess ..."

She broke off, biting her lip.

"Tell me what it is," I begged.

She shook her head.

"When Mr. Jarley comes, I will tell both of you. I have asked him to come as soon as he can."

I did not know what to think. I was uneasy; as I sat there, thinking about her astonishing words, she said suddenly:

"Did you find the notebook?"

"Yes. It had been put back in the exact place in which I found it."

"How strange! Perhaps *you* returned it and forgot that you did so."

"I would not forget such a thing, Selina!" I retorted, annoyed.

"May I see the notebook?" She held out her hand. "I would love to read it."

I went into the dressing-room. The jacket lay across the chair, neatly folded, where I had left it. I took the notebook from the pocket and brought it back to Selina. She examined it with interest whilst the milk grew cool in the cups.

I tried to find out why she had sent for Arthur Jarley; but she would not say. Clearly, something was on her mind.

Eventually, she smothered a yawn, laid the notebook aside and declared that the handwriting was too difficult for her to decipher.

She bent and touched her lips to my forehead.

"Dear Catherine," she said gently.

There was only warmth and friendliness in her voice; yet, could I trust her? It had never been in my nature to be suspicious of people and their motives; not until I had come to Sandleford.

I was very tired; the day had been mentally and emotionally exhausting. I should have slept soundlessly; instead, I drifted into heavy slumber, and then became enmeshed in a curious, waking nightmare that was the more frightening because I could not tell where the dream ended and reality began.

I thought someone awoke me; dragging me reluctantly from a fathomless darkness. I seemed to float, vaguely, in a thick fog, muddled, confused.

Someone was helping me from my bed, with firm but kindly hands. No, it was part of the dream. I shook my head, trying to clear the mists from my brain. It was not quite dark; the moon was up, filling the room with soft, grey light. I thought it was Milly who hovered around me; she was bending over me, putting on my slippers.

I had left the window open, and the curtains undrawn; the night air; flowing into the room, was cool against my forehead. I needed air; I was so hot, so full of sleep. My brain felt so muddled and I could not focus my eyes.

The hands led me gently towards the window. I looked down, feeling giddy. This room overlooked the back of the house, and was high above the long, flagged terrace with the summerhouse in the centre.

It seemed a long way to the ground. I was suddenly frightened, and tried to close the glass, but my fingers slid helplessly down the window-pane and I hadn't the strength.

I struggled desperately to come out of the nightmare, to be fully awake and aware of what was happening; but my thoughts were incoherent, and I felt stupid and dazed.

Who was in the room? Was it Alannah, who always came to me when I was in danger? No, Alannah was sound asleep, worn out after the day's exertions.

I knew myself to be in danger, as I had been before; but I recognised the fact only dimly and did not know how to combat it.

I turned from the window. I heard a strange sound; like the beat of powerful wings, close by. Instinctively, I ducked my head as something swooped past.

Whatever it was, it did not go out of the window. It was still in the room.

Sweat lay clammily on my flesh. I could not utter a sound, for my tongue seemed to fill my mouth.

The moon went behind a cloud; then the cloud passed away, and the moon sailed serenely into a patch of clear sky, making the room bright with its luminous light.

I saw the thing sitting on one of the bedposts; it seemed vast, a great hooded creature crouched there; in the light of the moon its two eyes looked back into mine, from above the cruel, curved beak.

It spread its wings suddenly, and they seemed to fill the room. As it screeched and rose into the air, I thought it was going to fly straight at my face.

Half-demented with fear, I dropped to the floor; the owl swooped low over me, so that its talons almost grazed my cheeks; I felt its wings brush against my hair, before it went out through the open window.

Every childhood horror I had ever known crowded upon me. Somewhere, in this house, a dreadful chain of events was being played out: first, the cat; now the owl.

Someone had brought it to the room. I would *never* believe that it had flown in of its own accord. Someone wanted to terrify me to the brink of madness, so that I might topple over into—what ...?

The mists were clearing from my brain, a little. Trembling, I tried vainly to pull myself to my feet. Someone lurked in the deep shadows that even the moonlight could not penetrate. I was aware of the presence, I heard a sound I could not place ...

The intruder moved away. There was a click as the door opened a little way; light flowed in from the lamps left burning in the passage beyond. I saw a hooded figure swathed in a dark cloak go swiftly through the opening and vanish, pulling the door closed as it did so.

The figure seemed to be bent, so I could not tell whether it was short or tall. The cloak muffled its outlines, so I could not say if it was a man or woman.

Why? *Why*? I beat my fists against my head, tears running down my cheeks. This was no ugly practical joke; it had sinister overtones.

When I heard the running footsteps in the corridor, I

knew, then, the nature of the sound I had heard: the hand that had coaxed me from my bed, the hand that had brought the owl into the room had tugged violently at the bell-pull before leaving, so that the household should be aroused.

I guessed which way my attacker had gone; to the West Tower, away into the safety of the secret entrance that gave easy access to this house. Wasn't that suggesting that whoever it was came from *outside* Sandleford? From Ashmead Grange? From the Folly?

The steps stopped outside my door; someone rapped on the panel.

"Miss Catherine. Are you all right?"

Grimly, I forced myself not to burst into tears; before I could answer, the door was opened.

Mrs. Treville stood there, in her woollen dressing-gown, grey plaits swinging to her waist. She had a lighted lamp in her hand; behind her was Milly, nervous and blinking.

"Whatever's wrong, Miss Catherine?" Mrs. Treville came in and set the lamp down on a table. "Why did you pull the bell like that? You gave us such a fright."

"I didn't pull the bell," I muttered. "Someone else did it. The person who brought the owl in here." I put my hands over my eyes. "It was horrible; huge wings flapping, and a great beak. I couldn't bear it."

There was silence. Mrs. Treville came across and helped me to my feet.

I felt her stiffen, as she glanced downwards.

I followed her glance, and saw that I wasn't wearing my slippers, as I had foolishly imagined.

I was wearing the red shoes that were to have been worn, for the first time, at the Ball.

It was the last straw. I bent down, my head swimming, and struggled to tear them from my feet.

"I won't wear them!" I cried. "I won't wear them again, ever! They're horrible and evil. I am *not* Anna ...!"

Mrs. Treville said something to Milly, who scuttled away as though glad to be gone. Then she took off the scarlet shoes and put her arms around me, rocking me gently as though I was a child.

"Now, now, love. You sha'n't wear them again if you

don't want to. Whatever did you put them on for …?"

"I didn't! I didn't! It was someone else …!"

Mrs. Treville made no answer; she sat me on the bed and soothed me with soft noises.

Milly came back alone, looking worried.

"The Mistress is sleeping heavy. Marie says she can't rouse her properly, and the Master's out somewhere …"

Down at the Folly, I thought. I lifted heavy eyelids and forced my eyes to focus on the bedside clock. The hands stood at a quarter to two.

"Now you go to bed, my lamb," Mrs. Treville said to me. "I'll sit with you. You're safe now. There's no owl, nothing here to harm you."

More than anything in the world, I craved sleep. I let them pull the sheet and blankets around me, and then closed my eyes.

My dreams were vivid and troubled. I was in the ballroom, under the painted ceiling, and the men I danced with had powdered hair and they wore velvet coats. *I* wore a great hooped skirt of scarlet satin, that matched my shoes.

I tried to tear the shoes from my feet and could not. A tall man took me in his arms. His eyes were as green as icy water, deep lines were cleft from his nose to chin, and above his hawk-like face his unpowdered hair was banded with silver.

I seemed to melt in his arms. I had no power over what I did. My feet scarcely touched the floor as we whirled in the dance together. His face, looking down into mine, was grave and unsmiling.

All the people we passed wore different expressions. Marie, by the wall, showed hatred for me. Selina and Seton stood side by side, watchful and unsmiling, as though I was a stranger they did not quite trust. Rufus looked at me with pity, and Agnes was there, laughing, as though it amused her to see me doomed to dance through all eternity as punishment for the sin of loving Troy Merrick.

I awoke, shivering, to a cold, grey morning. Mrs. Treville was sleeping, hunched uncomfortably in the armchair; but she stirred as soon as I sat up in bed, and hurried across.

"There, there, love. Just you lie quiet. I'll ring for Milly to bring you a nice cup of tea."

I heard the placating note in her voice. I knew what Mrs. Treville thought.

I had breakfast in bed. Afterwards, Milly helped me to dress, very pointedly refraining from making any mention of the events of the night.

When I was dressed, she told me that the Master and Mistress wished to see me in the library.

The summons was not unexpected. My knees felt weak, but I forced myself to walk slowly downstairs.

Rufus was waiting at the bottom; his eyes were filled with pity.

"My poor Catherine!" he murmured.

"What have you heard, Rufus?"

"That you have had a new and terrible nightmare. They found you with a pair of red shoes on your feet, crying out that there was an owl in the room."

"It was no nightmare, Rufus. It was real. Someone came into the room."

He said thoughfully:

"It's strange, Catherine. Smeech kept a pet owl, I don't know what became of it. Who would want to harm you?"

"I wish I knew. How am I a threat to anyone here?"

"Perhaps you have—unwittingly—annoyed someone with an unpleasant sense of humour."

"I am grateful to you, Rufus, because you do not suggest—as everyone else does—that these things are figments of an overwrought imagination."

"You seem to *me* to be a very sensible young woman."

Tears came to my eyes. I was immensely weary and desperately unhappy, but Rufus had restored a little of my self-respect.

He put a hand on my arm.

"If someone is trying to hurt you, then I shall soon find out who it is," he promised me.

I went to the library. I kept thinking about Troy, dancing with me, under the painted ceiling, whilst, in silver sconces, the candles wept tears of wax.

I thought suddenly: whoever came last night, did not come to kill. The owl in the room, the shoes on my feet, the violent tugging at the bell-rope to make sure that someone found me in a distraught condition—this was done to make it seem that I was unbalanced.

In the woods, someone had tried to kill me. That time, there had been no mistaking the motive. In my grandfather's study, there had been an attempt to kill me—and its consequences had only strengthened the belief amongst the members of the household that I was slightly mad. I had been found crying out that there was a black cat, that someone had attacked me; and there had been no signs of animal or attacker.

It was clever, I thought bitterly; cruelly, subtly clever. I could not fathom the motive—unless it was to ensure that I was kept under constant surveillance, guarded, watched, not allowed to go free from Sandleford.

I shivered, my hand on the door knob. I tapped at the door and Troy's voice called to me to enter.

The man with his back to the window bore little resemblance to the dancing partner of my dreams. His face was granite-hard, his eyes glacier-cold. Beside him, Selina sat stiffly on a small chair. She gave me a tired smile.

Milly had said that Marie could not rouse her mistress. Selina looked, this morning, as though she had been drugged: pale, listless, heavy-eyed.

I thought of the hot milk. It would account for my own state of mind when I had awakened, the lethargy in my limbs, the mental confusion.

We had both drunk from the same jug. Who had prepared the milk? A servant? Mrs. Treville herself?

"Sit down," Troy commanded curtly.

I sat facing him, like a child waiting to be reprimanded. Resentment burned within me; *I* had done no wrong.

"Perhaps you were over-tired after your outing yesterday," he said.

I thought of the happiness I had known on the previous day. It seemed a century away.

"Shall I tell you what happened?" I asked angrily. "Or will you believe it is all a fairytale?"

"I believe that you are under some kind of strain that makes you act so; however, by all means, let us hear your version of what you think happened to you."

"Think!" I flung the word at him. "I know, Troy! I am not a fool; neither am I unstable."

Selina looked at me pityingly, as she rose to her feet and left the room.

Troy said calmly:

"I think the events of the past weeks have disturbed a delicate balance within you, Catherine, making you overwrought and prey to strange fears and fancies. Dr. Garrod has recommended a specialist experienced in disorders of the mind. I shall arrange for you to go to London and see him."

I looked straight at him, too angry to be afraid of him.

"No!" I said. "I will *not* see your precious physician, Troy!"

He shrugged.

"Very well. However, may I remind you that I AM your guardian."

"That is my misfortune; the result of Aunt Vee's folly!" I cried. "If I chose to leave here, you could not keep me prisoner."

"Go then, Catherine. Leave this house. Wherever you go, I will follow; wherever you hide, I will find you, and have you brought back here. The law will uphold the decision that your Aunt made, no matter how much that decision displeases you."

"Aunt Vee did not know what sort of man you were. Perhaps the law will decide you are not fit to be my guardian!" I said bitterly.

"What do you mean?"

"What about the women you entertain at the Folly? Does such behaviour make you morally fit to be my guardian?" I demanded.

I knew I had gone too far. He stared at me, sombrely. He looked cold, remote and quite terrifyingly angry. I shivered inside, and faltered:

"Why must I stay?"

"Because *I* want you here, Catherine." His voice was so

quiet that I was bewildered; where there had been cold rage, there was now gentleness. How was it possible that any man could change mood so quickly?

I tossed my head.

"I will never submit to any man, Troy Merrick!"

He laughed, the last of his ill-humour thawing into amusement.

"You will find it necessary to do so, when you are married!"

"Then I won't marry! Aunt Vee didn't. She was quite happy."

"Ah, but *you* weren't meant to be an old maid, Catherine! You must have a man to warm your blood when winter nights are cold! If you have a husband who panders to all your whims, then you will have no respect for him. If you have a husband who does not give you your own way, then the sparks will fly!"

"Rufus has asked me to marry him." I looked thoughtfully at Troy. "Must we wait until I am twenty-one for your consent?"

"*Rufus?*" He looked outraged. "He's a *boy*, Catherine! I cannot imagine a more ill-matched pair than you two. Did he propose to you out of boredom?"

"A very ungallant remark!" I retorted.

"You can expect nothing else from a man who is not a gentleman!" Troy pointed out wickedly.

He took me by surprise. He pulled me close to him, half-angrily, half-tenderly.

"You need a MAN, Catherine!" he whispered. "Not a boy like Rufus Herries!"

The fire that his touch aroused was agony and ecstasy. If only I had known you long ago, I thought yearningly—how I would have RUN down the years to meet you. You, so old and so wise in the ways of loving, knowing how to rouse a fever of desire in a woman.

His face, with its anger and tenderness, was so close to mine that I could see the fine lines at the corners of his eyes, the skin taut over his cheekbones, the deepness of the grooves running from his high-bridged nose to the hard, disciplined line of his mouth.

And then his mouth was no longer hard.

His lips lay against my lips; they asked—and did not wait for an answer before they took mine.

I returned his kisses eagerly. I smelled the male scent of his skin, felt the sensuous touch of hands that moved slowly, as though time was of no account. There was green fire in his eyes.

His kisses came faster and fiercer; I wanted him too much to build a barrier of reason and commonsense against him. For a brief moment, I felt no shame. With his body so close to mine, we seemed to be one person, and I knew how effortlessly I would surrender.

I must NOT surrender! With a fierce mustering of the last of my willpower, I put him from me, and turned my head away, in shame for what I had almost done.

He stood back and looked at me, his face cold.

"You are like all other women, Catherine," he said contemptuously. "You tempt and tease without any intention of fulfilling the promises you make!"

"I would never make promises to YOU!" I cried, in anguish.

"Liar!" he retorted. "Your eyes, your body, made them willingly. If you are going to be a sinner, then, for Heaven's sake don't be a reluctant one. We should have enjoyed making love. There is nothing frigid about *you*; you may tell Rufus that I said so, if you wish."

I stared at him, lost for words. His frankness amounted to vulgarity, I thought, my cheeks crimson.

"Oh come, I understand!" He sounded weary. "Virginity is the dowry women bring to the marriage bed. Yours remains safe in your own keeping. No thanks to you, though—you were willing enough. Now—sit down, and tell me exactly what you think happened last night."

I stared over his head, and told the tale falteringly. I could not look at him.

He heard me out in silence. Then he told me to go, as though he had other things on his mind.

Agnes sent a message, asking me to have tea with her, the following afternoon. The invitation included Alannah.

We set out together; the afternoon was warm, the breeze gentle. Daffodils flaunted yellow ribbons everywhere. We went by way of the Chapel and called in there to pay our respects to the Lady of the Snowdrops. Alannah's hand was warm and confident in mine. By her glance, I knew she was aware of the events of the previous night. She looked grave and concerned for me; a look too old for such a child.

The sense that she was trying to communicate something to me was very strong indeed. I knelt beside her in the pew making my silent pleas for protection from harm. She moved close to me, her head touching my shoulder, and made soft, urgent sounds; but they were unintelligible.

I stroked her hair, feeling compassion and love for her.

"The words will come one day," I promised her. "We shall talk together."

She nodded emphatically.

We took the short cut to Ashmead, through the gate in the wall by which Seton wheeled Agnes over to Sandleford. The gate had been unlocked for us.

Seton walked to the gates to meet us. I thought how handsome he was; so golden and splendid. There was a likeness between him and Selina, almost as though they were brother and sister. Selina was very feminine; Seton's charm was entirely masculine. I thought of him as a man of strength who would never be deflected from his purpose; but though he was fascinating and compelling, he had none of the strong physical attraction that only Troy possessed for me.

"Catherine!" Seton shook his head at me. "I am distressed by what I hear."

"It is what you believe that matters. What do YOU believe?"

"You seem sensible and normal enough to me," he replied matter-of-factly.

He turned to Alannah.

" 'Morning Star' has a beautiful new foal. If you go to the stables, Jenson will show her to you."

Alannah went reluctantly, with many a backward glance at me; Seton's lips twitched.

"She has appointed herself your guardian, Catherine, and

would permit no one else to come near you, if such a thing was possible." He hesitated, and added gently:

"You are unhappy?"

"Uneasy. There are too many inexplicable things happening to me. Why should anyone wish to harm me."

"I find that hard to understand," he admitted, "for you are a truly delightful creature."

The small compliment pleased me; I smiled at him; but his face had a grave, abstracted look, as though his thoughts were elsewhere.

"On the other hand, perhaps you are a threat to someone," he added quietly.

"A *threat*?" I said blankly. "How?"

He looked uncomfortable as though he regretted having spoken. When I pressed him to explain, he said briefly:

"In keeping a promise, I find myself in an awkward situation."

"Keeping a promise to whom?"

"Selina."

"Is there something I should know concerning myself?" I demanded.

"Yes; but it is knowledge that could distress you. Though I gave my word to Selina I would say nothing, Troy Merrick has much to answer for."

With that I had to be content, for he would say no more, except for one cryptic remark.

"If love is the breath of life to a woman, then power is the breath of life to a man."

"Not to *all* men, surely?"

"Most of them," he said. "Goodness, how solemn we have become! Let us forget everything except that it is a very pleasant afternoon—and I have a most delightful companion beside me. Come and see the herb garden that is Agnes's pride and joy. How she would love to be able to show it to you herself. I tell her that, with patience, all things can be achieved. I am not sure she believes me."

He was an undemanding companion; a man of stature, mentally, as well as physically, for he could talk interestingly on a variety of subjects. One would never be bored in his company, I thought. Guiltily, I remembered Rufus; he had too light a touch on life for my liking, I often felt. He did not like to discuss any subject in depth, nor to be serious for long.

We looked at the herb garden, and the daffodils growing almost wild under a clump of trees at the bottom of the little park. I looked back at the house; Ashmead was a graceful, pleasant place; Sandleford was as forbidding as a cliff of grey granite.

Agnes was waiting for us in the drawing-room; but Seton was called away by an unexpected visitor on urgent business, leaving Agnes and myself alone. I thought she was too intense, taut as a bow-string, her movements quick and nervous.

I glanced around the room and congratulated her on the charm of its flower arrangements, the carefully-placed pieces of porcelain, the tables with their collections of silver miniatures.

She smiled, as though I had touched a responsive chord in her.

"It is pleasant to be able to please myself in such matters," she said. "All that you see here belongs to Seton, but he has given me a free hand in the house. In Mrs. Creighton's day everything had to be done exactly as she decreed and arranged as she dictated. When I cleaned this room, if I did not put everything back exactly as it was, I was punished."

"That sounds harsh!" I protested.

"Mrs. Creighton had a sliding scale of punishments, designed to fit any and every offence," Agnes retorted drily. "I would have to learn ten verses of the New Testament by heart—or spend the evening in my room without supper— and so forth, according to the crime I had committed."

"A child cannot commit a crime!"

"Mrs. Creighton would not agree with you. Attempting to justify myself was the greatest crime of all, classed as 'arguing'. For that, I invariably had a sound whipping. I could stand the physical pain; I hated the humiliation, as I grew older."

Impulsively I put my hand over her thin, dry one. I remembered the years of loving kindness shown to me by Aunt Vee, and wondered if resentment still smouldered far below the surface that Agnes presented to the world.

"I did not know my father," Agnes said calmly. "My mother refused to divulge his name to *anyone*, and Aunt Emma—Mrs. Creighton—never forgave such defiance, such wilful refusal to satisfy her curiosity. So she vented her fury on me, plus her resentment that her own life was dull and shapeless. Every day, I had to reaffirm my gratitude for all that had been done for me, and express shame at the circumstances of my birth. I knew the phrases by heart; I said them as one says Grace; each morning, after prayers, I would repeat those phrases to Emma and her husband."

"They sound like a pair of fiends!" I told Agnes indignantly.

"I don't think they were," she admitted honestly. "Narrow; sufficiently devoid of imagination to be cruel without realising it; determined to drive out any devils that might be lingering in me—always recalling what a sinful thing my mother had done in bringing me into the world. Worse than that, she had apparently been happy with the man who fathered her child. So, each evening at bedtime, I had to stand in front of Aunt Emma and her pious, God-fearing husband, listening to a lecture delivered on the dreadful sins of the flesh. I felt no sorrow, nor guilt for my lack of sorrow when they died."

"Not surprising," I said. "Seton must have been shocked at their treatment of you."

"He knew little about it, except that I was never allowed to play with him and Rufus and Selina; after all, he was only here for visits and holidays. I was too busy to have time to play, and considered by my Aunt and Uncle not fit to mix with other children."

Her eyes glowed suddenly; her face was triumphant. The fires, banked down in Agnes, smouldered into sudden life.

"Do you wonder, then, that I look forward to being mistress of this house that was the scene of so much humiliation and bitterness? Do you know with what joy I shall mould it as *I* please, when I am married to Seton?"

"I understand," I said gently.

She leaned forward, her eyes still bright, the hardness gone from her face.

"Don't misunderstand me, Catherine. THAT is not the reason I am marrying Seton. To me, he was always splendid—and out of reach. I was truly amazed when he asked me to marry him. I had no idea that he entertained so deep an affection for me that he wished to make me his wife! I still cannot believe in my own good fortune."

Seton joined us for tea; afterwards, he escorted Alannah and myself back to Sandleford.

"I am looking forward to the Ball," he said. "I expect you to save me more than one dance, Catherine. I have insisted that Agnes shall come. She refuses to wear fancy dress, of course; but she can watch the dancing and there will be plenty of people for her to talk to; she needs to be taken out of herself."

At the gate of Ashmead, we met Mrs. Scadden, the housekeeper. She had been out to post a letter, she said.

She was a tall, thin woman with a fuzz of greying hair that no hairpins seemed to tame. Her eyes were deep-set in her bony face. I thought: Agnes will look a little like her when she is old.

Seton exchanged pleasant greetings with Mrs. Scadden, who bobbed deferentially to him.

"It's grown cold, sir, now that the sun's gone in," she said.

"It is still too early in the year for the days to have any lasting warmth," he pointed out.

She nodded, pulling her cloak protectively around her.

The cloak was of coarse dark serge, fastened with wooden buttons, one of which was missing.

I sat in my room, and thought about it: Mrs. Scadden. She and Mrs. Treville were great friends, I had heard. There was nothing sinister about that.

Perhaps someone had borrowed her cloak.

Seton? Agnes? It seemed improbable.

A bed had been made up in the dressing-room that connected with my bedroom. Milly was to sleep there.

On whose orders, I asked?

"The Master's orders, miss. He says you are not well and need to be looked after."

"What he means is that he believes I am not in my right mind," I retorted.

Milly looked uncomfortable. It was not fair of me to strain her loyalty so, nor discuss the Master of the house, I realised. Besides, Milly's presence would at least ensure that I was left in peace at night.

Every day I prayed silently in the Chapel. I was twenty, and I wanted to live, even with the despair of loving a man I knew to be utterly ruthless. I prayed to be released from the power of that love, for, to me, it was underlined with shame and guilt.

There was another reason why I wished to stay alive: *Alannah*. For I knew that the deep affection I had for this child was returned in full measure.

I was not idle. Whenever I had the opportunity, I continued my search for the entrance to the West Tower; though only during the hours of daylight, and then I was careful to leave the upstairs door wide open.

Why should I expect to succeed where others had failed? Yet, it seemed just possible that, by chance, I might do so.

I saw little of Troy; since the day he had held me in his arms and kissed me so ardently, he seemed to have deliberately put himself out of my reach, and behaved with formal courtesy whenever we met.

He was away a great deal, and I wondered, often, if he came back secretly, to use the Folly. Sometimes, when I escaped the attention of the sharp-eyed servant, I would walk down that way.

I was still both fascinated and repelled by the place. The thickly crowded trees were secretive and menacing; there were fallen logs, rotting away in the rank grass and the very earth smelled sour. Only the path to the door of the Folly remained cleared, proof that it was regularly used.

I discovered a small gate in the wall, only a short distance from the shuttered grey tower. The gate was locked; but the lock was well-oiled.

How many carriages came up to those gates for their occupants to be admitted, I wondered? Thinking about it, I felt sick at heart; perhaps it was jealousy that upset me.

Yet I would not like to be Troy's wife, I reminded myself. If Selina had loved him deeply, she would have found the situation unbearable.

My searchings were taking me farther and farther afield. I would go out with Alannah in the afternoons, and they were pleasant excursions, as the weather grew warmer. We went to the village, along by the waterfall, to the Chapel, and, often, to Ashmead, where Seton made us as welcome as though we were the only people in the world he wanted to see.

The mornings were mine. I set Alannah some simple lessons to occupy her. I took a book, and I knew the servants—and Selina—believed I went to sit quietly in the summer-house, to read.

In reality, I combed the woods around the Folly. I did not know what I was searching for; perhaps I half-hoped that, one day, the door would have been carelessly left open, but this was never so.

I thought about Smeech and the owl; the memory of those great wings beating about my face, the talons almost in my hair, could still make me feel physically sick.

What I saw a few days before the Ball was far worse than anything I had experienced since coming to Sandleford.

I had gone down to the woods, determined to go to Smeech's cottage and discover if he still had a pet owl. It was sheer bravado, perhaps; but any kind of action was better, to me, than inertia, awaiting for yet another 'accident' to befall me.

The day was sunny, which made the sight so much worse. The damp, decaying smell of the earth stung my nostrils. The soft, moist ground received the imprint of my feet soundlessly. I walked warily, on the alert, and I carried a stout ash stick.

Above my head, the tops of the tall trees moved with a soft shush-shush in the breeze, as though they whispered that I was an intruder, and a puny mortal at that.

To the left of the Folly, in the opposite direction to the secret gate, the path curved and twisted. In the distance, just beyond a small clearing, I saw the place where Smeech lived, with its tarred roof and smoke curling placidly from the chimney. Beside it was a small broken-down shed, one side fallen in, and long fingers of ivy fastened around its rotting timbers.

I stepped into the clearing. The sun slanted down through the trees, washing everything in pale light. Everywhere around me, there was an unnatural stillness. No bird sang, no creature moved in the undergrowth.

I looked at the great tree, standing alone, in front of me, and understood why.

The trunk of the tree was patched with moss; its branches were gnarled, flung out like so many beseeching arms.

From every branch hung the bodies of birds and small animals, nailed there like hideous trophies.

I stared at the limp, dead things in horrified disbelief; the destruction of life had been wanton and wholesale. There were crows with jet-black wings, larks and robins, magpies and wood-pigeons; rabbits and stoats, squirrels and moles, hedgehogs; so many that I could not count them. It seemed for all the world as though the tree had put forth hideous, bloated fruit, where each pitiful body hung, head downwards, the birds with wings outspread as though they had deliberately been arranged so.

I could only guess how long some of them had been hanging there; I had sensed evil in Sandleford House, but here it was rampant. The stench of it sickened me; the silence was that of the dead, where nothing remains alive.

I turned away, retching. These birds had flown, singing, into the sky; the small, furry things had lived in these woods, made their homes here, run wild and free in sun and wind and rain, before being caught, cruelly done to death and strung up to rot.

I forced myself to walk past the tree; I came to Smeech's cottage, and stood outside the half-open door, calling his name, until he came out, blinking in the sunshine, his lower lip thrust out truculently.

He looked as foul as he did the first time I saw him. The same grimed, sweaty, unwashed skin, the greasy jerkin, the patched trousers and broken boots.

"Wha' dost thee want?" he demanded sullenly.

"You are *vile*!" I cried. "Loathsome!" I pointed back at

the tree. "THAT is the most dreadful thing I have ever seen in my life!"

"Tha' bain't seen much, then!" he retorted contemptuously. "Pests, the lot on 'em. Tha's me job, to keep down the pests."

"Not that way. To kill harmless creatures and nail them up there as though you were proud of what you had done."

"I be proud; why not?" he sneered. " 'Twas you ran to Master with tales about traps. Tha should mind tha own business. 'Tis nowt to do wi' thee what I does. Nor with HIM, neither."

He spat at the ground, and added:

"I were here in old Mr. Damon's time. HE let me be. Never came nigh these woods. Mr. Merrick pokes his nose in; same as thee does. He knows nowt of the land, nor of the ways of gentlemen!"

He spat again and I said angrily:

"I have met many a gentleman who had less claim to the title than Mr. Merrick! Do you think he would condone what you have done?"

"Ah don't know what tha's talking about. Mind tha' business."

He went into the cottage and fastened the door. I turned and hurried back through the woods, still feeling sick, remembering I had forgotten to ask about the owl.

I kept my head bent; so that as I came to the edge of the woods, I almost ran full tilt into Troy, who put out a hand to steady me.

"What the Devil are you doing here? You're supposed to be on the terrace, reading, Catherine!" he said fiercely.

"Go and see what I have seen!" I told him, weeping. "There is a tree of death down near Smeech's cottage. He has nailed birds and animals to the branches—dozens of them, hanging there. It is the ugliest, most horrible sight I have ever seen! And you permit it!"

"You make wild statements. I have not seen it; but I would remind you that life is full of cruelty and ugliness," he replied curtly.

"So it is, Troy. I hardly expected to be so grimly reminded of that fact, on YOUR lands."

"Go back to the house," he commanded, in a voice that allowed of no argument. "At once, Catherine."

As I stood there, too choked with anger and misery to move, he suddenly put up a hand and brushed away the tears from my cheeks.

It was a gesture of infinite tenderness, unexpected and endearing.

"Go, now," he said, more gently. "Don't cry, little one. I do not like to see tears upon your cheeks."

He turned and walked away with that seven-leagued-boot stride of his that carried him so swiftly and effortlessly over the ground.

I wanted to run after him, put my head against his breast, and let him hold me close to his heart. I knew the folly of such thinking. I hated myself for being so drawn to the man who was married to my cousin and was ashamed of my infatuation.

Milly was full of gossip, when she laid out my clothes for dinner that evening.

"Not even a week's notice, and him been here forty years. Not that I ever liked him, mind. Gave me the creeps, he did, miss."

"Who did?"

"Joe Smeech. The gamekeeper. I heard there was a terrible set-to between him and Master. The Master took a riding crop to him, 'tis said. Joe Smeech has gone, his cottage is to be burned, and there's been a couple of men chopping down a tree. They said he hung up dead animals and birds there, and the Master was in a terrible fury. Reckon, though, we've not seen the last of Smeech, miss. Vicious, he is ..."

I said nothing; I bowed my head and silently thanked Troy for what he had done.

Chapter Eight

Troy did not mention the subject of Smeech's dismissal to me; so I said nothing to him. Whether he acted to placate me, or because of his own revulsion at the sight of the tree, I did not know. Troy remained, as always, a closed book to me.

I spoke to Selina about Smeech.

"I think he will take his revenge," she said.

"How?" I asked.

"I don't know. He was employed here for a long time. What he did might have seemed perfectly justified to him."

"How can anyone justify cruelty?"

"*I* am not trying to do so, Catherine. I am trying to tell you what kind of a person Smeech is; a countryman, coarse and earthy. That is what Seton says." She put a hand on my arm.

"Don't go into the woods by the Folly, Catherine. You might come to some terrible harm, there."

In a sudden gesture of affection, she laid her cheeks against mine. I smelt the spiciness of clove carnations all about her.

"I could not bear it if anything happened to you. It is such a joy to have you here. Rufus told me he had asked you to marry him. Don't be angry with him for telling me; we are, after all, cousins, and we have shared secrets since we were children. It would be wonderful if you were Rufus's wife, living at Kilstock!"

"I haven't given him an answer yet," I said.

"Do you care for him?"

"I like him very much."

"Do you like Seton?"

"Yes."

"Seton is very handsome," she said.

"I know. When I look at him I think of a young Viking warrior. Or one of the Norse Gods, splendid and golden."

"Not dark and cruel like Troy."

"Cruel?" I said.

She shrugged.

"Is it not cruelty to flaunt other women as he does?" she retorted.

My days took on a curious pattern. I began to lose things. At first, it was trinkets: a pearl brooch, given me by Aunt Vee, a locket holding a photograph of my mother, a mother-of-pearl cachou box.

It was unpleasant. Milly was indignant and upset when I spoke to her about it; Mrs. Treville asserted that Milly was an honest servant.

Selina was upset; the staff talked amongst themselves, she said, about the extraordinary behaviour of poor Miss Fairfax. I could hardly blame them for their speculations, because all the trinkets reappeared at intervals. First it was the pearl brooch, discovered by Katy on the floor of the West Tower bedroom—and everyone knew I had what was considered an unhealthy interest in the West Tower rooms. The locket was discovered in the summerhouse, by one of the outdoor staff, and the broken cachou box was picked up from the kitchen floor by a housemaid, early one morning. The box appeared to have been smashed by being stamped upon by a heavy foot. The kitchen servants emphatically denied any knowledge of the damage.

The book on Magic was taken from my bedside table, and eventually found in grandfather's sittingroom with most of the pages ripped from it and scattered everywhere. The discovery shocked both Mrs. Treville and Selina. The red shoes vanished from my room—to reappear, one afternoon, placed neatly side by side in front of my bedroom door. Milly looked at them, round-eyed and declared that the Devil's dancing partner must have left them there.

"Don't be absurd, Milly," I said sharply; but how could I blame her for such remarks?

The harassment continued for some time. Things disappeared from my room and were found in strange places, often damaged as though by someone in a frenzy. Gowns were ripped; my table was overturned—even when the room was locked. Mrs. Treville ostentatiously handed her housekeeper's key to Selina; only I had a key, as Milly pointed out—for Selina gave her key to Milly, with instructions to retain it at night. Milly gave the key into my keeping by day—also on Selina's instructions; Milly locked me in my bedroom at night and slept with the key under her pillow. I knew she did not like having to sleep in the dressing-room and would far rather have been in the servants' quarters. The strain of it all showed in her face and I felt sorry for her.

There were nights when I slept dreamlessly, and peacefully as a child; nights when I was visited by terrible nightmares. Milly always insisted that I must drink the nightcap she brought, a special milk and honey posset prepared by her own hands.

Troy sent for me; his searching glance was full of pity.

"Do you still refuse to see the Specialist that Dr. Garrod recommended, Catherine?"

"Yes," I said emphatically.

"How stubborn you are. Your welfare is obviously of some concern to me," he said remotely.

"You care nothing for me, Troy Merrick!" I cried.

His green eyes were glacier-cold.

"You know that to be untrue," he retorted curtly. "Had I not been concerned, I should not have taken steps to see that you are cured."

"*Cured*? Of what?" I demanded.

"The malaise which you have, and which I believe to have been inherited from your grandfather."

"I am the victim of a subtle plot!"

"That, in itself, sounds like the remark of a mentally sick person!"

"Which is precisely the effect that was intended by whoever wishes to make it seem I am mad," I replied bitterly.

He frowned forbiddingly at me.

"Is this the way it was with my grandfather before he died?" I demanded.

"He was obsessed with the idea that Sandleford should be burned to the ground, but he never made an attempt to implement that idea. He quoted long passages from the books he read, and shut himself alone in his study for hours. He was not violent—nor forgetful—nor irrational in his behaviour."

"Am *I* all those things, Troy?"

"I am not *accusing* you, Catherine! Your old, peaceful way of life has been disrupted. You are not happy here."

"I could have been; if I had not been menaced."

"There is no *reason* why anyone should want to harm you!" he cried furiously.

"How can you be sure? Peace of mind means a great deal to me, Troy. Here, I have none. I don't want to stay. You know that."

"You will be comfortably placed if you marry Rufus," he said scornfully.

"I have not said I will marry him. It would be a way of escape. I am almost a prisoner here, Troy; my door is locked at night—on your orders, Selina tells me."

"For your own good. You could harm yourself. Also, I will not have the servants disturbed and upset. They cannot do a day's work unless they have a night's rest."

"Let me go from here, Troy," I pleaded.

"No," he said grimly.

"But, why, WHY?"

"I have told you; I want you here, at Sandleford."

"How selfish you are! I am in danger. That means nothing to you, then?"

A muscle quivered in his cheek, but he did not reply. The air seemed to be charged with a current of electricity. I felt the power of him as though he was some extraordinary being, not an ordinary mortal. I doubted if anyone, even Selina, had been able to read the book of his mind and heart.

On the day before the Ball, Selina came to me, with a letter in her hand.

"Arthur Jarley is coming, the day after tomorrow," she told me.

"Does Troy know about his visit?"

"No. On that day, he goes to Portsmouth on business. I think it best that he is not told. You must trust me, Catherine. I am worried about certain things concerning you and am in need of Mr. Jarley's advice."

She patted my shoulder gently. She was like Milly, Mrs. Treville, Katy, all of them: they behaved towards me with the forced cheerfulness people show towards those who are not normal.

If I live long enough, I thought bitterly, I may even become used to it; and I AM going to live; if only to trap the person who tries to trap *me*.

"Let's not think of *anything* except the Ball," she suggested gently. "I AM so excited! There is a Band coming to play for us, from London, and I have chosen red carnations and roses for the decorations in the Ballroom. We have not had a Ball in this house before, that I can remember. Marie says that the last time was when my mother was alive."

Marie had never spoken to me since the day she had told me about her past life. Her shrewd little eyes missed nothing, but she kept her thoughts to herself; she did not mix with the other servants and cared for her mistress with a fierce, protective loyalty.

I looked at her sometimes, and reflected on the hard leaness of her body. She was a tough woman. Her hands had a look of bony strength about them. I tried to imagine them pinning me down, striking me across the mouth. Had those hands thrown the lamp that was to have started a fire which was intended to suffocate me or burn me to death?

I obtained permission from Selina for Alannah to stay up for an hour later than usual, and watch the dancing in the ballroom with Katy, from a small alcove discreetly hidden away behind one of the potted palms.

Selina gave her consent with no show of emotion. The gap between Troy's wife and his love child was very wide. She never addressed the child directly, unless it was to scold her for a misdemeanour; yet, since I had come to Sandleford, Alannah did not run away and hide as she had once done with great frequency.

I could not tell what Alannah thought when she looked at Selina with those dark eyes of hers looking so enormous in her pale, pointed little face.

The house bustled with preparations for days. Extra staff had been engaged; servants hurried to and fro, polishing, cleaning silver; the great chandeliers in the ballroom had been taken down, piece by piece, carefully washed and dried and replaced—a tremendous undertaking.

There was to be a buffet supper in the old music-room which led from the ballroom; the tables were laid with fine white damask, the best porcelain, and sparkling crystal.

We were all caught up in the excitement—except Troy, who remained as aloof as ever. Alannah showed wonder and delight for it all; it was the first time we had ever seen a great house being prepared for a glittering social occasion. The kitchen seemed to swarm with people; the regular staff looked harassed and became short-tempered, because of all the extra work.

"Ah well," Milly said with a sigh. " 'Twill soon be time for the Fair, thank goodness."

"The Fair?"

"It comes every twelvemonth. One year, it's at South Meon, the next year it's at North Meon. It stays for two days, and we all get time off to go to it."

On the day of the Ball, men arrived early to prepare the ballroom floor, and a party of women came to decorate the place with flowers—great gilt baskets of the carnations Selina loved so much, and crystal bowls of roses, as well as the ferns and plants brought in from the greenhouses. The tables were set out, the damask cloth laid over them; a great number of people were coming, from all over the County. I was sorry that Anne, Troy's sister, would not be amongst them; she had politely declined, declaring she would be away from Hampshire on the day of the Ball.

Milly washed my hair, and rinsed it in a special infusion that Selina had instructed her to make; when my hair was dry, she polished it with a silk handkerchief. My long, dark tresses looked glossy and healthy; like Agnes, I bore no outward scars of what I had endured. I had slept soundly for two nights, untroubled by dreams and so the menace around me was less real and terrifying.

That evening, I put on the splendid red dress; it rustled richly around me, but somehow I did not feel happy wearing it, in spite of Milly's open admiration.

"It DOES become you, miss. You've the colouring for it. The shoes go lovely with it, too."

Nevertheless, she took the shoes from the wardrobe very gingerly as those she feared they had some evil power that even the contact of her hands could generate.

She slid them on to my feet. I felt a shiver go through me. Sharply, I reminded myself that I was wearing a perfectly ordinary pair of shoes that had been dyed to match my dress. Nevertheless I remembered that, somewhere in this house, Anna's red shoes were reputed to be hidden.

I stared at myself defiantly in the mirror; no shoes could have magic powers nor any clothes change the wearer's personality. As Milly had said, the gown suited me very well.

Milly took great pains with my hair; when I was ready to go downstairs, there was a knock at the door, and Selina entered.

In her hand, she carried a leather case; she opened it, and there on a bed of velvet, lay a magnificent pair of ruby and diamond earrings and a matching bracelet.

"Troy says you are to wear these," she said, as she handed the case to me.

"They are too valuable!" I protested.

"Nonsense. They belonged to our grandmother. I have a set exactly the same, set with sapphires instead of rubies. Troy will put them back in the safe, tomorrow. He says they will be yours, on your twenty-first birthday."

Her voice was expressionless. I looked at her sharply, wondering if she minded that Troy intended to give me the jewellery; but her smooth, unsmiling face was blank.

She smiled and her face came to life.

"Do you like my dress, Catherine?"

"It is beautiful," I told her.

She had chosen to be Titania, from 'A Midsummer Night's Dream.' Her deep blue dress was embroidered with tiny crystal beads like clusters of stars, and she wore a small silver crown on top of her shining golden hair.

"You are sure to be the Belle of the Ball," I told her, with perfect sincerity.

She smiled warmly.

"How kind you are to me. You look magnificent, Catherine. You are *much* better looking than the Anna in the portrait; and you are wearing your dancing shoes. Tonight you ARE Anna, and you will dance with the Devil himself!"

"Who *is* the Devil, Selina?" I asked. "How will I know him?"

"Oh, I can't answer *that*!"

She smiled mischievously; Milly was watching us, round-eyed. She was very impressionable, I reminded myself.

However, I was glad that the red dress was so becoming to me, making my skin seem paler, my hair darker.

Alannah came and admired it, stroking the fabric with her hands, looking at the brilliant jewels swinging from my ears. I thought she seemed sad as though I had become a stranger to her.

I kissed her forehead and held her close for a moment.

"Katy is going to see that you have some strawberry ice-cream," I whispered; and she gave me a delighted child's smile of sheer satisfaction, chuckling softly to herself.

I remembered what Selina had said, rather sharply, only yesterday:

"She could speak well enough if she chose! She just does *not* choose, Catherine. She is like Troy, secretive and deep and stubborn."

It was a splendid occasion. The house preened itself like a peacock. Troy and Selina stood side by side at the top of the splendid staircase and no one would have guessed that they were not two happily married people. Troy looked superb; he was head and shoulders above every other man, he was courteous, charming, attentive. I noticed how many women looked at him—and sighed, and looked again.

A tide of people flowed up the staircase: the men

handsome, the women laughing and happy, most of them eyeing me curiously as the introductions were made. I wondered what they had been told about me.

There was every kind of fancy dress; Rufus had come dressed as a Regency rake which suited him very well. Seton wore a black mask and a long black cloak lined with red.

"I am *le Diable*, Catherine!" he whispered.

"I always thought of the Devil as *dark*, somehow."

"Saturnine? With pointed ears well hidden? No, my dear Catherine. He is a golden fellow, splendid as the sun! I am *le Diable*, and you are Anna, so we must have this first dance together!"

He danced splendidly; I felt as though I was under a spell; I seemed to be lighter than thistledown in his arms, my feet scarcely touching the floor. I smiled to myself, thinking of the absurd fuss I had made about wearing the red shoes. All the things that had happened to me had no meaning, now ...

I saw Rufus staring at me; some time later, he claimed me for a dance and whisked me away, almost angrily.

"Seton Blair is paying you a great deal of attention!"

"Don't be ridiculous, Rufus! I have danced with him only twice."

"I want you to dance only with me!"

"That is foolish. I am not your possession."

"I wish to God that you were," he muttered fiercely, his lips close to my ear. "I scarcely ever see you alone, Catherine. I think you avoid me."

I sighed.

"That is not true. Don't you know what they say about me—that I am confused and forgetful and strange?"

"I am not interested in what is said. If you were married to me, and living at Kilstock, there would be no such stupid talk. This house has a bad atmosphere. Perhaps because its Master and Mistress hate one another. Your mind has been affected by those things."

Troy danced with me; ah, but it was not dancing, it was floating, gliding like a swan over a lake, held by him, guided, feeling myself take wings and soar higher and higher ... it was madness and excitement ... the strong, sensual current he generated ran through my body, making me different ...

He said:

"Perhaps Anna danced like this; and the Devil wanted her so much that he tried to seduce her; but his power was not enough."

"The power of love was greater than the power of darkness. She loved her shoemaker, so she was faithful to him."

"Would *you* be as faithful?" he mocked.

"Yes," I told him fiercely.

His eyes, his smile teased. Gone was the sombre man I knew too well; the dignified host, at his wife's side. This was Troy as he might once have been, before life hardened and sharpened him ... young and gay and infinitely desirable to a woman ...

The dance ended. Selina was close by, talking to several young men, but her eyes were on her husband and on me.

I saw Agnes, sitting on a small, gilt sofa. She wore a rose pink dress that gave colour to her pale cheeks. Her hair had been more becomingly dressed than usual.

Rufus was talking to her; whatever he was saying commanded her entire attention, besides making her look animated.

She can be very attractive, I thought, startled; I saw how she smiled up at him. He said something, quietly, that made her laugh, and then moved away. It was the first time I had ever heard her laugh in such a carefree fashion.

The smile lingered on her face, as I went up to speak to her, though her eyes followed Rufus; then she saw me, and greeted me very amiably.

"You seem to be enjoying yourself, Catherine!"

"It's the right occasion for enjoying oneself!"

"You look most becoming in red. Dramatic, startling; do you feel like Catherine or like Anna?"

"I am myself. I wouldn't lose my identity because of an old legend and a dress copied from an old portrait," I told her firmly.

"Ah, wise and practical Catherine!" she mocked lightly. "I see you are wearing red shoes, after all! Are you not afraid you will have to dance forever in them?"

I shook my head, thinking: is she just teasing? Or trying

to frighten me? One would never be sure, with Agnes. She was deep, like Troy.

Seton came to claim me for a dance. Immediately, I sensed the change in Agnes. The light died from her face; she was watchful and withdrawn. He scarcely glanced at her.

I wondered if they had quarrelled, as I whirled around the floor with Seton, to the beat of the music, the red dress rustling stiffly. I knew that I collected admiring glances; it was a new sensation and I enjoyed it to the full. My swinging earrings caught the light, and the diamonds and rubies flashed fire.

"How handsome you look!" Seton whispered in my ear.

"Fine feathers make fine birds!" I mocked.

"I am not thinking of your splendid plumage. I am sure Anna could never have held a candle to YOU."

I was enjoying myself; flirting on such a social occasion was quite permissible and very enjoyable. Tomorrow, we would all be circumspect again, I reflected.

"You are as light as thistledown," Seton added approvingly.

"That is because I am wearing magic shoes."

"You don't need them, Catherine; you were never lame," he pointed out.

Instinctively, I thought of Agnes, and glanced towards the small sofa where she sat; Selina was talking to her. A radiantly lovely Selina, Queen of the Night.

"I hope that Agnes is enjoying the Ball," I said.

"I am sure she is." His hand tightened on mine. "I am anxious to secure her happiness, Catherine. Her childhood was bleak; I know that my godparents were hard people, albeit upright and disciplined. Their harshness to her sprang from misguided beliefs."

"She has told me the full extent of that harshness."

"Then I am glad she has confided in you. She is reserved and does not make friends easily. She is like a tight bud that has never flowered; I believe that the bud will blossom when we are married. I am anxious to set a date for our wedding, though she seems reluctant to do so, and pleads for time. I care deeply for her, as I believe she does for me. I have heard a rumour, Catherine, that you and Rufus are to become betrothed."

"Rumour is premature; I have not made up my mind."

"Think well; marriage is a solemn undertaking, and it is for life," he pointed out. "Those who enter into it must be certain of their feelings for one another, certain of their ability to create a satisfactory relationship; their ideals must embrace the special responsibilities of parenthood."

I thought what an excellent husband he would make. I had already observed that he paid far more attention to the lessons in stewardship, given by Troy, than Rufus did.

As though he divined my thoughts, Seton said gaily:

"I am boring you, Catherine. We are much too serious for such a happy occasion. Life is short. Let's enjoy what it offers, to the full. Everyone is looking at you, enjoying the spectacle of Anna dancing with the Devil!"

Everyone? Troy certainly was watching us, with a scowl on his face. The undercurrents that were part of this house flowed strongly around me; deep, mysterious.

"Alas," said Seton, with mock dismay, "I am booked for the next dance with a very large lady who is dressed as a Dresden shepherdess. Why do large ladies yearn for such fragile trappings, I wonder?"

Seton had a spiky wit. He made me laugh, as we danced. Tonight, I resolved to forget everything that had made my life at Sandleford so strange and so menacing.

It was very late when the last guest departed. Selina, flushed and happy, declared it had been a great success and that we should entertain more often.

Seton and Agnes were staying the night. A room had been prepared for Agnes on the ground floor.

Selina put her arm around me when she kissed me goodnight.

"You shall NOT leave here—not even to live at Kilstock," she murmured playfully.

She was lonely, and I felt pity for her loneliness. There should have been children around her; they would have been some consolation for her sad marriage.

Milly had waited up to undress me, and brush my hair..

She looked tired and heavy-eyed, but she was eager to hear all about the Ball.

"You won't be wanting your nightcap tonight, miss," she said knowingly. "You'll sleep like a top."

"I expect so. Tell me, where do you prepare the nightcap, Milly? In the kitchen?"

"No, miss." She avoided my eyes, as she brushed out the long, heavy tresses. "In the little pantry along the passage. We always do the hot drinks there, as you know, for 'tis more convenient than the kitchen. We do morning teas and the like in the pantry."

I nodded. I knew that; Selina had explained it to me.

"Does Mrs. Treville put the ingredients out for you?"

"Yes, miss."

"Then you bring it straight to me?"

"Yes, miss."

"That's not true, Milly. I can tell. I've asked you before, and you hesitate and look uncomfortable. I want to know the truth. Something is added to my drink, before you put the milk in; I know that, because I sleep very heavily, and often awake feeling confused and strange."

"I'm not to say nothing about it." Milly closed her lips firmly.

"If you won't tell me, then I shall ask Mrs. Merrick."

"Best do that, miss."

The relief in her voice made me glance sharply at her; it implied that Selina held a key that could unlock the door.

Tomorrow, I will speak to Selina, I thought.

Milly stumbled, yawning, to bed. In my wrapper, I sat by the window, thinking about the Ball. How silent, now, the empty ballroom, with its lights out, the musicians gone, and the flowers already wilting. How silent the great house, all around me; but somewhere in it, was someone who watched and waited; a dark menace that had nothing to do with tales of Black Magic and cold evil.

That menace was directed towards me; sooner or later, I would find out who—and why. The small accidents strewn along my path were only a prelude to the final act of violence towards me, designed to send me hurtling to my death.

I shivered, feeling goose-flesh on my arms. It was *not* going to happen, I vowed.

It was almost dawn; already, the sky was lightening in the east. It was that hour, more witching, to me, than the conventional midnight hour; just before dawn, there is such utter stillness everywhere that the earth seems to have stopped breathing.

In the distance, dark firs were like black-cloaked figures, and the last of the stars had fled the sky. Below me, the garden was taking shape and pattern; I saw the pale ribbon of water that was the stream, the whiteness of the waterfall, the flagstones of the terrace.

A figure was approaching the terrace; a dark blur, muffled into a cloak. I drew back against the curtains, watching intently; whoever it was came along the path that led to the woods and the Folly. It seemed uneasy, somehow; its gait slightly stumbling and walking slowly.

My heart beat fast; obviously whoever it was intended to come into the house; how? Sandleford was securely locked. It was the duty footman's task, strictly enforced by Troy, to see that the house was secure when the occupants retired for the night.

The secret entrance in the West Tower; was there some entrance that way, I wondered?

Frustrated, I remembered that the door of my room was locked by Milly; and the key would be under her pillow.

My pulses quickened with sudden excitement. Milly had not locked the door; she had been so tired, poor girl, she had gone straight to bed after attending me. I could hear her snoring gently in the next room.

The figure reached the terrace. It turned to look back the way it had come, and, as it did so, the cloak slipped from its head.

Something about the blur of the face revealed for a split second was vaguely familiar.

The figure was that of a woman; I knew it to be so, for a hand went up quickly to tuck back a strand of pale hair that had been loosened when the hood had slipped.

The hood was hurriedly pulled into place again; my heart beat fast, as I went swiftly and silently to the door.

I opened it carefully; I had little time, for the first servants would soon be up and about. I hurried noiselessly over the thick carpet, and went down the shallow stairs as fast as my trembling legs would carry me.

I was almost certain of the identity of the night walker; I had to be *quite* sure.

I hurried past the study and the library, towards the East Tower and Selina's apartments. Just short of the East Tower, I paused and knocked lightly upon a door.

There was no reply. I had not really expected one. Slowly, I turned the handle and looked inside, reckoning that I had very little time to spare before the cloaked figure entered the house.

I could just make out the heavy furnishings; and the empty bed.

This was the room that had been given to Agnes. I had heard Selina's instructions to Marie to wheel her to this room and assist her to bed.

If I needed confirmation, it was in the rose-pink dress Agnes had worn at the Ball, laid over a chair; and in the wheelchair by the window, looking sinister and grotesque in its emptiness.

I closed the door again and moved a little way along the hallway; and there, in the deep shadows of a doorway, I waited.

I was on the alert; the appearance of the figure on the terrace might be part of an elaborate trap, though I did not see how it could be so? Who knew that I had sat at my window, instead of going to bed? No, the whole thing was too unwieldy and contrived, I decided.

The presence of Agnes on the terrace—if, indeed it WAS truly her—had some other explanation.

A figure came swiftly along the hall, keeping very close to the wall; the lighted lamps were burning low and the house was still heavy with shadow.

Such shadows gave good cover; the figure seemed to merge with them, until it reached the door of Agnes' room. Then the door opened and the figure stepped inside.

It WAS Agnes. Fleetingly, I had seen her face in the lamplight.

The lameness was in her mind, Seton had said. I wondered how long Agnes had been able to walk.

She had been coming from the direction of the Folly. Was she returning from some secret lovers' meeting? Who else had been there? Only Troy; it could not have been anyone else, for only he had the key to his secret retreat to which he took the women he could never bring to Sandleford.

Surely Agnes was not one of Troy's women?

Nothing was impossible in such a household as this. As for me, I was sick of secrets and half-truths, of fears and legends, and being menaced by someone who wished me ill.

I went across and tapped on the door, thinking: does she use the secret way my grandfather spoke of? Does it connect with Ashmead? Is that why there was a button missing from Mrs. Scadden's cloak—because Agnes had borrowed the cloak to wear and not realised that she had lost a button?

If that was true, then it was Agnes who had tried to kill me in the West Tower, and make it seem an accident ... death by fire ...

There was no reply to my knock. I had not expected one. I turned the handle and went in.

Agnes lay on her back, her eyes closed, her hair spread over the pillow.

I closed the door determinedly behind me, and went to the foot of the bed.

"Agnes," I said loudly. "I know that you are awake. I shall not go from here until you answer me."

She sat up in bed, then, and opened her eyes. They seemed to burn in their sockets with hatred or anger, I could not tell which. Her face looked old and sharp and her lips moved soundlessly as though she tried to choke down an emotion too fierce to control.

Finally, she said angrily:

"What do you want? Why are you here?"

"I saw you standing on the terrace, a little while ago."

"Are you mad?" she gestured scornfully towards the wheel-chair. All my life, I thought, the sight of an empty wheel-chair will haunt me.

"I *saw* you, Agnes. So then, I came downstairs and waited just along the hallway towards the East Tower. I watched you come down the hall. I saw your face, I *know* it was you, so why pretend you cannot walk?"

"You are mad!" she said bitterly. "They say you are deranged and full of fantasies. What you saw was built up in your imagination."

"You lie, Agnes. You KNOW that you lie!" I beat against the bedpost with my fist. "Is *everyone* here bent upon proving that I am insane?"

"I am tired," she said pointedly. "I wish to go to sleep."

"Of course you are tired. You have been out in the grounds when you should have been in bed, Agnes. Did you go to the Folly to meet Troy?"

A spasm of pain crossed her face; but she stared grimly at me.

"If you say that you saw me, who will believe you?" she demanded.

"Perhaps you have made sure that I will not be believed. Not only now, but in other matters. Perhaps it was you who tried to kill me in the West Tower. I pulled a button from a cloak, in my struggles, that night. Mrs. Scadden had a button missing from HER cloak. Did you borrow it, Agnes, that night when you came to the tower?"

"I never came to the West Tower, nor have I ever tried to harm you," she cried.

She lay back against the pillow and closed her eyes in a very pointed gesture of dismissal.

Of what use was it to rail at her? To cry out for the truth? She would tell me nothing. If I spoke of what I had seen, everyone would say that the excitement of the Ball had been too much for me.

I went back to bed, and did not sleep for a long time. I thought about Agnes. How often had she forsaken her wheelchair and for what purposes?

She had kept her secret very well from Seton, I reflected.

It was ten o'clock when Milly brought my breakfast tray.

"Sleeping like the dead, you was, miss. The mistress thought you'd like to have your breakfast in bed. They're all cleaning up still. I've told Miss Alannah you'll take her for a walk, if she's good; maybe this afternoon."

She fussed around me happily; I looked into her pinched little face and wondered if she was as transparently honest and simple as she seemed.

I felt the terrifying aloneness that comes from not being able to trust anyone. I listened whilst she chattered about the Ball, and, idly, I asked her if Mr. Blair and Miss Oakes had returned to Ashmead.

"Oh yes, miss. They went early. Miss Oakes wasn't feeling too well. I expect it was all too much for her, not being strong, poor thing."

I had no appetite; I looked at the sunlight filling my room, and remembered that today Arthur Jarley was due at Sandleford.

Troy would have already left for Portsmouth; the house seemed emptier without him, it shrank in stature; it was no longer a splendid palace for a king among men.

I put on my plainest dress, a dove-grey one I had worn in the days when Aunt Vee was alive. I dressed my hair severely in a knot on the nape of my neck, and put the ruby and diamond earrings back in their case.

My face, in the mirror, looked pale and tired. I was thinner than when I had first come to Sandleford. I felt very tired, as though I walked in a world as grey as my dress.

It was not simply the reaction from the long night's festivities. I had a curious sense of impending disaster; as though Arthur's coming would have a profound effect upon me.

Alannah came just as I was leaving to go downstairs; she seemed subdued and her eyes searched my face anxiously.

I held her close and kissed her, pushing the hair back from her forehead.

"We will go for a walk this afternoon," I promised.

Then I saw the small, dark bruises near her wrist; spaced so exactly that they had been four fingers and a thumb.

"Who did this to you?" I whispered angrily.

She shook her head; I thought how pinched and bleak her small face seemed to be.

I was determined to find this truth, at least this once. I went through every name.

"Selina?"

She shook her head.

"Troy? No. Agnes—Miss Oakes? Mr. Blair? Milly? Katy?"

Each time she shook her head.

"Marie," I said softly, at last.

She looked at me mutely. I knew then that it was Marie who had treated her so roughly. I felt ice-cold anger within me.

"Why did she do it, Alannah?"

The child's eyes were full of tears. I took my imagination to task and came up with an answer.

"Was it because you would not go to her?"

The child nodded fearfully.

"Don't worry," I said gently. "You must be obedient, you know. If she wanted you to come to her, I daresay she had good reason; but she had no right to hurt you. She will not do it again."

She clung to me for a moment. This was no house for a child to grow up, I thought; it was divided against itself, an unhappy and sombre place.

I went to the East Tower. Marie told me that her mistress was in the morning-room.

"It is you whom I wish to see," I replied.

She admitted me grudgingly to her sitting-room. There was an open workbox and a pile of Selina's filmy undergarments beside it. Plus a large portrait of Selina, in a silver frame.

I sat, uninvited, on the edge of a leather-covered chair. Marie sat opposite me. I found it hard to imagine that this woman had ever been a prostitute. She had none of the good-natured warmth or flamboyance I associated with such women.

I looked at the plain, bony face, the small, bright eyes. In her rusty black dress and with the smell of faded potpourri about her, she seemed as unreal as the portraits in the gallery upstairs.

"What is it, ma'mselle?" She was faintly insolent, as always.

I told her about the bruises on Alannah's wrist.

"*You* are responsible, Marie."

"Ah! How does a child that cannot speak, carry tales?" she mocked.

"What did you do to her?"

"Nothing!" She spat the word. "Such a fuss over so small a thing! When I was a child, I was beaten with the tawse for defiance and disobedience. I bid her come and she does not come. She stares at me—so—and does nothing."

"Because she is afraid of you."

"That is nonsense! Madame wishes to speak to the child. I am to bring her, she says; but the child will not come. She is sullen and wilful. Am I to plead and coax? I take her—so—by the wrist, and I say, you WILL come."

"You have no right to show force towards her. If you had cause for complaint, you should have gone to Mr. Merrick."

"Do you give the orders in this house, now, ma'mselle?"

"That will do, Marie!" Inside, I was shaking; and I was determined that she should not guess that fact.

"Have you forgotten that I saw you with the Master?" she asked softly.

"I have not forgotten. Don't threaten me, Marie. Tell your mistress, if you wish. If you touch Alannah again, *I* shall speak to Mr. Merrick."

"He will not always be so proud, that one!" she muttered.

"What do you mean?"

She hid her thoughts behind a suddenly expressionless face.

"They say, in the servants' hall, that you are strange in the head, ma'mselle."

"Perhaps YOU can answer that, Marie. Perhaps it is you who takes my things and hides them and then returns them so that it seems as if I am confused?"

I watched her closely. Not a muscle in her face moved; then she laughed, a harsh, humourless sound.

"Indeed you are strange, ma'mselle. Let those with time to toss about like a child's ball, play tricks if they will. I look after Madame. It is all I wish to do. All I have time to do."

"Supposing Mr. Merrick sent you away from here."

"*Never!*" she whispered fiercely. "He would not dare!"

I stood up; the conversation led nowhere. It was like beating one's head against a wall.

I left the room with as much dignity as I could muster.

"Let him take his bastard back where she belongs!" Marie muttered, closing the door sharply behind me.

I walked to the main hall; one of the servants was looking for me. Selina was waiting for me in the morning-room.

Arthur Jarley rose to his feet as I entered; the sight of him took me back to yesterday. I heard Aunt Vee's voice again and saw her smile; I walked beside her through the rooms of the tiny house in the sleepy Dorset village.

Tears filled my eyes; Arthur held my hands, looking concerned.

"My dear child," he murmured, distressed.

Selina was beside me, concerned.

"What is it, Catherine? Tell me!"

"Nothing that time will not cure. I have too many memories of a life that was peaceful and pretty as a summer day," I said wrily.

Selina gave me a glass of sherry; she sat me down opposite Arthur. I looked up into the kind, anxious face, and my forebodings returned.

Selina stared over our heads.

"Mr. Jarley, I have sent for you because I am deeply troubled and have wrestled with my conscience until I am exhausted. There is no one else in whom I can confide; but Catherine has told me that you looked after her Aunt's affairs, and therefore I feel you may be concerned with her welfare—as I am."

She sat with her hands clasped tightly in her lap; she was silent for so long that Arthur said, at last:

"What is this matter on which you want to consult me, Mrs. Merrick?"

"It concerns my grandfather, as well as Catherine. We all believed him to be penniless. He was not. He was a very rich man who refused to spend one penny of his money on a house he detested."

"How do you know this?" Arthur demanded, astonished.

"I overheard a conversation not meant for my ears, between grandfather and Troy. I was outside the door of grandfather's room. Troy told grandfather that he had traced a grand-daughter, Catherine Fairfax.

"Grandfather wanted to know what Troy thought of Catherine." She gave me a brief, dry smile. "Troy's report was guarded, but favourable. Grandfather listened, and then said that he had decided to leave his entire fortune to the unknown Catherine!"

She looked directly at me; a wide-eyed, candid look.

"I was not jealous, Catherine. Astonished; angry to learn that my childhood had been spent in near-poverty because of grandfather's obsession about Sandleford—but that was all. I had the house. It was all I had ever wanted. Troy had not only restored it, he had made a handsome enough settlement on me, to keep me in comfort all my life. I did not need money; women do not crave wealth and power, as men do."

"I had no idea …!" I stammered.

"I know that. Troy has never told you the truth. Grandfather's money will by yours when you are twenty-one; if you die before your twenty-first birthday, then the entire fortune goes to Troy."

Chapter Nine

It was several seconds before I grasped the full implication of her words. Arthur stared at us both, frowning.

"Catherine should have been told!" he said curtly. "She had a right to know that she was her grandfather's heiress."

"I am aware of that fact," Selina said calmly. "After grandfather's death, I told Troy what I had heard. He was extremely angry with me, and forbade me to mention the matter to *anyone*. He said he did not wish Catherine to know the truth until she had been here some time. I have felt, lately, that he does not intend *anyone* to know the terms of grandfather's Will."

"Who was your grandfather's lawyer, Mrs. Merrick?" Arthur asked sharply.

"He distrusted solicitors, and would never employ one. He drew up his own Will and made Troy the sole executor."

"Even a home-made Will requires the signatures of two witnesses, if it is to be valid," Arthur retorted.

"There were two witnesses. One was Mr. Seton Blair. The other, my servant, Marie. It is because of Mr. Blair's increasing concern that I have finally decided to confide in you. He insists she should know the truth, no matter what Troy decrees; he feels that Catherine's safety is more important than loyalty to my husband."

"Safety?" I cried, my heart pounding furiously. "What do you mean?"

"You have been in danger on more than one occasion since you came here, Catherine. I have believed—as Troy insists—that you are overwrought and unhappy and not always responsible for your actions. It was Seton who felt there might be another explanation."

"No!" I whispered, horrified. "You must not *think* such things! Troy is rich and powerful enough, in his own right!"

"He is greedy. Hungry for money and power. He lives lavishly, keeps mistresses in comfort, is having a new fleet of ships built. Will even *his* wealth run to such expenditure?"

"You are quite sure that this Will exists?" Arthur said to Selina.

She nodded.

"Mr. Blair is here, in this house, to tell you himself. I asked him to return to Sandleford after he had taken Agnes back to Ashmead, as I thought you might wish to question him."

"I do; also your servant. We must first establish the existence of such a Will; then its validity," Arthur said, in his precise, legal way.

Selina touched the bell-rope. I went across and stared out of the window. The day seemed to have become clouded over with menace. I could not breathe, and each heartbeat was loud and painful.

"It is such a monstrous thought," I said aloud. "I cannot bear it!"

I could not see Selina's face; but her voice was full of pity.

"My poor Catherine, you believe yourself to be in love with Troy. I have seen it in your eyes and have grieved for you, knowing that he has encouraged feelings in you that he has no right to arouse. I know Troy's tremendous charm, the magnetism that is part of him, and his way with women—for I, too, have been his victim, remember."

Her frankness, in front of Arthur, embarrassed me. I heard him move restlessly in his chair. A servant came into the room and Selina gave instructions for Marie to be brought to her; and a request sent to Mr. Blair to come to the morning-room.

Marie came into the room with a rustling of skirts. She stood in front of Arthur, her hands folded at waist-level: a thin woman, in rusty black, her eyes bright and hard in her sallow face.

I listened intently to her replies to Arthur's brief questions.

"Yes, m'sieu. I remember well. The Master requested me to sign a paper."

"Did he seem quite coherent?"

"I do not understand."

"Did he speak clearly? Did he explain what it was?"

"Oh yes. He said it was his Will. That I must sign and Mr. Blair, also, each whilst the other was there."

"Did you read the writing on the Will?"

Marie lowered her eyes.

"No, m'sieu, I did not. Mr. Fairfax told me there was no need. When I sign, he thank me, and I am given a sovereign for my trouble."

When Arthur had done with questions, she walked stiffly from the room, with a single, piercing glance at me. I could not tell what she was thinking.

Seton was ushered in; he walked across and kissed my cheek. I wondered if he could feel how I trembled. He was kind, not in the light-hearted, teasing way that Rufus was kind, but with a deep concern for me.

"I am sorry," he said simply. "This is causing you great distress. It is a bad business."

"Did you read Mr. Fairfax's Will before you signed it?" Arthur asked him.

"I would never sign any paper without first reading it," Seton replied firmly; and I saw a gleam of approval in Arthur's eye.

"Can you remember what you read?"

"Yes. It said that Catherine Fairfax, daughter of Daniel Fairfax, was sole heir to everything that Damon possessed, on her twenty-first birthday. Until then, everything was to be held in trust for her, and the sole trustee was Troy Merrick. If she died before her twenty-first birthday, Troy was to have everything except Sandleford House—which, in accordance with tradition, passed to the child of Damon's elder son."

"Did the Will surprise you?" Arthur asked casually.

Seton shrugged.

"Naturally. We all thought Damon was penniless. There had been a rumour that Troy had traced a child of Daniel's; but as Damon had not seen this grandchild of his, the sudden decision to leave her everything was rather surprising. Damon was a strange man; full of moods, whims, impulses. Only in one thing did he remain constant: his intense dislike of this house. He considered Troy a fool to restore it so lavishly, but said that if Troy chose to commit such folly that was HIS affair."

"Did Mr. Fairfax seem lucid when he asked you to sign the Will?"

"Perfectly. Weak; tired, yes; but his wits were in their proper place."

"Did you not think it strange that Miss Fairfax was unaware of her position when she came here?"

"Yes. I was concerned about it. Several times I mentioned the fact to Mrs. Merrick. She told me that her husband had been adamant that he did not wish Catherine to be told the truth until *he* decided it was time to do so. I thought it odd; particularly in view of the fact that Catherine has, on more than one occasion, seemed to be the victim of circumstances that *could* have been accidental, and yet were quite inexplicable."

"No!" I cried.

His look held infinite pity. I saw compassion in Arthur's eyes. Had I not told myself, often enough, that someone wished me harm, wished it to seem that whatever happened to me was the result of my own instability of temperament?

Ah, but that was before I knew Troy was involved. I would not believe ill of HIM.

Who would benefit from my death? Only Troy.

All roads led back to him.

My thoughts ranged wide. Rufus? He had nothing to gain. Seton? Was it too wild to consider some unholy alliance between him and Agnes? Did HE know she was able to dispense with her wheelchair whenever she chose?

Selina? Was she less innocent, less candid than she seemed? She had her house, money, position, friends. My death would not resolve *her* unhappy marriage.

It was not love I felt for Troy, I told myself. It was a terrible craving. Pain and ecstasy. A fire that could destroy. I was no match for a man so ruthless, one who would never remain faithful to any woman.

Selina came across and put an arm around my shoulders.

"Catherine, dear, you look ill. Let me take you to your room."

I let her lead me away. My limbs had no will of their own. I was trying to escape from a tortuous maze without an exit, being pursued by something that moved ever closer to me, as I grew more and more exhausted ...

Selina turned back the coverlet, and sponged my clammy hands and forehead with eau-de-cologne.

"Try to rest, dear. I will send Milly to sit with you. I knew this would be a great shock to you, but Seton said it was my duty to send for Mr. Jarley."

I thought of strong hands reaching out to overpower me. Of nightmares, and a disordered room, a swooping owl, a cat weaving around my bare, cringing flesh. Subtle forms of cruelty, to pave the way so well ...

I put out a hand and caught hold of Selina's wrist.

"What is it, dear?" She bent over me, her face concerned.

"I've remembered something. The milk that Milly brings me every night. Something is added to it to make me sleep heavily. Then I'm awakened from that deep sleep, and things are strange and confused."

She stroked my hand between her fingertips.

"Dr. Garrod prescribed powders to make you sleep. You disliked medicines, you said; you did not need anything. You were adamant. Dr. Garrod said they would be tasteless in milk. Each day, Marie fetches just one powder from his surgery; each night, I give it to Milly to put in your milk. It is an excellent and very mild sedative. I took it, for some time, after grandfather died, and found it very helpful. However, if you feel unhappy about it, you shall not have any more."

Who knew that I took the powders? Selina, Marie, Milly, Dr. Garrod, Troy. Everyone.

I put my arm across my eyes to shut out the light. Selina drew the curtains, dimming the room.

"That's better. Try to sleep, Catherine."

"When will Troy be back?" I asked.

"Not for some days. The first of his new ships is almost ready for the sea. It is a matter of pride with him that he sees to all the details himself. After his business is done, I am sure he will find other diversions—and return here when he pleases, as he usually does."

Her voice was dry, without bitterness; she had long since accepted him for what he was, I thought.

"I don't want grandfather's money!" I cried.

"You have the right to live to inherit it!" she retorted.

She closed the door quietly behind her. Seconds later, Milly tiptoed in noisily, her shoes squeaking, her print apron rustling. She settled herself comfortably in the armchair; I supposed that she reckoned that watching was much to be preferred to working.

I slept, fitfully, and my vivid, half-waking dreams were filled with pain. When I finally awoke, and sat up, shaking away the memory of dreams, Milly asked:

"Can I get you something?"

"Is it late?" I asked.

"It's lunch-time, miss; if you'd like something sent up ..."

I shook my head, pushed back the coverlet, and swung my legs to the floor. When I tried to stand up, they supported me firmly enough.

"I need fresh air," I said.

Milly left me alone. The quietness seemed accusing; how *could* it be Troy who tried to harm me? How could it be anyone else? Back and forth went the shuttle of my thoughts.

I washed my face and tidied my hair. When Selina came into the room, I was ready to go out.

"I thought I'd take Alannah for a walk," I said.

"Why not?" She smiled brightly. Though I searched her face I could find nothing there to make me suspicious.

"It will do you good," she assured me. "Mr. Jarley has gone. He asks me to tell you that he intends to pursue certain enquiries with all possible speed and vigour. Those are his own words. He is angry and perturbed. He intends to ask Troy why the truth was kept from you."

"I intend to do that, myself."

She looked uneasy.

"I think you should leave it to Mr. Jarley, Catherine."

I made no promises. I intended to tell Troy that he could

keep every penny of the Fairfax money. Having told him that, I would leave Sandleford and never return. Guardian or no, he would *not* force me to come back, I thought fiercely.

Yet, I remembered his boast to find me, no matter where I went, and I felt the tears burn behind my eyes.

I went to fetch Alannah, thinking: if it is Troy who is responsible for what has happened to me, then at least I am safe whilst he is away from Sandleford.

Alannah clung to me, as though she would never let me go. Her fear communicated itself to me; she looked as though she had not expected to see me again, and I thought: I am going to miss her very much.

"Cook is packing a hamper," I told her, "and we are going to drive to the top of the hill, for a picnic, because it is such a lovely afternoon."

Her eyes danced; she made a small gurgle of pleasure.

Selina had insisted on ordering the coach for us, though I would have preferred the governess cart. It WAS a lovely day: very warm, with a cloudless sky.

I knew that Selina would have come with me, had I not been taking Alannah; I couldn't blame her for feeling as she did, about Troy's child.

Rufus came up at the last minute, scowling at me.

"Am I not invited?" he asked.

"Of course," I said.

Rufus sat down beside me, and Alannah was opposite him, looking very small on the upholstered seat, her feet not touching the floor. She was in a happy mood, pulling off her tam-o'-shanter as soon as we were out on the road, and waving it out of the window.

"You have been avoiding me all the morning," Rufus murmured accusingly, in my ear.

"I have not. I saw nothing of you."

"I rode early to Kilstock. There is some dispute amongst the men, as usual. Sometimes, I think I will wash my hands of the whole business."

"And live forever at Sandleford? You wouldn't like that, surely?"

"I would go and live where the sun always shines. Where the sun is blue and warm. Somewhere old and beautiful, like Greece. How you would enjoy Greece, Catherine!"

"Has Selina told you the reason for Mr. Jarley's visit today?" I asked.

"She mentioned it at lunchtime. She worries considerably on your behalf. Really, you must have annoyed the ghost of Anna for her to persecute you in such a fashion!"

I glanced sharply at him. Was he making light of it merely to comfort me? Or did he not see the seriousness of the situation? He had stated that he believed me to be perfectly sensible, and that fact had comforted me more than his light-heartedness could ever do.

"YOU don't believe in the power of ghosts to trouble the living," I told him.

"Oh, but I do, my dear Catherine. Have you not heard of mischievous, unpleasant spirits? Poltergeists. They have great powers, I am told; they can hurtle objects through the air; that is but one of their accomplishments. I assure you, however, that none exist at Kilstock."

I laughed; but my laughter was followed by a sigh. How well did I really know Rufus? I was beginning to distrust everyone with whom I came into contact.

Perhaps I was looking for a scapegoat because I could not bear to face the obvious truth that Troy wishes himself rid of me, in order that Damon's great wealth would pass to him.

If Selina died childless, then presumably Sandleford would pass to Troy and he would become one of the most powerful men in the South of England.

Rufus found my hand and held it in his own; his glance was full of affection. How tempting a prospect was the thought of being mistress of Kilstock. I should know love and security, peace of mind; all these would be mine. Living in a haven from the torment of my thoughts about Troy, with a loving, undemanding husband.

Would I never be free of Troy, I wondered, with a moment's anguish?

At the top of the hill, the coach was halted. The coachman spread a rug for me, and set the picnic basket beside me. Alannah had brought a big, coloured ball with her, and I watched Rufus toss it into the air, calling to her to run and catch it.

It was a small island of pleasure in a troubled sea of events, I thought. The sun was warm on my head; the town spread below me, with its skirt of blue water, shimmered in the soft heat-haze. I lay back, feeling the rough grasses tickle my cheek, and thought: I wish I need not go back to Sandleford. It is always cold there, and full of shadows.

Cook had packed a generous basket, and we were hungry. Rufus came, panting, to fling himself down on the rug, declaring that Alannah was too energetic for an old man like him; and Alannah, laughing, caught a corner of her skirt in each hand and danced a jig for us.

"Who taught you to do that?" I asked.

She stopped suddenly and the folds of material dropped from her fingertips. She looked so sad for a moment that I knew as clearly as though she had answered: *my mother*.

We stayed too long; the sun strayed behind a cloud, and the breeze had a chill edge. Rufus stood up and held out his hands to us.

"Time we were going," he said.

We were a silent trio, returning to Sandleford. As we turned in through the gates, I shivered involuntarily. Alannah's hand found and held mine firmly.

I looked down into the child's face; it suddenly seemed older and wiser, as though sharpened by knowledge. It was an illusion, gone in a moment.

I had an awareness of shadows folding themselves thickly around me; a feeling that all that happened to me in the last few weeks was only an overture, and the curtain had not yet risen …

Selina had left a message that she had gone to Ashmead to have tea with Seton and Agnes.

I thought, grimly: Agnes will not come to Sandleford, if she can help it; she does not want to see me, because of what I know. Is she afraid I shall give her away?

The next couple of days passed peacefully enough. I gave as much time as possible to Alannah, knowing how much I should miss her when I left Sandleford. I talked to her, and told her the tales that Aunt Vee had told ME as a child, I made her smile with stories of my escapades; when she laughed, I counted it a great victory.

We went to the Chapel, and I knelt there, sending up my small, muddled prayers for guidance, for safety for Alannah, all through her childhood in such a house. I looked at the woman whose feet were half-hidden in small white flowers, and thought: at least the prophecy of the snowdrops has not come true, this time. There has been no death in the house.

Then the Fair arrived in the village; overnight, the peaceful green was transformed. The booths went up, and the sideshows, the caravans came, the lean dogs, the grubby women and sharp-featured men who were not real gypsies at all, but travelling tinkers and showmen and fortune-tellers. The night they arrived, we heard music, borne on the evening air. It was the sound of steam-organs; a tinny, strangely mournful music that made me sad.

Alannah was excited; but her excitement turned to disappointment when she discovered that Selina had no intention of letting her go to the Fair.

She looked pleadingly at me, as though I could wave a magic wand; Selina was adamant. It was no place for a child. None of the household from Sandleford ever went to the Fair; only the servants, she pointed out.

I could not explain this to Alannah. I thought: if Troy was here, *he* would have taken her, and they would both have enjoyed it.

I wanted to go; something in its earthiness appealed to me, though I was half-ashamed of that fact. There would be drinking when the naphtha flares danced in the blue dusk; I thought of the wooden balls being hurled at coconut shies, the voices of the showmen outside the booths, shrieking girls in swing-boats, petticoats flying; and, over it all, that strange, sad music that sang so coldly in my blood.

The staff were allowed to go to the Fair after their day's work was done. It was a great event in their lives. Milly whisked, singing, through her work, and came to see me when she was dressed to go out. She wore her best grey coat and skirt that she wore to Church on Sundays, and a jaunty hat with a feather trim. Pinned to the lapel of her coat was the little silver and mother-of-pearl brooch I had given her.

I went along to sit and read to Alannah; but she turned her face away so that I should not see the tears, and I knew she was still bitterly disappointed at being shut out of the fun and excitement.

In the end, I went to bed early; I lay there, wakeful. The night was hot and I opened the window a little, though Milly declared that night air was a bad thing.

I drifted off to sleep to the faint echoes of fairground music.

Much later, I awoke to hear the sound of tapping. It was faint and faraway, as though it was part of a half-waking dream. The Devil's dancing shoes, I thought, coming from the direction of the West Tower. A sound made by someone with a macabre sense of humour; but surely the unseen dancer knew that the West Tower rooms were empty, and that the joke—if it could be called such—was pointless, in consequence?

I lifted my head from the pillow, frowning, and propped myself on one elbow. The sound seemed intermittent; more like a signal; but it was very faint indeed and after a few moments, it faded away altogether.

I heard soft footsteps outside my room. Swiftly, I slid from my bed; I heard the stable clock strike twelve, the chimes borne clearly towards me on the still air. Milly would be back from the Fair by now, sound asleep in the room next to mine, and I did not want to waken her.

Of course, I thought, dismayed, I won't be able to open the door! Milly will have locked it, as usual, a precaution against intruders, so far as I was concerned—a precaution against nocturnal wanderings, so far as the household was concerned.

Nevertheless, I tried the handle; to my surprise, it gave under my touch. Milly had obviously forgotten the usual routine.

I recognised the back of the figure, walking down the corridor, towards the main staircase.

"Rufus!" I called.

He turned sharply. Was it wariness on his face? Or guilt? In the dim lamplight, I couldn't be sure. I thought he came reluctantly back to where I stood in the bedroom doorway.

I realised that I wasn't wearing a wrapper; what did it matter, I thought? My high-necked, long-sleeved nightdress was as respectable as a gown, so far as I was concerned.

"What is it?" he demanded, his voice quiet and sharp. "Why aren't you asleep, Catherine?"

"I heard the sound of tapping," I said.

He tilted his head in a listening attitude; so did I; but we could hear nothing.

"I *did* hear it, Rufus."

I searched his face, silently asking for an explanation as to why he was prowling around the house at such a late hour. He saw my look and said:

"I couldn't sleep. *I* thought I heard a very faint tapping noise, too. Well, you know the old legend. I thought of the dancing shoes and the West Tower. I went along and looked. There was nothing, no sound. I decided I'd go downstairs and get a book, to send me back to sleep."

His voice was full of its usual light mockery. He smiled and whispered mischievously:

"If anyone should see us they'd think it a *very* compromising situation! You appear to have been entertaining me, in the manner in which men have always been entertained by the fair sex, and now you are bidding me goodnight. Oh, Catherine!"

I managed to smile, though I felt strangely uneasy and depressed.

"Who would be wandering around, so late?"

"One of the servants back late from the Fair," he suggested promptly.

"At midnight? Hardly likely."

"Does it really matter?" He bent and kissed my cheek. "Go back to sleep, there's a good girl."

I went obediently; quietly, I slid between the sheets. Milly was a sound sleeper, and probably her evening's gaiety had tired her out.

I was awakened by the sound of curtains being drawn back. The room was full of sunlight, and there was a tray of tea by my bed.

It was Julia who had brought the tea.

"Where is Milly?" I asked.

When Julia turned from the window, I saw that her eyes were full of curiosity, her mouth pinched into a virtuous little button of disapproval.

"Where's Milly? We'd all like to know that, miss. She wasn't on duty this morning, and Mrs. Treville sent me to look for her. I came in, earlier, but you were sound asleep. Her bed hasn't been slept in."

I pushed back the covers and went into the dressing-room. Milly's bed was smooth and unruffled.

"Perhaps she went to her old room in the servants' quarter?"

"No, miss. We've looked there. Everyone's been looking. She must have stayed out all night."

"I shouldn't think she'd do such a foolish thing; she knows it would mean instant dismissal," I pointed out.

"Where is she, then?" Julia wanted to know. "We've looked *everywhere*."

"Did anyone see her at the Fair?"

"Oh yes. She went with Betty and Katy, but Betty met her young man there, and Katy came home early because she had a headache. Milly said she was going to stay on and she'd be back before eleven. Betty's young man brought her back at half-past ten; they never saw Milly. *No one*'s seen her, miss. Do you reckon she's run off?"

"Why would she do that? Isn't she happy there?"

"Oh, yes, but, well you know ..."

"I don't know, Julia. What are you trying to say?"

Julia flushed and looked embarrassed, mumbling something about Lallie being in trouble.

"I'm certain Milly wasn't in trouble!" I said sharply.

"Oh yes, miss, I'm sure, too, but I got to thinking ..."

She whisked off, with a rustle of starched print. I got to thinking, too, and was perturbed. Milly wasn't flighty and I didn't think she would have risked dismissal.

Selina was at breakfast, looking fresh and pretty in a crisp new dress. Her hair shone like gold, her cheeks were pink, she held herself regally as she sat at the head of the table. I thought what a fool Troy was to spend so much time away from her.

"You've heard the gossip, of course?" she said resignedly to me.

"If you mean about Milly being missing—yes. Aren't you worried, Selina?"

"The house has been thoroughly searched, and the grounds are being combed, at this moment. I don't see what else I can do. It's my belief she didn't return to the house from the Fair. If harm came to her on the way home, then it is not a matter for us; I have sent word of her disappearance to the village constable."

I thought: how capable she is. How well organised. This morning, she seems truly mistress of the house, in her own right.

"Isn't anyone responsible for checking the servants in when they have been out at night?" I asked.

"Usually. At times like this, when the Fair is in the village, we are more lenient. Mrs. Treville was tired and went to bed early. Kellatt checked last night that all the doors and windows were secure; that was at eleven-thirty, his usual time. The door to the servants quarters was unlocked, so he secured it."

"Then you wouldn't know if Milly had come in or not?"

"I rather think she did *not*," Selina said quietly. "Where could she hide?"

"Grandfather mentioned secret passages, in his notebook," I argued.

"Catherine!" Her voice was sharp. "That's an old tale, full of nonsense!"

"*You* believe the old legends," I insisted.

"Yes, but that's rather different from the idea of Milly straying into secret passages in the middle of the night," she pointed out.

I felt foolish. I *was* foolish. Selina was clearly very worried, and I wondered if, after all, she wouldn't have preferred to delegate the worry to her husband.

"When is Troy coming back?" I asked.

"The day after tomorrow, I believe. If he decides to stay away longer, he won't bother to inform me," she said, with a shrug of her shoulders.

Alannah was having a riding lesson; afterwards, Kellatt

was going to take her to the Home Farm to see the new litter of piglets. The morning was mine. I had a great deal to think about.

I sat on the terrace, in the sunshine, listening to the soft hiss of the waterfall; even the voice of water sounded sinister, here. I began to understand my grandfather's hatred of the place. If the Black Mass had often been celebrated in the West Tower, then surely Sandleford would never be a peaceful house, for all that Argus Fairfax had built his Chapel and dedicated it to the Lady of the Snows.

By lunchtime, I had made my decision.

"I shall leave Sandleford before Troy returns," I told Selina.

Rufus was lunching with us. His eyebrows rose, he looked at me sharply, but said nothing.

Selina looked distressed.

"Catherine, you *cannot* do that! I have told you, Troy will find you and have you brought back!"

"Let him fight for me, if he wishes—in a Court of Law," I told her. "My mind is made up. I shall go back to Dorset and ask Arthur Jarley if he can find some employment for me. I hardly think Troy will try to remove me by force."

There was a long silence. Rufus was watching us both, in turn, but he seemed to be waiting on Selina's reply.

She stared down at her plate. Her fingers with their sparkle of heavy rings, were trembling almost uncontrollably. She looked up, with tears in her eyes.

"I don't want you to go," she said frankly. "Yet, how can I keep you? If it is true, as we suspect, that Troy wants the Fairfax money, then ..." she bit her lip and shook her head.

"You cannot go, Catherine!" Rufus urged. "You have an alternative. Take it!"

"I need to be completely free, Rufus, to think over many things," I said calmly.

Selina turned to Rufus and said unexpectedly:

"How little you know of my husband, Rufus! He has a terrible craving for more and more power, more and greater wealth; an ambition that drives him relentlessly, like a ship driven before the wind. He will not rest until he gets what he wants."

"I do not believe Troy would use devious methods to get his way," Rufus replied.

"He would use ANY methods. It is better for Catherine to go from here, where she will be safe."

Rufus looked at me; his face was more serious than I had ever seen it. For once, he could not find anything of which to make a jest.

"I shall leave in the morning, before Troy returns," I told them. "I will leave a letter of explanation for Troy, telling him I do not want the Fairfax money, and that I have decided to seek employment."

I left them sitting there and went along to the West Tower, but the door was locked. In any case, Milly would never have gone to these rooms late at night, I reasoned. She called them 'creepy' and disliked being there alone, even in the daytime.

There was an air of unrest throughout the whole house. Milly had not been found, and the village constable, florid and important, stood in the hall, his helmet beneath his arm, when I went to collect Alannah for her afternoon walk.

Rufus waylaid me in the picture gallery; he was standing before Anna's portrait, regarding her quizzically.

"Catherine," he caught hold of my hand. "Wouldn't you like to eat strawberries, sugar and cream, sit on a cushion and sew a fine seam, as the old nursery rhyme says? All yours, Your Majesty. You have but to say the word."

"I wish that I COULD say it, Rufus," I admitted frankly.

His sudden anger astonished me; I had never before seen him angry.

"And why can't you marry me? Because Troy draws you like a magnet. You have a most expressive face, Catherine Fairfax, and do not easily hide your thoughts away. You will never marry ME, because HE holds you in the palm of HIS hand. What can come of your foolish passion? By all accounts, he has sinister designs upon you. He wants your money."

"You have no right to say such things!" I cried.

"Is it so hard to face the truth?"

"What IS the truth? Only that my guardian does not choose to tell me I am heiress to a fortune."

"A fortune that reverts to him should you die before you are of age!"

The anger suddenly went out of him, as he spoke. He shrugged, his eyes bright and mocking.

"I cherish a hopeless passion for you, for which there seems to be no remedy. However, I shall learn how to cure myself, for I don't propose to die of love!"

I sighed.

"You will find a mistress for your house one day, Rufus. Someone whom you can love as you love me, today; and who will return your affection as it deserves to be returned."

He smiled wrily.

"You make pretty speeches, Catherine!"

"I am sincere," I told him.

"I believe you." He bowed low, kissing my hand with a flourish that was faintly mocking.

Unhappily, I went along to the Nursery. Alannah was waiting for me, a sheet of paper in her hand. On it, she had drawn an enormous sow and nine pigs.

I knelt and put my arms around her.

"That's very good, Alannah. So you enjoyed your visit to the Farm?"

There was no need to ask. Her eyes sparkled and she gave the small chuckle that never failed to delight me. She thrust the paper into my hand, and her look said: this is a gift for you.

"Thank you," I said, as I kissed her forehead.

I wanted to forget Troy; I was determined to do so; but trying to forget this child was going to be the most difficult task of my life. With all my heart, I yearned to be able to take her with me.

She seemed so utterly defenceless, so alone. Selina ignored her; Seton was always pleasant to her, but he must have seemed a rather remote person who had not often come into contact with children.

I reminded myself that Rufus and Agnes were kind to her. So was Troy—when he was at home; but they were all adults, and their world was different from hers. Perhaps because I was younger than any of them, I felt closer to her. I loved Alannah dearly, not merely because she was handicapped, but for the warmth of her affection.

I knew I had to tell her I was leaving Sandleford. Just as well I was going quickly; she wouldn't have time to anticipate my departure. Children were resilient, their memories short; once I was gone, she would soon forget me.

I chose to tell her when we were in the Chapel.

"Alannah, I am going away from Sandleford, tomorrow. I—I won't be coming back," I said, putting my arm around her.

I felt her stiffen. This was far worse than the terror I had known inside the West Tower.

"Troy will take care of you. Perhaps he will let you come and stay with me one day," I added.

She flung her arms around me and held me tightly as though to forcibly prevent my leaving. I saw the piteous look on her face, and hated what I was doing.

I drew a deep breath and looked at the tranquil figure in the stained-glass window.

"I will see you again, Alannah," I said, my voice loud and clear. "I *will*. I promise."

She refused to be consoled; she was subdued for the rest of our walk, and clung tightly to my hand. She went reluctantly to nursery tea. I wanted to weep for her.

"You shall come to my room this evening," I said, as cheerfully as I could. "And stay with me until bedtime. Would you like that?"

She nodded; Katy looked at me hopefully.

"I'm going to the Fair, miss," she said.

"That's all right, Katy. If Mrs. Merrick has given you permission to go, you can tell her I will be looking after Alannah and I'll see she goes to bed."

I went down to the drawing-room. Selina poured tea into paper-thin cups. She was very pale and quiet; I asked if there was any news of Milly.

"None. It's a complete mystery. People don't just—disappear. All kinds of wild rumours are flying around the servants' hall. First Lallie, now Milly, they are saying; this is an unlucky house because of what was once done here. I don't believe that. It is a beautiful house. I love every stone of it; its legends, its oldness, its nooks and crannies."

"It seems chill and sombre to me," I said frankly. "I don't feel at ease here."

"You have too much imagination, Catherine," she chided. "Well, I shall miss you. Must you go so soon? Troy will be angry when he returns and finds his ward has defied him and gone her way. No one ever defies Troy."

"Then I shall be unique," I replied lightly.

"You will forget him." She bent towards me, her violet eyes very bright. "You will meet someone else; or perhaps you will find that your feelings for Rufus are deeper than you believe them to be. Troy will bring you no happiness; he has brought none to ME."

"I shall never return to Sandleford," I told her.

"Never is a long day, Catherine. Troy will vent his anger on me, when he discovers that you have left here."

"I am sorry," I said. "I would not willingly have caused you distress."

She shrugged.

"Oh, I am well used to his rages," she said philosophically. "I would not like to predict that he will not use every means in his power to have you brought back here. As your legal guardian, he has a very strong case."

I shivered, suddenly. Troy would leave no stone unturned, I knew.

"You cannot leave here without going over to Ashmead to say goodbye to Seton and Agnes," Selina said. "We will walk over together. I should like some fresh air, and it will do you good also. I don't think you should stay here alone."

I hesitated.

"I have promised to play with Alannah," I explained.

"You spoil her. Troy must make proper arrangements for her to have a governess. I shall insist upon it. She will become impossible when you leave. I am sure you can spare time to say goodbye to your friends."

Selina was very quiet as we walked to Ashmead. Agnes received us; she was sitting by the open drawing-room window when we were ushered in. Her hands lay listlessly in her lap; I was horrified to see how ˙l she looked—pale and drawn, eyes sunk in their sockets.

Selina was all concern.

"Agnes, you should be in bed; has Dr. Garrod seen you?"

Agnes shivered and shook her head.

"I have a slight chill, no more," she said briefly. "Is there news of Milly? Has she been found?"

"I am afraid not," Selina told her.

"Something has happened to her!" Agnes cried, in a great state of agitation.

Selina looked taken aback.

"What is wrong with you, Agnes? We have no information at all about the wretched girl. I am sure nothing has happened to her; I am extremely angry at the distress she has caused us, and, when she returns, I shall tell her so."

Agnes stared down at her hands, and I saw how they trembled.

Seton's entry into the room was a relief. He looked with concern at Agnes and said, ruefully, to Selina:

"I have told her that she should be in bed; but she defies me! Women are stubborn creatures."

Agnes did not look at me. I felt great pity for her. She had been the drudge, worse off than a servant for many years, shut off from the carefree childhood world that Rufus and Selina and Seton had inhabited. It had left her warped and twisted; who could blame her? Everyone around her believed that she was unable to walk. She had their sympathy and attention so long as she perpetrated that myth. I had exposed her and she hated me; it was simple and not sinister, at all.

"Catherine is leaving Sandleford," Selina said.

I saw the dismay in Seton's face.

"Why?" he asked me bluntly.

"I think it better," I said calmly. "I am seeking independence. I intend to become a governess. I do not like to be idle."

"Troy will never countenance it. Are you planning to return and claim your inheritance when you are twenty-one?" Seton demanded.

I thought it an odd remark. Too personal to be in keeping with his character. However, I answered with a non-committal shrug and a smile. There was a deep, cold silence.

Agnes was so still she hardly seemed to breathe. Selina said sadly:

"Tonight is Catherine's last night with us."

"*Tonight*?" He looked sharply at her, and she nodded.

"You're leaving tomorrow?" His look flashed quickly over me. "So soon?"

"Having made up my mind, there is little point in delay," I said.

His look disconcerted me. The atmosphere was claustrophobic and I was anxious to be away. Equally, Agnes wanted to be rid of us; that much was obvious.

I said that I could not stay, as I had promised to spend my last evening with Alannah. I took my farewell of Agnes and her hand lay limp and cold in mine, her eyes looked through me.

Seton walked to the gate with us, alternately expressing regret that I was leaving, and concern over Agnes.

"Something ails her. She has not been herself for several days. Mrs. Scadden has been full of Milly's disappearance today—servants' gossip flies fast—and I have had to ask her not to mention it in front of Agnes."

"Why?" I asked.

"Agnes seems obsessed by it; she has a morbid appetite for all the details Mrs. Scadden can supply. One would almost think *she* was responsible for Milly's disappearance."

"Milly?" Selina said lightly. "I think she has run off with the blacksmith."

"You are quite wrong; he was hard at work at his forge when I saw him this afternoon," Seton retorted; and their laughter chimed together on the evening air.

We reached the end of Ashmead lands; Seton put his hands on my shoulders, looked deep into my eyes, and then kissed my cheek.

"I am sorry that you are going away, Catherine," he said.

I did not see Rufus again that evening; Selina told me that he had gone to dine with Dr. Garrod and to play Chess with him. He would not be returning until very late.

I thought: he has arranged this deliberately, because he is angry with me.

Selina had seemed quite well on the walk home, chatting about many things, continually expressing her regret at my decision to leave after we had known one another such a short time; but once inside Sandleford, she drooped.

"I have a headache," she declared. "I think I may have taken a chill. These warm days, so early in the year, are not to be trusted. I shall go to bed early. What will you do, Catherine?"

"I must pack. I shall spend some time with Alannah, and then put her to bed. I would like to leave after breakfast tomorrow."

"I'll see that the coach is here, when you are ready. Troy has taken the big carriage. Kellatt himself shall drive you to Dorset. If Troy is angry, I don't care."

She slid a hand through my arm and rested her head on my shoulder.

"I'll see you at breakfast," she promised. "You know, I feel sure he won't let you go so easily as this. He'll find you and force you to come back."

I had an early, cold supper; the servants were anxious to be off to enjoy the last night of the Fair—with the exception of Mrs. Treville and one young footman.

Mrs. Treville announced her intention of going to her sitting-room for what she called 'a good read.' The house had never seemed so empty, so quiet, or so full of a menace that hid itself in the gathering shadows. I would go to bed early, I decided. Not that harm would come to me, surely, on my last night here?

With bitterness, I reflected that nothing had happened to me since Troy had left for Portsmouth.

I wrote a brief letter to Troy, telling him that I did not want the Fairfax inheritance and had no intention of returning to Sandleford.

I had little enough to pack. I left out the red ball gown I had worn, and the red shoes. The gown was lying on the bed when Alannah came to the room.

She took off her house shoes, and solemnly wriggled her feet into the red shoes. They were much too big and looked ridiculous; she could hardly walk in them.

She held the heavy folds of the ball dress against her, and

pirouetted in front of the mirror. I thought: she is thoroughly enjoying herself. Children love dressing-up.

"Here, then!" I gave her one of my hats, with a little cascade of feathers down the back; a ribbon scarf and a pair of long gloves.

Delighted, she put them all on, strutting like a peacock, up and down the room, until I rocked with laughter and forgot that I was going to miss her very much in the lonely days ahead.

She suddenly kicked off the shoes and ran from the room; a few minutes later, she was back again, carrying one of the huge peacock fans from the wall of the dressing-room in the West Tower.

The spread of vivid blue feathers almost dwarfed her, as she bowed solemnly, holding the fan in front of her.

I had never liked the fans. I looked at the exquisitely enamelled head, the minute, glittering stones outlining the cruel, curved beak, the jewelled eyes. There is something ominous about such birds as peacocks and owls, I thought.

The peacock fan that Alannah was holding was probably valuable. I watched her turning this way and that in front of the mirror but the big fan was too difficult for small fingers to grasp properly, and she soon tired of it. She tossed it down on the bed and looked for something else with which to amuse herself.

"I am sure you shouldn't be playing with this," I told her. "I'll put it back on the wall."

I was surprised that the door leading to the West Tower apartments had been left unlocked; but Selina had said that the servants were always more careless when the Fair was in the village and it took days to re-establish a proper routine, afterwards.

I walked into the room with my head held high. Oh, I was brave enough, then! Tomorrow I was leaving Sandleford forever. Never again would I hear the sound of the Devil's Dancing Shoes beating out a measure, somewhere within these walls.

Alannah had needed to climb on to a chair to reach the place where the fan hung; even then, it must have been quite a stretch for her.

I stepped up on to the chair, fan in hand; as I straightened, I trod on the hem of my skirt; I was jerked so sharply that I almost overbalanced.

Instinctively, I put out a hand to save myself, and grabbed at the small stone knob on which the fan had been hung; and so, by such small, insignificant acts, the course of a whole life is changed.

The knob yielded under the unexpected pressure of my hand; I looked at the stone and saw that it was carved into the shape of a lion's head, an exact replica of the stone lions guarding the entrance to the house.

I righted myself, relieved that I had not damaged the fan; as I replaced it in position, I heard a noise behind me.

It was the noise of stones moving on one another; of masonry sliding into position.

At once, I knew what it was. I had searched for so long …

I scrambled down, ran across and opened the heavy cupboard doors. Where there had been a wall at the back of one of the cupboards, there was now an oblong of darkness through which came a draught of cold air. Yet I had tapped those walls until my knuckles were sore, and they had seemed so solid.

It was still daylight; but there was only darkness beyond the opening and I needed a light.

Fumbling and impatient, I lit the candle in its silver holder that was always kept in the West Tower rooms. I lifted it high, as I reached the opening, and peered downwards at a flight of steps.

I found a rusted iron handrail and grasped it tightly. I took the first two steps cautiously, peering through the gloom.

There was something huddled against the wall near the bottom of the steps. A pale blur; I went down two more steps, and saw that it was the body of a woman in a grey costume. Her hat lay beside her, and her sandy hair was tumbled about her shoulders.

She had blood in her hair and on her temple; one of her shoes was missing from her foot, and, as I peered through the gloom, I realised what had become of it.

She was holding the shoe tightly in her hand; as though she had been beating out a signal for help on the wall.

I had to go on; I had to make sure that she was dead. I flinched every step of the way. This was worse than the tree of death.

"Milly?" I called, foolishly.

I bent and touched her cheek. It was ice-cold. Her wide-open eyes had a look of terror in them.

She was dead.

Chapter Ten

Numbed with shock, I stared down at Milly, imagining her beating on the wall with her shoe, using the last of her strength; alone and terrified in utter darkness.

The thought was not to be borne. The compassion I felt suddenly was a physical pain; but there was no time to think of the implications of what had happened. I had much to do; and the first task was to tell Selina of my discovery.

I lifted the candle high and peered through the gloom. The passage in which I stood was wide enough to allow two people to walk abreast. The floor beneath my feet was firm, and when I put my hand above me, I almost touched the roof, which appeared to be made of stone. The whole place seemed quite dry, and there was a current of air coming from somewhere.

Slowly, I walked up the flight of stairs; at the top, I paused, my heart almost stopping; beyond the opening through which I had come stood Alannah, wide-eyed and curious.

How careless I had been! She rushed across to me, her face alive with excitement. I caught hold of her arm to prevent her from rushing through the opening, and shook my head, summoning a smile.

"There's just a small space down there," I lied. "It's very dark. You must wait until Troy has been to see that it's quite safe. He will be back tomorrow."

I hated lying to a child. She looked disappointed and rebellious as I closed the door of the cupboard firmly behind me. I didn't go across and move the knob that would have shut the aperture at the back of the cupboard, for I was anxious that Alannah should not see how it worked.

"Bedtime," I said firmly. "Come along."

She looked obstinate, thrusting out her underlip and backing away. She pointed at the cupboard, and her glance was suddenly pleading. If she had been old enough and able to speak, I think she would have said she felt cheated.

I had an inspiration.

"How would you like to sleep in my bed tonight, Alannah, instead of in the Nursery?" I suggested.

She looked slightly mollified, and nodded.

I fetched her nightclothes from the Nursery, and helped her undress. I sponged her face and brushed her hair; watched, as with folded hands and bent head, she made her silent prayers. Then she climbed between the sheets of the big bed, pecking my cheek half-heartedly, as though still annoyed with me for spoiling what she looked upon as a great adventure.

I was in a fever of anxiety and impatience to get to Selina. I dared not let Alannah see that. I waited until she closed her eyes, and her breathing became slow and even; then I tiptoed from the room, and made my way with all speed to Selina's room.

Marie answered my knock at the door; her face was dour.

"What is it?" she demanded insolently.

"I must speak to Mrs. Merrick immediately!"

"That you cannot do ma'mselle! She is sleeping."

"The matter is of the utmost urgency."

"It must wait."

"It cannot wait. You *must* waken your mistress!"

Marie effectively barred the way, shaking her head emphatically.

"Madame has taken a sleeping draught for a migraine. It would be most unwise to awaken her. That, I shall not do. Neither will you, ma'mselle."

It was useless to argue; and pointless, I realised, to rouse Selina, if she was sleeping as heavily as Marie insisted.

What was I to do, I wondered frantically? Rufus was out. I did not wish the servants to be told of the discovery before the household knew. The Master of the house was away. I felt utterly alone; there was no one to consult, no one to trust.

Except Seton, I realised.

I hastened to the servants quarters; only Simkins, the young footman was there, in his shirt sleeves, carefully pressing his uniform jacket.

He looked nonplussed when he saw me; I must have seemed strange to him, wide-eyed and dishevelled as I was.

"Put on your jacket," I said, as calmly as I could. "Go at once to Ashmead and request Mr. Blair to come here immediately. Tell him I must see him on a matter of the greatest urgency."

Simkins, looking curious, obeyed. When he had gone, I leaned against the wall, closing my eyes; it was a relief to have delegated such a terrible responsibility to someone as capable as Seton.

It seemed an eternity before Simkins returned.

"Mr. Blair is not at home, miss. I gave your message to Miss Oakes. She said she would give it to him as soon as he returned."

"Did she say where Mr. Blair had gone?"

"No, miss."

I decided that if Seton did not come soon, I would send Simkins to Dr. Garrod's house, to ask him and Rufus to come to Sandleford with all speed.

Having made my decision, I felt calmer, and went along to my room. Alannah appeared to be sound asleep.

I needed to be busy; I could not bear waiting in the silent house. The place seemed to be full of eyes, watching to see what I would do, and I was acutely aware of the dead girl lying in the passage.

I wanted to know where the passage led. So I went back to the dressing-room, deciding I would have some time to explore it before Seton came. I relit the candle and went down the steps, trying not to look at the figure huddled pathetically against the wall.

The passage was a long one. It sloped downwards, twisting and turning; some way along I found the source of the air current; there was a small grating above my head, with one bar missing. The grating was half-covered in ivy, strands of which had recently been broken away. I heard the faint neigh of a horse and I realised I was near the stables. This was the way that Kellatt's cat had entered the tunnel and got into the study, frightening me.

I came, at last, to an oak door, heavy and very thick. It was securely bolted and barred on the far side.

I was sure that the door led directly into the Folly; the secret path by which smugglers had found safety and fugitives eluded justice; the road for those who did not wish it known that they enjoyed celebrating the Black Mass. I imagined them gathering at the Folly, supposedly for an evening's revelry, and then being shown the secret way to the West Tower. It was simple and clever.

Perhaps Troy had found it useful, I thought bitterly; he was the only one who used the Folly now.

I put my ear to the door and listened; only silence surged back. Troy was in Portsmouth and had not yet returned with a woman to keep him company.

I had a sudden, violent premonition of danger; it was so strong that I began to hurry back as fast as I could, along the passage, my progress hampered by clinging skirts, and the fact that I did not want to create sufficient draught to extinguish the candle.

As I rounded the last bend, and came within sight of the stairs, I heard hurrying footsteps, far behind me.

Instinctively, I quenched the flame with my fingertips and flattened myself against the wall. The footsteps grew nearer, and the walker carried no light, which meant whoever it was knew every inch of the way.

My mouth felt dry, my skin prickled. I held my breath as the footsteps came abreast and someone brushed past me. There was a sound of breathing, and a small flurry of air as a cloak moved against me.

The figure mounted the stairs and stood, for a moment, silhouetted in the opening. Then it put up an impatient hand and thrust back the hood of the cloak.

As soon as I saw the colour of his hair, I recognised him. I almost cried aloud my dismay and disbelief.

He walked into the room; his voice carried back clearly. "Well? Where is she? What has happened?"

"Where is she? How should I know that? I came straight here to wait for *you* to carry out the plan we made. I have taken the necessary precautions, because this is your last opportunity and this time you must not fail me. If she leaves here tomorrow, we will have no other chance ... I have locked the Nursery door in case the child should waken, and posted Marie outside it. I have given Simkins a sovereign and told him he may go to the Fair.

"Catherine came to my rooms, Seton, in a state of great agitation. She demanded to speak to me, and Marie gave the answer she has been instructed to give whenever she knows I am going to meet you at the Folly. Dear, faithful Marie, who approves of my having a lover whom she calls a 'gentleman'!

"I guessed that Catherine must have found out that Milly met with an accident. Curiosity killed the cat. Curiosity killed Milly and Lallie, but you really should be more circumspect in your love-making, Seton, and not make so much noise that servants investigate. We should have used the Folly not risked discovery by staying here."

"Milly had been drinking," Seton pointed out. "She enjoyed herself well, but not wisely, at the Fair. Otherwise she would not have been bold enough to come and investigate, as you put it. As for being circumspect, how you would hate that; and you, my dear, omitted to lock the door to these rooms. That was careless of you!"

His voice was drily matter-of-fact.

"Well, then, where *is* Catherine?" he asked.

"I have said I don't know. Probably in her room. *I* cannot go and fetch her, for I am supposed to be prostrate with migraine, and have no wish to arouse her suspicions too soon. *You* must go, Seton. It seems she sent Simkins to fetch you, so it will appear that you have come in answer to her summons. She will bring you here—or you will bring her. Whichever it is, I will be waiting."

Beads of sweat trickled down my forehead and ran into my eyes. If Seton went to my room, he would discover that Alannah was not in the Nursery as they both imagined.

The thought that they might harm the child was inconceivable.

With trembling fingers, I groped for the matches in my pocket, and relit the candle to guide me on the remainder of my journey. Seton was talking to Selina, his voice low and caressing, as I walked through the opening and faced them, trying to muster enough dignity to cover the fact that I was terribly frightened.

"I am here," I said.

They looked startled; but not at all perturbed. Why should they? I was utterly at their mercy.

I was both repelled and fascinated by what I saw.

Selina sat on a small gilt sofa. Hers was the beauty of corruption. She was naked almost to the waist, where her wrapper had fallen back to show the rounded contours of her body and the whiteness of her limbs.

The wrapper was of transparent, rose-pink silk, flounced and beribboned and elaborately trimmed with pink feathers on the long, trailing sleeves. On her feet she wore scarlet velvet slippers with tiny gilt buckles. Her lips were reddened, her cheeks rouged. Her eyes glowed with pleasure at the sight of me; her lovely golden hair lay over her shoulders, down to her waist, in shining bands, and all about her was the spicy scent of clove carnations.

I didn't know, until that moment, how coldness and sensuality could go hand-in-hand; not until I looked at the woman who had pretended to welcome my presence at Sandleford.

Then I looked at Seton. *Le Diable*, he had called himself, on the night of the Ball. All down the years, painters had depicted the Devil as dark and saturnine; on the contrary, the Devil was fair, like Seton, with thick, shining hair sweeping almost to the collar of a cloak that I recognised as Mrs. Scadden's. He seemed to glow with a white incandescence; there was a light of savage pleasure in his strange turquoise eyes, corruption in his smile, a sensuality to match Selina's in his face.

Under his cloak, he wore evening dress and a white silk scarf. He dropped the cloak, unwound the scarf and said softly:

"So you *were* in the passage, after all! How did you find the entrance?"

I was not going to tell him; I was still fearful for Alannah's safety.

"You won't harm me!" I said. "Mrs. Treville is in the house!"

"An old woman," said Selina lazily. "She has gone to her room, at the top of the house. There is no one, no one within call, my dear cousin!"

"I sent for *you*!" I said bitterly to Seton, "because I believed you were the one person I could trust. YOU killed Milly; and Lallie!"

"Of course," he said gently, "we could not risk people discovering the secret way that we found when we were children. It has always been useful; our best-guarded secret. It will be YOUR last resting-place. You set the scene yourself. Your case is packed, and it will be put in the passage with you. You have written a note for Troy saying that you are leaving Sandleford and do not propose to return. It will be thought that you left tonight, instead of in the morning—for reasons of your own. Later—much later—your body will be taken from the passage and found in circumstances that will cast suspicion on Troy."

I almost dropped the candle. He took it from me and put it on a small table. It gave the darkening room an eerie light and his closeness made me want to retch as I had done at the Tree of Death.

I shook my head at them both, in utter disbelief.

"Why?" I whispered. "*Why*?"

"Little country cousin from Dorset, do you really think I would let you live to inherit Grandfather's fortune?" Selina asked contemptuously.

"If I die, the money goes to *Troy*!" I cried; and one thought burned like a flame in the darkness of my mind: Troy has never tried to harm me!

"Yes. The money will then be Troy's," she agreed calmly. "*You* have to die *first*, Catherine; for, the day after you came here, Troy saw you in the Chapel with the child; he was touched by your piety, it seems. He told me, then, that it was his intention to hand over everything he possessed to you, then to go to Australia and never return here. He is already in the process of making over his wealth to you; he is with his lawyers in Portsmouth, for that purpose, as Seton has confirmed. There are ways and means of discovering these things, if one pays for them; just as Smeech was paid handsomely to see no one came near the Folly that Seton and I used. How naïve you are, Catherine! It was bad enough that Grandfather should leave you his money whilst *I* spent my childhood in near-poverty. The moment I heard you were coming here, I planned your destruction. Troy did not want you to be told you were Grandfather's heiress—because, he said, it would prejudice our relationship as cousins. He wanted you to become accustomed to Sandleford and the kind of life you would have as a wealthy woman, before you knew the true facts. He believes that money can corrupt."

"I don't want any of the money!" I cried.

"Troy and Grandfather between them, decided otherwise. So they signed your death warrant. The money is rightly MINE—to share with Seton. To make us both rich and powerful beyond anything YOU can conceive! We cannot risk having you live long enough to collect such riches and so take them from US!"

She stretched out a hand to Seton; he pulled her to her feet and she leaned against him, coiled into the shape of his body so that they were almost one, lust in every line of their blended limbs.

"Why did you not marry Seton?" I demanded bitterly.

"He had only Ashmead, Catherine." She smiled at him, and he bent his head, kissing the long line of her throat. "He is not a rich man. Seton was a boy who went away and came back a *man*!" She sighed deeply. "A man I wanted as passionately as he wanted me. We knew that nothing could ever match our desire for one another. But I was married to Troy, who had given me Sandleford; Troy, who had made a handsome marriage settlement on me …

"He was stupid, Catherine. He took me to the Folly, on our wedding night. For weeks it had been the centre of preparations. He showed it to me so proudly. The walls and ceilings had been painted with scenes from the great love stories of history. He had bought a huge gilded bed with a silk canopy for our wedding night; he said he wanted to make it the most perfect setting possible in which to consummate our marriage."

I hated the sound of her laughter. Tears scalded my throat; my heart ached with love for Troy, who had been so cruelly rejected.

"Consummate our marriage, indeed! I told him that the only thing his money could buy him would be a Mistress for Sandleford, not a wife to share his bed. I told him I would sit at the head of his table and entertain his guests—but no street urchin, from amongst the hovels and whore-houses, no back-street guttersnipe, was going to father a child of MINE!"

She laughed again, as she added:

"He had laid the table ready for our wedding-night feast. He strode out and left it, swearing never to go near the place again. I had another key made, just as I had another key made to fit your bedroom door. Having a key to the Folly has been most useful to Seton and myself. It is so easy for me to use the passage—Seton comes to the side gate and uses the key to the Folly door that I gave him. It is our pleasure-house, Catherine. Should Troy be so foolish as to try to assert his rights as a husband—which he has done occasionally—then Marie knows how to keep him away from me."

I looked contemptuously at Seton.

"Your betrothal to Agnes was a pretence!" I cried.

"It was—expedient," he answered smoothly. "It was an excellent way of ensuring that no one suspected the relationship between Selina and myself. In due course, the engagement will be terminated. You can hardly imagine I would marry THAT pitiful, whey-faced creature!"

I turned to Selina. "You lied when you said Troy took mistresses to the Folly!"

"Oh, he has mistresses, Catherine. Alannah is proof of that, though he tells me she is not the child of one of his mistresses. How I laughed at him when he told me. He struck me, then, Catherine. For the first and last time. It was then I began to plan his death."

Seton said pleasantly:

"As his widow, Selina would be rich. The discovery that

your grandfather was very wealthy and had left his money to your, complicated matters. Then Troy decided to add more to your riches; to him that hath shall be given! Once you are destroyed it will all revert to Troy, and then it will be easy. We must have *everything*, you understand. Not just a portion of the money. Selina's marriage settlement is a pittance compared with what *you* would have inherited!"

"Was it you who tried to kill me, in the woods?"

"Yes. The child saved you. We set the scene. The snowdrops outside your door—Selina's gift. The sound of dancing shoes, made by tapping on the back of the cupboard, designed to make you uneasy and afraid. Again, you were fortunate when I tried to kill you by fire, in the study. Kellatt's cat got into the tunnel, and followed me, making me clumsy ..."

"We decided there were better methods," Selina murmured. "It must be made to seem that you were unbalanced, sliding into madness, so that your death could be a result of your strange state of mind. Who would believe there had been an owl in your room? We borrowed it from Smeech. Who believed you had been attacked? No one. Things were lost by you and found in strange places. You broke things, you were careless and forgetful ... you had to be given sleeping draughts—one each night. For three nights, I saw to it that you received a harmless dose of cornflour in your milk, so that the powders could be saved up, to give you, tripled in strength, on the fourth night. You awoke in a strange, confused state that would make whatever happened easy to accomplish."

"Why did you send for Arthur Jarley?" I demanded.

"That was clever of me, Catherine. It meant that doubt and suspicion could be sown in fertile ground. With your death, Troy's wealth will be vast. Only he benefits from your death. It might be questioned that your death was an 'accident' cleverly manipulated by Troy. No suspicion would ever be attached to either of us. When Troy dies, soon after YOUR death—it might seem that he has taken his life out of remorse for killing you—it is a question of setting the scene properly, Catherine!"

"Troy!" I shouted his name triumphantly. "He will not be easy to destroy."

"You would be surprised, Catherine. It is merely a question of planning how results can best be achieved. There is always the element of luck to consider, but there comes an end, even to such as yours!"

She looked towards Seton, and nodded. He was holding the scarf in his hands, the ends hanging loose. The world spun and rocked giddily for a split second. What hope of escape had I? He could easily pursue me through the tunnel, if I ran that way. I would never get past them to reach the door to the bell if I tried that way of escape. I was completely trapped.

"Afterwards," Selina said to Seton with lazy pleasure, "we will make love, you and I; on the splendid lacquer bed that Troy bought for Catherine. It will be our own private celebration."

She was completely relaxed; only Seton was slightly tense. She moved away from him, lighting the lamps, declaring that the candle-flame was too meagre, she wanted to *watch* ...

It seemed the ultimate in evil; Selina, cool, smiling in anticipation of pleasure in watching me die. Of the two, she was the more ruthless; Seton was so utterly infatuated with her and would do whatever she told him.

"Riches!" she whispered, as though to spur him on. "Such as few people know; WE shall be the richest people in the whole of England! The most powerful!"

I saw the naked greed in her eyes. Seton is *not* the Devil incarnate, I thought; neither is Selina the embodiment of all the evil that has ever flowed through this house in a dark tide. They are just two depraved people, possessed of a terrible lust for one another, and an overmastering greed that had trampled on reason.

Perhaps they were mad. I did not know. Certainly, they had played their parts well; the stage was the poorer for the loss of such an actor and actress as these two had been throughout my stay at Sandleford; for I remembered how affectionate she had seemed to me, how readily Seton had offered friendship.

Seton came slowly towards me, as though he had all the time in the world. Fear held me paralysed.

He was so close I could have touched him. He lifted the scarf, smiling at me, his eyes a blaze of brilliant blue.

"No!" I cried, instinctively putting up my arm to shield myself.

It was then that I saw the small figure in the doorway behind Selina. Alannah, in her nightgown, her dark hair hanging over her shoulders, eyes huge in her white face.

I stared at her, in horror.

She was in danger as great as mine. I shut my eyes and prayed frantically. I heard Seton say:

"We are being kind to you; you won't be left alone in the dark, to die, as Milly was. You won't know anything when we leave *you* in the tunnel. It will be more merciful this way."

I felt the smooth silk slide over my neck; and then a voice I had never heard cried out, high and shrill.

"*Please! Please don't hurt her ...!*"

The hold on the scarf slackened and I clawed it away. Alannah was screaming out the words over and over again.

"*Please! Please don't hurt her ...!*"

Long afterwards, I discovered that they were the last words she had spoken when she had seen her mother raped. They were the first words she ever spoke to me, and even in the midst of the horror of that night, I rejoiced at the miracle for which I had prayed; I had not dreamed that the miracle would save my life, by startling Selina into savage anger.

"My GOD!" she cried violently. "So she CAN speak! How long has she been there? How much has she heard?"

"Alannah!" I cried. "RUN! Go, quickly, quickly!"

She hesitated, and I nodded frantically towards the door of the bedroom, behind her.

She turned and ran through the bedroom.

Selina started to laugh, as she watched the child struggling with the door.

"You waste your time! *I* have the key!" she retorted. "You must have been here all the time! Now you can keep your precious Catherine company down there in the dark! No one will ever find YOU—or Milly! Only Catherine.

After Catherine has been taken out, we shall seal the passage for ever."

Alannah began to cry, as she realised her struggles were in vain. My heart was breaking for her; I called upon every ounce of strength I possessed.

"Get her, Seton!" Selina said lazily. "Get her and put her down there to wait for Catherine!"

"Don't hurt her!" Alannah shrieked again.

As Seton moved, I made a wild lunge at him; I fell, and, in doing so, brought him down with me to the floor.

He was up in an instant, trying to hurl me aside, but I grabbed at his legs; Selina, seeing what was happening, kicked out viciously at me, the toes of her red slippers catching my face and my head with considerable force.

Dazed with pain, I managed to struggle to my knees, grabbing at the small bamboo table, on which I had placed the candle, to support myself.

Selina knocked my hands away; in doing so, she made the table rock violently, and the candlestick slithered to the edge, catching the thin, trailing sleeve of her wrapper.

She cried out and snatched her arm back; but the feathers smouldered and the ribbon trim blazed as they were caught by flames she fanned in the agitation of her movement.

"Keep still!" I cried getting to my feet.

She did not hear me.

"Oh God!" she cried. "Oh God, help me!"

The flames had laid hold of the flounces on her skirt, as she moved recklessly in her panic. She was trying to tear the burning silk from her flesh as I picked up the cloak Seton had been wearing, to wrap her in it and so smother the flames.

She would have none of the cloak; as I went towards her with it, she screamed, backing away towards the bedroom, as though she feared I was going to attack her. Now her hair was alight, and she appeared to be clad in ribbons of flame that clung to her limbs.

Seton, white and trembling, made no move to help her. Where, now, the splendid golden Diable, I thought bitterly! He was as nerveless as a terrified boy, helpless in his terror.

Alannah crouched, weeping, against the door she could

not open. The acrid smell of burnt feathers stung my throat. Every movement Selina made fed the flames with air and made them leap joyously, catching hold of drapes and hangings in the room around her.

Completely naked, her burning hair a golden aureole around her face, Selina shrieked out in terror and agony, as she flung herself across the room and hurled herself against the windows with terrible force.

There was an explosion of shattering glass; for a moment, Selina swayed in the opening, whilst the night air rushed in; then she toppled forward and skimmed downwards, swooping like a bird of fire through the night.

As she plunged to her death, there was a moment's silence; then the sound of a horse galloping furiously along the drive.

The rider dismounted and ran across to where she lay, spreadeagled on the flagstones by the lily pool. He knelt and touched her, his head bent. Then he rose to his feet and stared up at the window, where I stood, unable to move.

I saw that he had a silver streak in his dark hair; and his face was the face of an eagle, proud and fearless.

"Oh Troy!" I whispered. "I thought I would never see you again!"

The last two things I remember, still remain clearly printed on my memory:

Alannah, holding my hand tightly; and the sight of a red velvet shoe, lying on the carpet.

It looked pathetic; one of the buckles had been torn from it. I bent and picked it up and held it in my hands, feeling grief for Selina.

There was no sign of Seton; he had gone back the way he had come. I was so desperately tired, I wanted to sleep forever ...

"I had to break the door," Troy told me. "Not an easy task, strong though I am."

I lay between cool sheets; there was a bandage on my forehead. The room was masculine and unfamiliar.

"Where am I?" I asked.

"In my bed."

"What time is it?"

"Long past midnight. Go back to sleep," he commanded.

"Not until I have told you what happened."

He stared down at me, his face dark and sombre; tears poured down my cheeks: for the sheer relief of being alive, for the joy of hearing his voice and seeing his face again.

"Very well, if it won't wait until morning," he said.

"It won't."

I told him; slowly, carefully, because I was tired and did not want to forget anything. By morning, it would seem as confused and strange as a nightmare.

Troy listened without a vestige of expression on his face. When I had finished, he laid a hand on my bruised cheek.

"It is over," he said quietly. "For us both. The pain, the bitterness, the despair. Selina is dead, and everyone will say it is part of the curse, the old legend. I did not know about Seton. I had suspected, for some time, that she had a lover and I thought it was Rufus. A man can be strong and clever, rich and successful; yet he is a fool in the hands of a woman, as I have been."

I shut my eyes.

"I don't want the Fairfax money, Troy."

His hand brushed away the tears.

"You will have it, nonetheless, Catherine; and learn how to use it wisely, for the good of others as well as for your own pleasure. You will see that money, rightly used, can be a tremendous power for good. It is something I shall enjoy teaching you."

"Why did Grandfather leave it all to me?"

"Because Selina told him, as she told me, that she would never bear a child of MINE. Damon was incensed. I did not want to be mixed up in this sorry business, but he liked and trusted me. Money corrupts, power corrupts; that is why I was determined not to tell you about your inheritance until I felt the time was right. It is perfectly true that I was astonished when I learned, just before his death, that Damon was a rich man."

I opened my eyes and looked into his brilliant emerald ones, wondering why I had ever thought him cold. I remembered how I had distrusted him. I thought of the hurt, the loneliness, the humiliation he had borne, beneath the proud surface.

"I am no saint," he told me frankly. "I have had mistresses, though I never used a woman badly, nor have I cheated any man. I have something to tell you that should make you very happy. Alannah is not the daughter of one of my mistresses. She is your half-sister."

I stared at him dumbfounded.

"*Half-sister*? How …?"

"Your father is alive and well, living in Australia. I traced him through a letter I found, after Damon's death. The letter was several years old and said that, having confirmed his first wife's death, Daniel, your father, planned to remarry. He had gone to Austrlia, made money, repaid his debts and was living comfortably in Sydney.

"I went to Australia and met your father, before you came to Sandleford. He was astounded to learn that he had a grown-up daughter, as well as Alannah. He was in poor health, recovering from the shock of his wife's death. It was MY idea that Alannah should come here and get to know you."

"You should have told me long since that my father was alive!" I cried.

His smile was wry.

"Should I, Catherine? You were not particularly well-disposed towards him. You considered he had behaved badly to your mother. Daniel freely admits that it must have seemed so, but he was at his wits' end and forced to leave the country; had he known about your mother's condition, he assures me he would never have done so. I believe him. Your grandfather had never answered his letter from Australia nor had Damon admitted HE knew of your existence. Daniel is angry about that, I assure you. He is adamant that Alannah shall never touch the Fairfax money. He wants to see you. I have looked forward to telling you the truth; perhaps I am child enough, Catherine, to enjoy playing the role of conjuror, who pulls delightful surprises from his pockets!"

The admission touched me. I was overcome with joy; I had a family!! A father! A sister!

I had judged my father too harshly, I admitted; Troy had shown more understanding. I bent my head, my eyes full of happy tears.

"There was a bond between Alannah and myself from the beginning," I whispered. "I thought it was because she was YOUR child. It is even more wonderful to discover that she is my sister!"

The sun was shining when next I awoke. Troy had gone; Agnes sat by my bed, composed, but very pale, her eyes red-rimmed with weeping.

"Troy has told me everything," she said quietly. "I have seen the secret entrance. Seton has disappeared. I loved him dearly, Catherine."

"I know, Agnes dear," I said gently. "The fact that he was not worth the devotion you showed does not detract from that love."

"I should have known it was too good to be true that he could look at ME!" she said with intense bitterness.

"You must not say that Agnes. You have gifts to give that a man, one day, will be proud to receive. The Creightons tried to teach you to despise yourself. Don't let them succeed! You should be proud that you have shaken off the fetters that they put upon you!"

Her smile was twisted.

"Proud? That I cheated, pretending I could not walk when I could leave my wheelchair when I chose? At first, I did not want to admit I could walk because, whilst I was an invalid, there was so much kindness, so much attention given to me. Are you not disgusted?"

"No. These are perfectly natural feelings. You had never known what it was to be taken care of and looked after."

"You have not heard it all. Through being able to walk, I discovered that Seton was meeting Selina. At first, I could not believe it. I told myself I was exaggerating a childhood friendship. I—I used to watch; one night I followed him to the Folly."

"The night of the Ball?"

She nodded.

"When I realised what was happening, I was beside

myself with a rage and jealousy that I did not know how to control. I blamed Selina; she put an evil spell upon him, she had some dreadful hold over him. I kept planning how and when I would expose them; and all the time I had to pretend there was nothing wrong. I swear I never thought of him as a man who would kill, until I found the brooch."

"What brooch?"

"The one you gave Milly. I knew you gave it to her, because I met her, off-duty, in the village one day, wearing it, and she was full of praise for you, when I admired it. The day after Milly was missing, I went to Seton's room with my mending-basket; and there was the brooch, or a piece of it, caught in his scarf. I didn't know what to do."

I said quietly: "Remember he was kind to you, Agnes. When a man is infatuated and greedy, he loses his reason; but YOU need only remember his kindness."

She drew a long, shivering breath.

"There was something—odd—in his expression when he looked at Selina as she said that tonight was your last night here. It was as though a message passed between them. There was something horrible in the room, for a moment; but that evening he went out, wearing Mrs. Scadden's old cloak. I had discovered that he always borrowed her cloak when he was going to the Folly. I thought about the brooch, and the strange feeling, and I didn't know *what* to do; so I sent one of the servants to find Troy, and bring him here. He was staying with his sister Anne, as he always does when he is in Portsmouth. He said he borrowed a horse and rode like the wind.

"I was glad I had sent for Troy, when Simkins came with your message. I had the feeling that harm was being planned for you, though I couldn't know how or why. Seton *wasn't* to blame, as much as Selina was, whatever you may say, Catherine. She *forced* him to do what she wanted, by promising him a share in your inheritance and Troy's money. SHE was the evil influence at Sandleford; a very powerful force for wickedness."

"No, Agnes," I said. "She was a greedy woman; she hated me because I was robbing her of a vast fortune. She was cruel to Troy, she was unfaithful; so are many, many people. That does not make them the incarnation of evil; you mustn't think about such things. In time, it will all seem less dreadful than it does at this moment. Let us talk of happier things; Alannah can speak! Isn't that wonderful?"

She smiled faintly.

"She has been making up for lost time; she chatters to me all day long."

None of us saw Seton alive again. Three days later, his body was found in a lonely copse, some miles away, a shotgun beside him. In his pocket was a written confession of his part in the affair, admitting that he and Selina had caused Milly's death by flinging her down into the passage, but declaring that Selina alone was responsible for Lallie's death.

Agnes, locked in her own terrible grief, refused to see anyone for some time. I knew she had saved my life, and Alannah's, by sending for Troy, when all her instincts must have cried out against betraying Seton, whom she loved so fiercely; for, after Selina brought about her own death, I am certain that Seton would have panicked, killed us both, and put us in the passage, to prevent us from telling anyone what had happened that night.

Seton had left Ashmead to Agnes. No one is ever utterly evil, I told her. He had seen to it that she was provided with a home.

Dr. Garrod insisted that I should stay in bed for several days. I saw little of Troy, for he was kept busy. He came occasionally to inquire after my progress, but he seemed withdrawn and aloof.

"Milly has been buried in the Chapel grounds," he told me. "The passage has been blocked and sealed off. It is certainly the one your grandfather searched for; I had no knowledge of its existence, or the use to which Selina and Seton put it."

"Did you love Selina very much?" I asked sadly.

"No. I loved a Golden Princess, who did not really exist. We should not put people upon pedestals, Catherine. Damon once told me that he knew the real Selina; that no one else did."

I saw the pain in his face and longed to comfort him.

Rufus was deeply distressed by what had happened.

"Selina and Seton and I were children together. She was always strong and wilful—but it's hard to believe she could kill ... she must have been mad ... the servants are saying that it's the curse of the Devil's dancing shoes."

"Servants talk nonsense. It's a nine days wonder that will soon be forgotten. I feel so sorry for poor Agnes. Please go and see her, Rufus. She might talk to YOU."

Alannah was a great comfort to me; the first time she came to my room, I held out my arms to her.

"Troy has told me that we are sisters. I am so happy, Alannah! Are you glad, too?"

She nodded, and buried her face in my breast. I held her close, stroking the dark hair.

"You have seen a lot of bad and unhappy things, Alannah. They are all over now. The memory of them will go away, just as you forget nightmares. When I am well enough, I shall come with you to Australia and meet MY father who is YOUR father, too. I want you to tell me about him."

She chatted away happily to me; only once did she refer to the incident of Selina's death: that was when she told me how she had only pretended to be asleep when I looked in on her, and had then crept back to the tower room to explore the secret place; but she had heard someone coming before she had time to open the cupboard and had hidden behind the curtains at the top of the stairs leading to the study.

She had seen Selina enter the room, and had been frightened; running out of hiding only when she heard me cry out.

"Now we will promise each other not to speak of it again," I whispered. "You can *speak*, we have so many *good* things to talk about and so many plans to make."

The first day I was up and dressed, Mrs. Treville and Kellatt took Alannah to the farm.

I was sitting idly in the window, thinking that summer had come overnight, when Troy entered the room.

As always, I felt his power and his magnetism; and something else that I had never sensed before. I could not look at him; I felt a joy more exquisite than anything I had ever known.

He came across, gently lifted me to my feet and held me against him.

I recalled some lines of a poem I had once read:

> '*Some part of thee I have seen,*
> *In every lovely thing,*
> *And if this heart that sings today*
> *Waits upon tomorrow's pain*
> *Yet still you will be,*
> *A candle burning,*
> *In the darkness of eternity.*'

Troy was the end of all desiring, the harbour at the end of all my voyaging. If I were blind, I thought, I would know if he was in the same room; deaf, and I would feel his voice deep within me. He touched depths I had not known existed in my heart; he would draw me across continents and seas, wherever I was, by an invisible cord, strong as steel, fine as silk.

Troy Merrick. A pirate, a buccaneer; a boy full of dreams; a tender young lover; a man proud, sensitive, arrogant and fierce.

"I love you, Catherine Fairfax," he said. "Do *you* love ME?"

"You must know the answer by now," I murmured.

"I want to hear it from your lips."

"I love you, Troy; now and until the end of my days."

He kissed my lips; quietly, at first, and then with a warmth, a passion that made radiant promises for the future.

"Then we shall be married," he said. "I must warn you I am not an easy man to live with. I am no gentleman."

"I'm glad to hear it."

"So you'll marry a guttersnipe?"

"No. I'll marry Troy Merrick, who is the most wonderful and exciting person in the world."

"Dearest Catherine; you won't send me away empty-handed on our wedding night?"

"No," I said brazenly. "I'll give you sons; and daughters; and love you for ever."

Our lips, our hands, our eyes met, in happiness and tenderness.

Epilogue

Looking back, now, all that happened at Sandleford seems unreal.

I am in my cabin, waiting for my husband of a few hours, to join me. The cabin has been filled with flowers, on his orders. He is impatient of last-minute tasks that keep him from me, but, being Troy, he will not leave anything undone.

Worn out by the excitement of a wedding day, Alannah is asleep in her cabin; we have become very close during the last few weeks, which we spent in Anne's house at Portsmouth; for I did not want to stay at Sandleford a moment longer than necessary.

Marie was never the same after the death of the mistress whom she protected with such fierce loyalty. Her mind suffered and, because she cannot live outside in the world again, Troy made arrangements for her to be comfortably cared for in a private nursing home.

Rufus and Agnes came to our wedding; Agnes seems to be much better, and I see the beginnings of a good friendship between her and Rufus—who has finally forgiven me for choosing Troy as a husband.

No one ever saw Smeech again; but a strange thing happened, the day after Alannah and I went to Portsmouth. The Folly caught fire. I could imagine the flames singing as they danced, and the scorching heat like a fiery wind out of Hell. I was glad that I had not been inside the place where Troy suffered such disillusionment and humiliation.

I saw the blackened, roofless stump of the tower 1 ex day.

"I am glad it has been burned down," I told Troy.

Some time afterwards, Smeech was convicted of causing several serious fires in the neighbourhood; and though he would not admit to causing the fire at the Folly, I am certain that *he* did so and that it was *not* further evidence of the Devil's curse on Sandleford, as the servants insisted.

"What are we to do with Sandleford?" Troy demanded.

"Make it into a museum. Let people come and see it, full of all your treasures, for *we* shall never live in it again. There is one thing I would especially like: to have the gates of Sandleford Park opened every year, when the snowdrops are out, so that people may look at them, and go into the Chapel to see the Lady."

Troy agreed with me that it would be a splendid idea.

Now I am waiting for Troy, here in this cabin. We are casting off, putting out of harbour and I can feel the gentle rise and fall of water beneath 'Sea Witch'; soon, she will greet the open sea, beyond the Harbour, like a bird in flight; and Troy and I will go on deck to watch the lights of England fade into the distance.

I am thinking of all the strange, foreign countries we shall visit on our journey across the world. I am thinking of the joy of meeting the father I thought was dead. I am thinking of all the years that lie ahead …

Now, I think only of HIM, as I hear his footsteps outside the cabin door; I turn from the mirror, and he is there, an expression on his face I shall remember until the day I die.

I hold out my arms to him; my happiness is almost too much to bear.

"Catherine?" he says softly. "My dearest love …"

I don't think that we shall go on deck, after all, to see the fading lights and taste the salt winds on our lips.

(The End)